"I am inclined to accept the offer," Alex said.

Ebony took a deep breath, closing her mind to everything except the need to be with her child. "You will allow Sam and me to stay together? Wherever you take us?"

"The safety of your child and your access to him will depend entirely upon my access to you. At all times. Do you understand me, my lady?"

Shocked, she looked up to search for a trace of the laughter that would explain his demand. But there was no laughter, only the hard blue steel of his gaze.

The breath left her lungs in a shudder, leaving her cold and numb. She had little choice but to accept. If she wanted Sam at her side, she must stay by this man's side, literally, and without argument. "Yes!" she said. "And you, sir, are a *devil!*"

* * *

The Widow's Bargain
Harlequin Historical #717—August 2004

Praise for Juliet Landon

The Knight's Conquest
"A feisty heroine, heroic knight, an entertaining
battle of wills and plenty of colorful history flavor
this tale, making it a delightful one-night read."
—*Romantic Times*

Juliet Landon

The Widow's Bargain

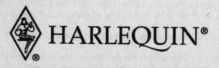

HARLEQUIN®

TORONTO • NEW YORK • LONDON
AMSTERDAM • PARIS • SYDNEY • HAMBURG
STOCKHOLM • ATHENS • TOKYO • MILAN • MADRID
PRAGUE • WARSAW • BUDAPEST • AUCKLAND

ISBN 0-373-29317-8

THE WIDOW'S BARGAIN

Copyright © 2004 by Juliet Landon

First North American Publication 2004

www.eHarlequin.com

Printed in U.S.A.

Available from Harlequin Historicals and
JULIET LANDON

The Knight's Conquest #673
The Widow's Bargain #717

Please address questions and book requests to:
Harlequin Reader Service
U.S.: 3010 Walden Ave., P.O. Box 1325, Buffalo, NY 14269
Canadian: P.O. Box 609, Fort Erie, Ont. L2A 5X3

Chapter One

Galloway, Scotland. 1319

The dry forest floor muffled any sound made by feet that for the last hour had rested on stirrups to reach Castle Kells by sunrise. Last night, Sir Alex Somers and his men had seen the castle from across the other side of the loch, glowing pink and orange on its high throne and looking down a sheer cliff into the mirrored surface below. Built on a spur, it was effectively sealed off on two sides while, at its back, mountains and forests cloaked it against the north winds. Further along the glen, the land sloped into green pastures where dark ponies grazed and blue smoke rose vertically from a cluster of thatched bothies. Now they viewed it within hailing distance, but well hidden, with a burn beside them that tumbled its way through the boulders into a deep pool some twenty feet below, roaring softly in tune with the pines.

'We can bide here a while,' said Sir Alex to his companion, 'if we keep well back into the trees. I don't suppose it'll be long before he returns.' His soft

Lowland accent made his words sound more like an observation than a threat.

The companion, Hugh of Leyland, not quite so tall, not so broad or brawny but as agile as a polecat, brushed a crumb off his doublet of faded brown and unhitched a leather bottle from his belt. He accepted the strategy without question, but there were details that could do to be aired before the action began.

He took a swig of water and wiped his mouth with the back of his hand. 'He has a son, do you say?'

'Had,' said Sir Alex, cryptically. 'Killed in a raid a few years ago. He has a wee grandson, though.'

'Living here, with Sir Joseph?'

'I believe so.' The blue eyes searched as he spoke, eager for any sign of movement near the gatehouse or along the track that led to the distant woodland.

They made an impressive-looking twosome, like a pair of tawny lions who knew each other's ways, who were not averse to a friendly scrap in an overflow of excess energy but who would have defended the other to the death, as would the men who waited silently behind them. In his prime, at thirty-one, Sir Alex Somers was physically robust, wide-shouldered, deep of chest, and possessed of a face that invaded women's dreams in situations where neither of them had any business to be. The colour of dark hazelnuts, his thick hair bounced in uncontrollable spikes that touched his forehead and curled over the scarf around his well-muscled neck. But it was his eyes that turned female knees to water, for they were the same intense blue as a cloudless summer sky, and far less innocent.

'That might be useful to us,' said Hugh, his second-in-command. 'We take the wee laddie and use him as bait, ransom, whatever. A squawking bairn will always get his grandpa's breeks in a twist. Does the bairn have a ma?'

'They usually do, Hugh.'

'I'll find out. Leave it to me.'

Sir Alex found no amusement in Hugh of Leyland's predictable efficiency in finding a woman. They were both adept at that. But there were some, like Sir Joseph Moffat of Castle Kells in Galloway, for instance, who would think little of sacrificing their own kin, if need be. They had heard enough about the man to make them think so, a local Justice of the Peace, landowner, horse breeder, raider, rogue and thief, and those were the more honourable aspects of his character. Sir Joseph would not be kept awake at night by his conscience. 'Best not to depend on it, though,' he warned. 'It'll take a fair bit to put the scarers on a man like Moffat. He's had more years of practice than most in these parts, Hugh.'

Hugh leaned against a tree and watched his friend saunter forward like a large cat, as at ease out of doors as in the finest halls of Europe. Hugh had been with him for nine years, as long as any other man in the hundred-strong company. He was two years younger, a paler tawny, curly-haired man, built like a wiry athlete, merry-eyed and unashamedly thankful for the women who threw themselves under his feet just as willingly as they did under Alex's.

Sir Alex squatted down upon his haunches and peered over the steep rocky precipice ahead of him, beckoning Hugh to come and see, to keep down and be quiet.

Hugh crawled forward, intrigued. 'What?' he whispered.

The burn hurtled and splashed between mossy

boulders and leapt over a shining brown ledge into a secluded pool, foaming inside a dark circle. A neat pile of clothes lay over on the dry rocks, and a shriek of laughter rose above the clatter of the water, drawing grins from both men.

'A lassie!' Alex said.

'Two lassies. Look…see! We're in luck.'

As he spoke, two pairs of shining pink arms came into view upon one of the flat rocks, then two dark heads with helmets of wet hair followed by glistening shoulders, backs and haunches. Heaving themselves upwards, they shed water like otters, twisting to sit upon the rock and kick at the swirling ripples around their ankles. Their hands twisted at dripping ropes of hair to wring out the water, throwing handfuls of it over their shoulders, revealing every curve of their slippery torsos now highlighted by the new sun. Gold and pink and sleek, they preened like mermaids in their sheltered lair.

'Now that,' said Alex, 'is worth riding all this way to see. Are they castle lassies, d'ye think?'

'Sure to be,' Hugh said. 'Hell, Alex. Do we have time for it?'

'Silly sod. You know we haven't. And we have to stay hidden. Will ye take a look at the black-haired one, though? She's a stunner, Hugh. Wheew!' He blew between his teeth softly. 'What a body. And a face to go with it.'

'I'm looking at the shorter one, like a little ripe berry. They're too good to be village lassies and too happy to be laundry-maids. They'll be seamstresses, that's what.' They fell into a stunned silence, noting from the cover of a convenient hart's-tongue fern every perfect detail of the glorious scene. And when they felt a movement at their backs, they found that a small crowd of their followers had also wormed their way forward, their eyes staring out of their sockets at the sight.

The women stood to collect their clothes, moving into a position where, with one glance up at the rockface, the silent audience would be revealed. Quickly, Alex, Hugh and every man withdrew like a collective shadow back to the horses, almost too overcome to speak.

'Well,' said Sir Alex at last, 'that was an interesting start to the day. Think you'll be able to keep your mind on the job?'

Hugh grinned. 'Maybe we'll be able to weed them out when we get inside the castle.'

'There'll not be time for that, lad. The men will likely keep the women out of the way. Still, I'd like to take another wee look at the black-haired one, dressed or undressed. We'll see.' He glanced at the streaks of light that had begun to filter through the trees where they hid. 'Move the men back into the shadows now, Hugh. And keep a man posted over there to watch the track and the gatehouse. The rest of us had better mount up. We all know what's to be done, eh?'

'Oh, yes,' Hugh said, placing a foot in the stirrup. ''Tis a lovely morning to be raiding a castle.'

From Lady Ebony Moffat's chamber on the topmost floor of Castle Kells, the views across the loch were to the south and east through groups of windows that were little more than slits in the eight-foot-thick stone walls. The apertures widened into wedge shapes with built-in stone benches on three sides, deeply cushioned. One such space in the corner had been curtained off to create a garderobe in the thickness of the wall, and in another corner was a door that led spirally downwards to the next level.

The cushions had not, of course, been made for young Sam Moffat to jump up and down on in excitement, nor had the windows been made just that size for him to squeeze his head through to look sideways towards the woodland path. Consequently, when a man's shout was heard from the stairway to say that Master Sam's grandpa was coming in, Sam found that it was more difficult to reverse into the room as easily as it had been to go out of it. For a moment, there was panic in his little breast. 'Mama!' he yelled. 'I'm stuck again!'

Tempted to use the next half-minute to teach him a lesson, after the hundredth time of telling, Lady Ebony lifted her faded blue wool surcoat off the bed and slipped it over her head. After seven years, it still fitted like a glove over her linen bliaud. Her sister-in-law Meg was already making her way to the door. 'I'll follow you when I've freed him,' Ebony called. 'You do on down.'

'Are you sure?' said Meg. She had seen it before. It was his ears.

Ebony smiled, adjusting the surcoat across her shoulders. 'As Sir Joseph's daughter, love, you must be there or he'll want to know why. You go and show an interest. I'll bring Sam down in a moment.'

It didn't take as long as usual to free him, for now he had learnt how to press his ears flat and twist. Nor did he have time today for the soothing noises from his mother when his Grandpa Moffat would surely have brought something back for him from his night

raid which, to Sam, was as innocent as a trip to the
market. He skipped off, reddened about his six-year-
old ears, his eyes as grey as granite, blond-haired,
slight-framed, bursting with an unpredictable primi-
tive energy. After three years, Sam rarely asked about
the father he so closely resembled.

It did no good for his mother to protest at Sir Joseph's frequent gifts to his only grandson, a pony that
no one had taught him to ride, money that he was not
allowed to spend, clothes from another child's back,
toys and trinkets salvaged from someone's home. Her
initial objections had been disregarded, and she could
not bring herself to tell her child that his grandpa
gleaned other people's property by force, mostly at
night, plundering across the Scottish-English border
to torch houses, kill the men, lift the cattle and bring
them up on to Scottish pasture. There was only so
much one could expect a child to understand at six
years old, and as long as they were obliged to live
under Sir Joseph's protection, Sam must be taught,
first and foremost, to respect his elders.

His cries of excitement could be heard echoing
down the stairway and disappearing into the maze of
chambers, halls, stairs and passageways that was now
his world; hers and Meg's too. It was unsafe for them
to venture out when raiders passed so frequently in
both directions, perpetuating feuds that had escalated
alarmingly in the five years since the Scottish victory
at the Bannockburn. Now, there was not a household,
large or small, that did not fear the raids, though these
would be fewer now that the hours of darkness were
less. Perhaps this would also be Sir Joseph's last raid
till the autumn, when they might begin to live more
normally than this.

Sharing none of her son's urgency, she sat on the window-cushion and rested her head against the wooden shutter, her eyes scanning the pattern of massive oak beams that supported the roof. Woollen tapestries clad the walls with colour and warmth. Polished stools, a table, chests, and a canopied bed provided every comfort, and a fire at one end was protected by a hooded chimney with the Moffat coat of arms carved into it. The castle was cool at all times of the year, and this chamber was one of the most private in a place where privacy was at a premium. She had no cause to bewail a lack of comfort, and her inclination was to stay up here well out of the way rather than to be seen condoning her father-in-law's lawlessness.

Not wishing to let Sam out of her sight for too long, she relented at last, taking up a piece of damp linen and spreading it over a chest to dry before removing from it a strand of moss that had caught in its fibres. Still damp, her hair was hurriedly bundled into a caul of gold net and pinned carelessly on top of her head in a style unknown to fashion. At Castle Kells, what did it matter how one looked and, in Scotland, who except the nobility cared a damn about fashion in these uncertain times? She took a quick look round and went down, descending the steps slowly with her skirts held up. It would take her quite some time to reach the great hall.

The unusual absence of men made Ebony wonder if Sir Joseph's return was in some way out of the ordinary. She quickened her step. He had taken about thirty men with him, this time, but still she would normally have encountered members of the household at every turn, as she had done earlier that morning.

The guard who always stood in the window niche overlooking the courtyard was missing. She peeped through the arrow-slit, but it was set too high to show her more than the gatehouse on the opposite side and yet, even as she watched, an archer on top of the tower took aim at something below him. Before he could complete the draw, however, his arms went up and he fell backwards with an arrow in his throat.

'Reivers!' Ebony whispered. 'It's the reivers! God have mercy on us.' Reivers. Border raiders. Murderers and thieves. Merciless destroyers. How had they got in? And where was Sam, her precious child? Panic rose in her breast like a sickness. Men such as this had killed her Robbie three years ago; she could not let them take Sam, too.

Picking up her skirts, she ran like a hare, flying through arches and open doorways, leaping down steps to reach the great hall on the first floor. Breathless, her heart pounding with fear at what she might find, she threw open the door at the side of the high table where covers had already been laid, silver trays, spoons and knives set, but no more than that. People were everywhere, huddled in groups guarded by men whose assortment of weaponry was fearsome, their expressions menacing.

With her mind set on only one goal, she barged her way past them. 'Let me through!' she yelled. 'Let me through, damn you! Sam! Where is my child? Sam!' Distraught, and screaming his name, her calls cut across the hall already bristling with tension and fear. Hitting out at the barriers of arms and bodies, kicking and elbowing men aside like skittles, she searched for a sign of Biddie, Sam's young nursemaid, in a congregation of unknown and familiar faces and a terrified crowd of household servants, cooks, grooms, pages and all.

At the far end of the hall near the great chimney-piece stood another group of strangers who had turned at her noisy entrance. Biddie's white wimple was easy to spot, her face contorted and pleading. Her loud cry held all the anguish and terror of one who has failed in her duty. 'Mistress!'

Ebony charged towards her but, even in her panic, was no match for the man who caught her and swung her hard against him, catching at one arm and hand. Before he could capture the other, she swung it back and threw her force behind a blow to his head, the sound of the impact cracking through the hall like the snap of a whip. 'Let go of me, you churl!' she shrieked. 'My child…where is he?'

Ahead of her, the group parted to let Biddie through. A large and powerfully built man followed close behind, his eyes opening wide with surprise before quickly narrowing again, concealing their bright blueness. 'Not exactly the reception we'd hoped for, Hugh,' he said quietly to the man with the reddening cheek, 'but it's an interesting start, eh?'

Ebony heard none of this exchange as she took Biddie's plump arms and shook her. 'Where *is* he?' she said, her voice on the edge of tears. 'What have they done with him? And Meg?'

Biddie's mouth twisted. She was barely twenty years old, but dependable and devoted to Sam. 'Nothing…I don't think,' she whispered. Her large liquid eyes glanced across at the door. 'They took him into the courtyard. He'll be all right, mistress.'

But the enraged lioness was not prepared to accept that, hurling herself bodily into the group of men who, by chance, stood between her and the courtyard door. No time for asking, pleading or remonstrating; her only thought was to reach Sam before he was harmed.

Intrigued, and astonished to find a clothed version of the black-haired mermaid they had carried in their minds since sunrise, the men allowed her to get as far as the door, which was guarded. She turned like a creature at bay, her eyes both tearful and blazing with fury, her hands ready to claw at the man who faced her. 'I want my child,' she croaked. 'I *want* him. Let me go to him.' Her voice shook, almost running out of air.

'The fair-haired wee laddie is *yours*?' the man said in surprise. 'And you are…?'

'I am Sir Joseph Moffat's daughter-in-law,' she snapped. 'And who the devil are you, sir? Do reivers admit their names these days, and do they still terrorise women and children like the cowards they are?'

'You're a Sassenach!' he said, ignoring the questions. 'This gets more interesting by the minute. What's an Englishwoman doing in this den of thieves?'

'Never mind the courtesies. Get my child here to me *now*, if you please. What have you done with him?'

'Nothing. Yet.'

The courtyard door opened to admit two people, one above the other, the uppermost one bending his little head to duck beneath the point of the arch, his little hands clutching at the white hair of a gaunt and elderly man clad in padded waistcoat strapped with baldric and sword-belt. Sam's legs straddled the man's neck and dangled on to his shoulders. He was giggling.

He caught sight of his mother at once. 'Mama!' he called. 'I'm riding Josh. Look at me! I'm going to show him my pony.'

She would have flown to him and dragged him bodily into her arms, but she was caught back by the tall man and held with such force that she was unable to escape him, and such was Sam's excitement that his attention had gone from her in the blink of an eye. While she was never able to remember exactly what the man said to her at that moment, she understood that she must not show Sam her distress. 'Yes, love,' she called. 'Don't be too long, will you?'

With a merry wave and a grin, Sam was jogged through the company and out at the other side of the hall in the direction of the stable yard, while tears of relief and dread filled Ebony's eyes. 'Don't take him away,' she gasped. 'Let me go to him.' She tried to shake off the restraint of the man's hands but to no avail, and the outer door was closed with a terrifying finality as Sam's head ducked once more.

'Now, my lady. You've had one answer. It's time I had some.' The man had scarcely taken his eyes from her, but now he allowed her to distance herself from him, bristling like a wildcat. 'Give me your name,' he said, harshly.

'My name, sir, is Lady Ebony Moffat,' she replied, angrily brushing a tear away from her chin. 'Reivers don't usually—'

'And your man? Where is he?'

'My man was killed by the likes of you.'

'When?'

'Three years,' she whispered, hanging her head.

Her hair had fallen into a black silken bundle at the nape of her neck, and damp strands still clung to her throat. Her grey eyes, black-lashed and almond-shaped, were set in a perfectly oval frame, high-cheeked and fine-boned, like an elf, and now her pale full lips trembled with distress. 'My father-in-law has had us live here since then. Where is he? Where's Meg?' She saw the man's eyes link with those of the man she had struck, then return to hers, showing her a flash of blue that she could only liken to steel. The man was obviously the leader of this mob, yet his manner was soldierly, his men disciplined, their actions ruthless, but nothing like the murderous rabble who had raided her home and burned it down. They were, she supposed, all different in their methods, even if their aims were the same.

'Sir Joseph is wounded,' he said with a distinct lack of concern, 'and your sister-in-law is tending him.' Sidestepping, he barred her way as she made for the stairway. 'You'll not find him there. And she's perfectly safe.'

Fiercely, she tried to push him away as if he were a youth. 'You've wounded him? So who's to be next? Damn you…take what you want and go! Leave us in peace! What is it you want…food…cattle…?'

He held her back again with infuriating ease. 'No great hurry,' he said. 'No one is going to ride off to get help. No one is in a position to resist, and Sir Joseph is hardly going to defend anything for a while. We shall take the men and hostages away, and the castle is in our hands for as long as we need it. We'll leave when we're ready.'

'Not my son,' she pleaded. 'You'll not take him away?'

The man she had struck was not inclined to negotiate. 'He's the old man's grandson,' he said from behind her, 'and grandsons make useful hostages. The old devil will be more inclined to co-operate when he knows we have his wee bairn, won't he?'

She whirled round to face him as the last words left his lips, hurling herself at him in a frenzy of rage. 'Lout!' she screamed. 'Murderous, thieving lout!'

But before her nails could reach their target, the man who had recently held her fast did so again, and she was pulled hard against his chest, lifted off her feet, and thrown over one broad shoulder like a sack of oats, then carried, squirming, shrieking with rage and beating at his back, towards the small door at the dais end of the hall where the white covers were still untouched on the table. One of his men, grinning, opened the door and closed it behind them and, with the sound of its slam against the frame, Ebony knew that, once again, her worst nightmares had returned.

Her strongest instinct was to give in to the blind panic that engulfed her, to scream, bite, kick and fight against the overwhelming fear of losing her child. Utterly consumed by a nameless black terror that saturated her limbs with the strength of ten, she lashed out like one demented. Even so, her efforts made very little impression upon the solid bulk of the man who held her painfully hard against the stone wall of the deserted passageway with his hands, body and legs, keeping his head out of range of her only free weapon.

He let her fury subside and gradually wind down to a standstill, and she knew at the back of her tormented mind that the time had come for something other than mere appeals to their better natures, for they were not in the business of concessions. Tears streamed down her face and neck, sticking her loosened hair to her skin, and her head dropped forward onto his padded doublet, too heavy for her to hold up. 'My son…my son…' was all she had breath to say. 'I cannot lose him.'

At last, she became aware of his body pressing against hers, and perhaps it was that that helped to remind her that she had hardly looked at this man, would hardly have recognised him if she were to see him again. Now, she raised her head and saw through her tears that he was clean-shaven, that he was regarding her impassively, that his mouth was well formed and unsmiling, and that his air of healthy virility might have had something to do with his white teeth, which showed as he spoke to her.

'Steady,' he said. 'Steady now. Your son's safe enough, but I need a hostage. He need not be gone for ever.'

She shook her head wildly. 'No, not him! He's all I've got.'

'He's the only grandson?'

'Yes,' she wailed, 'and he's my only child, too. If you must take him, then take me with him. He cannot do without me, nor can I do without him.'

'I don't take women.' His tone was brutally uncompromising.

Then what *would* he take? Could she bribe him? Shame him? The master-at-arms had shown her once how to use a dagger, but today she had seen no need to wear one. She would not make that mistake again. Sardonically, he had also advised her that, if ever the need arose, she should offer reivers anything she possessed to buy herself time, or life. *Any* currency, he had stressed. Bargain with them. Life is more important, he'd told her, not needing to explain what life was more important than. His advice at the time had seemed to be a particularly masculine way of looking at things, though now the gravity of what she knew she must offer seemed trifling in comparison to her need. 'Please…please, you *must*,' she whispered, forcing herself to look at his eyes to show him what she was saying.

'Must?' he said. 'What *are* you saying, exactly?'

'I'm saying,' she said, looking away, 'that you can…'

'Can what?'

'…can have me…whatever you will…if you'll only let me go with him, or leave him here with me. I *beg* you not to take him from me.' The words sounded as foreign to her as if coming from someone else's lips, and he was silent for so long that she began to wonder if indeed she had said them. Yet it needed an effort of will, after that, to look into his eyes. 'Unless…unless there is something else?' she ventured, hearing the absurdity of her question. What else did she have that such a man could possible make use of?

The pressure on her wrists was suddenly released and her hands, freed of his cruel grip, fell numbed to her sides. His body arched away from her as he leaned with his hands on the wall at each side of her head, making a barrier too large and powerful to evade, though it seemed likely that her offer had now passed the stage of evasions.

She noticed how fine lines scored the corners of his mouth—made, she supposed, by commands and a life out of doors—and she had little doubt that, if he had indeed understood the nature of the bargain, he would be weighing up the implications, for there was a wealth of experience in the eyes that roamed leisurely over her face and figure. If there was triumph or greed in his expression, then he was hiding it well. Nevertheless, his hesitation mortified her.

'I see,' he said. 'So we are bargaining, are we?' His eyes rested upon hers at last, searching behind the tears.

She resolved to have strong words with the master-at-arms for initiating this charade. 'Yes,' she whispered, looking away. 'It's all I have. It's worthless compared to my bairn's life, but it's yours if you want it. You see, I have lost my shame.' Which was a lie he would hardly recognise.

'Your bairn's life is not at stake, lady. He's a surety against reprisals. Quite a prize. So have you been used to offering yourself—' his words were interrupted as her hands came up between them to rake savagely at his face, but her wrists were caught again and twisted away behind her back '—to reivers?' he finished.

'No, sir!' she snarled, glaring up at his laughing eyes and incensed by the insult. 'The gift I kept for my late husband will always be his, no matter who else must be paid off. You could have claimed to be the first, for all the good it would do you, but I'll not offer it again to have its value questioned so. You are a reiver and not worth the breath it takes, nor will you ever know what it has cost me to offer my body to a common thief and murderer. Forget it! I did it for my child, not for your amusement.'

'Yet only just now you told me it was worth little,' he said, softly, holding her close to him. 'Is there some confusion here, perhaps?'

'Not to a woman. Worth and cost are not the same thing, but that's not something a man like you would understand too easily.'

'That's as may be. Yet I am inclined to accept the offer. Does it still stand?'

Now it was her turn to hesitate as the enormity of the bargain began to grow and fill her with dread. She would have to go to bed with this stranger, or to allow him some appalling intimacy here in the passageway, whichever he had more time for. The consequences could well be disastrous, too awful to think about. She had been near no man except Robbie, for three years remaining completely uninterested in any man's arms except during the darkest hours of the night when she wept into the pillow. This man would care as little for her lost experience as for her conscience, her reputation, or the long-term effects.

'Well?' he said.

She took a deep breath, closing her mind to everything except the need to be with her child. 'You will allow Sam and me to stay together? Wherever you take us?'

'The safety of your child and your access to him will depend entirely on my access to you. At all times. Do you understand me, my lady?'

Shocked, she looked up to search for a trace of the laughter that would explain his demand. But there was no laughter, only the hard blue steel. 'At *all* times? Not…not just *once*?'

'Not once, no. For as long as I want you. Is your son worth that to you?'

The breath left her lungs in a shudder, leaving her cold and numb. Put like that, she had little choice but to accept that, if she wanted Sam at her side, she must stay by this man's side, literally, and without argument. 'Yes, he is!' she said. 'And you, sir, are a *devil*!'

'Then we have a bargain, do we?'

With her teeth clenched, she tried to push herself out of his arms as a picture of dear Robbie appeared before her like a reproach. 'Yes, we do. And now do I get to know the name of the man to whom I've just sold myself?'

But her struggle was ill timed as his arms moved across her back, tipping her head sideways into the crook of one shoulder where her cheek came to rest on his quilted doublet. He gave her no other warning of the depth of his hunger and, as his lips closed over hers with their bargain still upon them, she braced herself for the sudden and inevitable roughness, the display of lust that she had occasionally caught in men's eyes. Prepared to be hurt, she held her breath during the first tender exploration by his mouth, the tasting, savouring, the incredible gentleness of his dominance until it became clear that pain was not his intention, nor were her initial fears borne out. She had expected brevity, too, while his men waited upon his reappearance, but his kisses were unhurried and in no respect perfunctory, nor were they in any way comparable to the gentle kisses that Robbie had taken or offered her. And when he released her at last, she discovered that her eyes had been closed and that there were fresh tears upon her lashes.

'My name,' he said, 'is Somers. Alex Somers at your service, my lady.' There was no ambiguity in his meaning.

'Master Somers,' she said, finding her voice far away down some rusty channel, 'you are—'

'I am *Sir* Alex,' he corrected her.

'I see. And I suppose that was a prelude, was it? Are you about to take me here against the wall, or do we have to…?'

His teeth showed evenly as he laughed and pulled her back to him, halting her supposition before it staggered to an embarrassing conclusion. 'Here? Now? Is that what you want, lady?'

Oaf! Lout! 'I do not want you at all, sir. I want my child,' she snarled.

'And I would prefer a more comfortable setting,' he said, pressing his nose close to hers, 'where we could take a more sedate approach to the matter. Your chamber will do well enough, when things have settled.'

'How knightly. How chivalrous. I should have known.'

'That I don't take half a bargain when I can have it all? Yes, lady, you should. You will come to know me better than that, in time. Now I suggest you take a filial interest in your wounded father-in-law.' He released her from his embrace, pointing down the passageway. 'Second left.'

'That's the steward's office,' she said, wiping her damp cheeks.

'Yes. That's where Sir Joseph is. He'd have been dead by the time they'd carried him up to his chamber.'

'And you didn't want that?'

'Not particularly. He has information I need.'

'Then why wound him?'

'He came back wounded from his raiding, lady.'

'You lie!'

'No. Go and see for yourself. His wounds are hours' old.'

For a moment, she stared at him. 'And what about my child?'

'He's having the time of his life. He'll come to no harm.'

'How can I be sure of that?'

In one swift and practised movement, his fingers pulled the net off her bundle of hair, spilling it in a black glossy tide over her shoulder. She saw his eyes darken suddenly and once more she found herself in his arms with neither the time nor the wit to protest. His hand buried itself deep in her hair as his second assertion of authority came fierce enough to take her breath away, making her cling to him for support.

His reply was breathless and husky, as if he was fighting for control. 'Until our bargain is sealed, my lady, you can't be sure, can you?' he said. 'So don't go where I can't find you.'

Chapter Two

Even as the door closed behind him, the relief of being allowed to stay by her child's side was being eroded by doubts that her bargain with such a man could be the action of a sane and intelligent woman. During the most humiliating and degrading conversation of her twenty-three years, Ebony's mind had been crystal clear in obtaining one thing at any price. Now, she found that a cold fear was setting in like a Scottish mist, chilling her to the bone and waking her to the significance of her first bid and of his raised stakes, resulting in an abominable bargain that could tie her to his side indefinitely unless she took prompt action to release herself and Sam. Escape? Yes, there were ways out of the castle other than the gatehouse. She had not fled from one mob of reivers simply to be caught up in this devil's crowd, and nine years was not too long for her to forget her way home.

At fourteen, Ebony had been more than eager for a new life in Scotland. Coming from Carlisle, just over on the English side of the border, to Galloway's glorious mountains and lochs had meant a complete break from her widowed mother, Lady Jean Nevillestowe, who had willingly accepted an olive branch from a Scot to cement a prestigious family connection. Sir Joseph had no problem, he had said, with the idea of an aristocratic Englishwoman for his newly knighted only son Robert. And though the two countries had not been on the best of terms in 1310, it was not so uncommon for the English and Scots to unite at board and bed, ignoring dissenters whom Sir Joseph could stare down with his pale prominent eyes.

So she had gone to live with the Moffats of Castle Kells to prepare for the time when she would wed Sir Robert, and by the age of seventeen she had been deemed old enough to accept him as her husband and to bear him a son almost immediately. Tragically, their idyll lasted only three years, their manor being in the path of English reivers during one of their raids from across the Solway Firth. The last image Ebony had had of her dear one was silhouetted against the roaring flames as he pushed her, Sam and Biddie out of a low upstairs window. The house and its contents had burned to the ground with Robbie in it while the three survivors had fled to the nearby woodland where the thick bracken had hidden them all night. At daybreak, trembling with shock and cold, they had set off in their shifts along the loch side to the castle. Sir Joseph had found them, the man who last night had been inflicting the same fate on someone else as she and Sam slept safely. Had he found the culprits at last and taken revenge for his son's life? And were his wounds the result?

Since that appalling event, her main concern had been to keep her small son safe from further harm and to find ways of redirecting his cries for the father he adored. Lately, he had stopped asking for him, but his nightmares continued to be fuelled by his insensitive grandfather who saw no harm in nightly warnings that, if he didn't go straight to sleep, the reivers would come and get him. Needless to say, he rarely did fall asleep quickly, and never alone, and now he was in the very hands of those ghouls who were cleverly disguising themselves as his friends. Whatever bargain she had made with them, she saw no dishonour in making an effort to outbid Sir Alex which he, no doubt, would call going back on her word.

As far as she knew, this was the first time that Castle Kells had suffered a raid. She had begun to think it would never happen, being so well fortified and protected by the loch and the mountains, and Sir Joseph a reiver himself and more than able to look after his own. Now that he was out of action, she had not for three years felt so vulnerable or so out of her depth.

Stuffing the caul from her hair into the pouch at her girdle, she forced her shaking legs to move reluctantly down the stone-flagged passageway to where the laird of Kells was apparently suffering a dose of his own medicine. Believing Sir Alex to have been exaggerating the seriousness of Sir Joseph's injuries, she was unprepared for the ravaged body that lay motionless and grotesquely spread out upon the trestle table in the steward's confined office where his rolls of parchment were squashed beneath tatters of burnt clothing.

'Meg...oh, Meg!' she whispered. 'Dearest. I'm so sorry.'

Meg's fresh, smooth face was almost as white as her father's, her blue long-lashed eyes sorrowing at the plight of her disabled protector. 'The first day of May, Ebbie,' she said, quietly, 'and this is what we get. Who would have thought, this morning, when we…?' Her voice broke, her arms opened and dropped helplessly to her sides. Always so tidy and prim with the air of an efficient red squirrel, Meg at twenty-four years old was not one to break easily. With a father as difficult to please as hers, and a life constrained by her environment, her natural stoicism had been honed to perfection, a barrier against melodrama in any form. This was one of the few times that Ebony had seen her distraught.

She held out her arms and took Meg into them, rocking her. 'Shh, love,' she crooned. 'Hush, then. 'Tis all right. We'll get through this.' She caught Brother Walter's dour expression over Meg's shoulder as he shook his head and frowned as usual, which was his habit whether he had good reason or not. As Sir Joseph's chaplain and physician, this was probably the only time he had tended his obstreperous master without having to fight him about the treatment.

His pessimism appeared to have affected the usually buoyant Meg. 'Perhaps,' she said, 'but Father won't. Just take a look at him.'

The terrible wounds were much worse than Ebony had supposed and now she understood Sir Alex's wry comment about carrying him up flights of stairs. He was badly burned, and unconscious.

Brother Walter surveyed the mountainous, hairy, scorched body, then offered his verdict. 'Nay, but I dinna ken when I've seen worse na this, m'lady. 'Tis bad. Verra bad, I tell thee. Clooted him across his back, it did.'

'What did?' Ebony said.

'Flaming timbers, m'lady. His back's worse na his front, ye see.'

Instead, Ebony saw only the irony of Sir Joseph's timing after the numerous occasions she had wished him to hell without the slightest hope that he would ever oblige.

'But what I dinna ken either,' Brother Walter grumbled as he carefully peeled away a charred sleeve off one arm, 'is why that crood shoulda come here, of all places. I ken Scots raid their own side when it suits 'em, but na-body'll traipse all the way up this glen unless there's a ver' guid reason. If they hoped to kill the maister while they were about it, then they must be wearisome glad the noo.'

'I believe they may not be,' Ebony said, rolling her sleeves up. 'It's information they're after.'

There was the sound of muffled sobbing from the corner where Meg's maid, Dame Janet, stirred a pot of lotion, hardly daring, even now, to come too close to the man who cared not for too many females in his household.

Meg stared at Ebony, seeing for the first time the streaks of tears that had left their mark upon her cheeks, the disordered hair, the swollen lips that had howled and pleaded and been ruthlessly kissed. 'Ebbie! You've been weeping! Oh, my goodness…what happened? Did they harm you, pet?' She took her sister-in-law's hands in hers. 'Tell me!'

'No, nothing,' Ebony said. 'I was bothered about Sam, that's all.'

'And you found him? He's safe? And Biddie?'

'Quite safe, love.' Her eyes held less than the truth, and Meg was quick to see it.

'You mean, safe at the moment? What, Ebbie? You

must tell me. D'ye mean they're going to take him?' She shook Ebony's hands.

Tears welled up again as the words were forced out angrily. 'Sam *and* me. I made them promise not to take him without me. I believe they're planning to stay till tomorrow so they can get Sir Joseph to speak.' She glanced again at the blistered skin and the blood-soaked rags, not daring to say what was in her heart. 'But heaven knows where they'll take us.'

'Then you must take Sam away,' Meg insisted. 'Now. This minute.'

'How can I do that? I cannot leave you like this, Meg, when you need me more than you've ever done. What d'ye think they'll do to *you* when they find I've taken Sam off? They'll kill you.'

'They won't!' Meg shook the hands again, harder, her tone as decisive as ever. 'Course they won't. And I can cope on my own, anyway. If they were going to strip the place and fire it, and kill all the men, they'd have done it by now and gone. But *you* must get away, Ebbie, and take Sam to safety down the glen. You know what my father would say if he could hear.'

Neither of them was prepared for the shock of Sir Joseph's touch upon Meg's skirt, the fumbling clench of his fingers over the woollen fabric, the tug as her hand claimed his. 'Father,' she whispered. 'What is it?'

The swollen cracked lips breathed a command. 'Take…Sam!'

'Yes, Father. Ebony will take him, I promise. Are you…?' But the effort was too much for him to sustain and he relapsed into his dark agony-free world once more, leaving his daughter speechless with his pain. 'He heard us. You heard him,' she said at last. 'Now you have to go. I promised him.' There were tears on her lashes.

'When it gets dark,' said Ebony. 'Then we'll go. Now, Dame Janet, do we have any of that fern-root salve for these burns? What's in that jar you have there?'

Dame Janet handed it to her. 'Fern-root and butter, m'lady,' she said, pulling the linen cover off. 'It's as good as anything, but we need more bandages.' Her head shook, sadly.

'I'll go and find something,' Meg said.

'No,' said Ebony. 'I know where the oldest sheets are. You stay and plaster him with this.' Stay where it's safe, was what she meant.

It was a great pity, she thought as she closed the door, that Meg's mother was not here to help. In 1317, the terrible year that followed Robbie's murder, Sir Joseph's wife went to heaven with a broken heart. And who was to blame her? Life with her boorish husband would be no picnic without her beloved son to take her part. Sir Robert Moffat had never approved of his father's unlawful activities, but had been in no position to prevent them when almost every sheriff, governor, warden and assistant warden, keeper and laird was open to bribery, blackmail and treachery of every kind. The years since the battle at Bannockburn had been lean ones, floods, crop failure, famine and disease had been nationwide, and raiding had become an accepted way of staying fed. Robbie would never have abducted a child or bargained with a woman's honour.

He and Ebony had been friends as well as husband and wife, with never a word of conflict between them,

and only Biddie and Meg knew of the bitter tears she
shed at night, longing for the courteous comfort of
his arms. That morning at daybreak, she and Meg had
gone down to bathe under the waterfall, Meg insisting
that, on this of all days, they must look into a still
pool to see the reflections of the men they would
marry. None of the pools had been still enough and
they had given up, laughing at their distorted faces.
But Ebony had been glad not to see, for it might have
shown her Davy Moffat's face, Meg's cousin.

Taking care to evade Sir Alex, Ebony took a longer
route through the maze of passageways to reach the
stable yard via a door in the kitchen-garden wall,
which she and Meg used to take them along their path
to the waterfall. She picked up a basketful of beets
and cabbages left by the garden lad in his panic, passing the men and grooms who tended the beasts that
seemed to have multiplied with alarming speed since
the morning. Sam was with Biddie and the grandfa-
therly Joshua and, though he spared his mother time
for a quick hug, he was not inclined to be diverted
from learning how to pick his pony's hooves clean
and to brush his fetlocks.

Still distinctly on edge after her earlier conflict,
Biddie was eager to comfort her mistress with the
whispered information that Sam believed the reivers
to be the king's troops who had come to demand Sir
Joseph's men for another battle against the English.
A muster, they called it, at Newcastle-upon-Tyne.
'Which is why they're so fierce,' she said, round-eyed
with the well-rehearsed innocence she used to
sweeten the truth.

'King's troops!' Ebony scoffed. 'And he believes

it, of course.' She took Biddie's arm and led her away from Joshua's sharp ears.

Biddie tipped her white-wimpled head towards the yard. 'Course he does. They've just marched the men away who went raiding with Sir Joseph last night as well as those who didn't. Sam watched them go. Well,' she said, noting Ebony's disdainful expression, 'he's better off believing that than the truth, isn't he? We can do without the extra nightmares. And look at him now. No one's ever bothered to show him how to do that before.'

They watched the man called Joshua, gnarled like an oak, brown-armed, white-haired as a prophet and as fit as any of the younger men, though he must have been the oldest. His face was a weathered parchment, his eyes a lively brown, his mouth ready to smile. Biddie's attention was riveted equally upon the two pals as she monitored their new relationship.

Ebony turned her back on the two of them. 'We've got to get him away from here,' she said, keeping her voice low.

The large eyes swivelled in her direction at last. 'Escape, you mean? Before they take Sam with them? Are they really going to do that?'

There was no question of telling either Biddie or Meg of the bargain. 'Yes,' Ebony said, looking away. 'As soon as it gets dark, we have to take him down to the waterfall and into the boat. It was there this morning when Mistress Meg and I bathed.'

'And what about Mistress Meg and Sir Joseph?'

'They say we must take him. Both of them. If we go before dark, we chance being seen. If we delay, they may find the boat and take it away. It's got to be tonight, Biddie. I have to go and help with Sir

Joseph now, and you must go up, if they'll let you, and gather together what Sam will need to keep warm, and some food. Hide it in the stair-passage so that we can collect it once we're out of sight.'

Loyal to the roots of her hair, Biddie would never have questioned her mistress's motives and, if she secretly wondered when Ebony had last shown a streak of indifference to Mistress Meg's needs, she was hard-pressed to remember. After all, Sam's safety came first, and time was not on the side of heroism. 'If they take Sam,' she said stoutly, 'they'll have to take me too. But I could go on my own, you know, and get help from further down the glen. They could be here by daybreak tomorrow.'

'You can't go in daylight, Biddie. You'd not stand a chance.'

Biddie pulled her wimple down, leaving it in white folds around her neck as a nest for her brown curls. 'Not even if I take this off?'

'No, love,' Ebony smiled. 'We cannot spare you.'

Bandaged around the laird's wounds, the strips of torn linen sheeting did little for him except to make him more decent. As the task continued, Ebony's conviction that she could not leave Meg one moment before she must increased with each passing hour. Meg had lost her mother and brother in the space of one year. Her father was strong but, even if he survived, would likely be disabled and she would be left behind at the castle with only a skeleton staff of household servants and no defence. Even her father's retainers had been marched away, and though he and Meg had insisted and Meg had promised, Ebony knew that her premature departure would be heartless.

She went about her business, saying nothing of her doubts, and Meg fell silent with foreboding.

There were other men who needed Ebony's care, men whose injuries were too severe to make the journey with the others, and although she caught sight of Sir Alex on several occasions, she avoided his company at the mid-morning meal that was served later than usual. She, Sam and Biddie ate alone. She was torn by conflict and indecision, burdened by the price she had agreed to pay for a place at Sam's side, yet telling herself that it was nothing compared to the thought of losing him. Women had done more than that in the past. Much more.

Usually loud with laughter and shouting, the crashing of doors and the excited baying of hounds, the castle was now eerily quiet under the new command of competent men formidable behind flint-hard expressions that watched from every vantage point, every door and arrow-slit window. Still puzzled by their restraint, she went from office to store, from treasury to muniment-room, from chapel to kitchen to stable to see what, if anything, they were preparing to take away on the morrow, but saw only the evidence of their thorough examinations, nothing of looting or destruction. It was as he had said: they were taking their time.

The situation showed no improvement on Sam's noisy return to his mother and nurse after almost the whole day in Joshua's care. He had, he told them in non-stop breathless chatter, been allowed to help the bowman to make him a small bow and then the fletcher to make him arrows. Then they had sat him upon Josh's great horse while it was being groomed, and someone had fashioned a small sword for him to wave. None of which impressed his safety-conscious mother.

'Have they no thought for the danger, for pity's sake? What on *earth* are they thinking of?' she scolded. 'Is that their idea of how to look after a child of six? I should never have allowed him near them. Idiots!' They were in the kitchen and heads had begun to turn at the unusual spectacle of Lady Ebony in a fret. 'What would your Grandpa Moffat say to that, I wonder?' she went on, preparing a dish of chicken pieces and cold stuffing for Meg and Brother Walter.

'He'd say they were cloot-headed bastards, Mama,' Sam chirped, helping himself to the crust of the bannock on the tray. 'But Josh doesn't have a cloth head. He's nice.'

It was not so much the sentiments that Ebony deplored, but the fact that he was able to voice them with such pride in his vocabulary. Her eyes met Biddie's in astonishment. 'We have no way of knowing,' she said in unmistakable reproof, 'whether their parents were married or not, so it's best not to use that word until we can be sure, Sam Moffat.'

Unabashed, Sam broke another piece off the bannock and popped it into his mouth. 'Will they tell us, then?'

'Probably not. And it would not be polite to ask them. Now, leave that alone. You've had your supper. Come with me upstairs.'

'May I not go and see Grandpa and Aunt Meg now?'

'Not at the moment. He's sleeping. Biddie will take this to Aunt Meg.' Sam was hauled away, protesting,

but still full of excitement about the usually banned
activities he had shared with the men, an enthusiasm
his protective mother could not recall him ever showing in Sir Joseph's forbidding company. He was also
utterly exhausted and, by the time they had reached
the upper chamber, his remaining energy took him
only as far as the bed where he flopped, one gangling
arm and one leg barely making it to the surface.

Ebony sat by him, holding back the natural impulse
to undress him and tuck him into the bed where he
slept with her and Biddie each night. He would need
to be dressed if they were to go within hours. 'Sam,'
she said, stroking his soft hair. Sleepily, he crawled
over the coverlet and snuggled into her embrace and,
while she deliberated what to tell him or indeed
whether she could bring herself to leave Meg in such
a sorry plight, his eyes closed, the light began to fade,
and it was time to light the candles.

Her torment was resolved as Biddie reappeared.
'Biddie,' she said. 'We're not going.'

The young nursemaid looked as if she had mis-
heard. 'Not...?' she said.

'Not,' said Ebony. 'I can't leave Meg tonight. It
wouldn't be right. She needs us.'

Biddie came further into the room and sat on a
stool by the side of the chest from which their clothes
had been taken. 'But they're to take you and Sam
tomorrow, anyway,' she said. 'Aren't they? And
didn't Mistress Meg say you should make a run for
it? You're thinking it's too dangerous?'

'It's not the danger, Biddie. It's Meg, mostly.'

'Mostly.' The maid recognised uncertainty as well
as anyone. 'And Sam?' she said.

'Well, look at him. We'll never get him moving again after the day he's had. He went out like a light with not even a story to soothe him.' Sam had not moved, his long slender legs dangling like ropes off her lap, his little toes pointing inwards, his thumb nowhere near his mouth, so far.

'But the bag of food and clothes is on the stairway to the kitchen-garden door,' said Biddie. 'I hid it behind the empty baskets. If you're sure we're not going, I'd better go and bring it back before anyone finds it. Besides, we'll need it for tomorrow.'

'I think it's for the best. And when Sam's in bed, I'll go down and tell Meg we're staying. She's as exhausted as the rest of us, poor lass. Light some candles before you go.' Ebony looked down at her sleeping child, sure that she had done the right thing, but aware of some uncertainty about the reasons she had given to her maid. Were there others that she could not interpret? Was her decision entirely unselfish? Did it matter, after all?

In the soft dancing glow of candlelight, the large chamber was redefined, restoring muted colour to the wall-hangings and darkening the lancets of sky beyond the windows. Suspended over the bed, the canopied tester almost dissolved into the low beams above, and the pale blue bedcurtains had now changed to the deep aquamarine of an evening sky, her linen pillows the cream of beestings, the cow's first milk. Carved roundels stood out sharply on the sides of her prie-dieu, and tomorrow she would have to leave it all behind for a new life with a mob of thieves. But tonight, she must allow Sam and Biddie to sleep in peace.

The opening of the door came fast upon a peremptory knock, making both Ebony and Biddie jump with fright. 'You!' Ebony snapped, angered by the uncomfortable lurch behind her breastbone.

Sir Alex stepped inside and swung the heavy door closed behind him, sending a rush of fear through Ebony's arms, making them tighten upon Sam's heavy form. It was the first time she had seen him at a distance, time to notice his long legs and well-muscled thighs encased in leather chausses, his wide shoulders and the haughty set of his head, the sheer power of him as he stared her down even from yards away. 'Well?' she said, though her voice had suddenly lost its cutting edge as he approached the bed, holding up the linen parcel of clothes and food that Biddie had supposedly hidden.

'Well indeed,' he said, companionably, placing himself on the bed by her side. He laid the parcel between them and undid the knot with strong workmanlike fingers, laying it open to reveal Sam's small-clothes and extra shoes, a woollen blanket, a shawl, two bannocks, half a chicken, a wedge of cheese and three apples. 'You'll not get far on this, will you?' he said. 'Not with *his* appetite.' He glanced at the sleeping child with a smile. 'And you'll break both your necks carrying him down those stairs in the dark.' He tipped his head towards the doorway.

The clothes and food were, she knew, totally inadequate, but it was all they could carry. And now, with Sam still clothed, she would never be able to convince her captor that they had decided against escape. 'We weren't going to,' she said. 'We were not going anywhere.' She could see in his dismissive glance that he did not believe her.

'No,' he said, reminding her of a condescending

uncle, 'it was never a possibility, was it, with so many hawk-eyed men around? They don't miss anything, you see, nor was I fooled by your agreement. You're not the kind to stick to a bargain if you can see a better one ahead, are you, m'lady?'

It was on the tip of her tongue to say that all's fair in love and war, but she dared not lay herself open to more of his scorn, knowing the adage not to be true. 'I have no place for luxuries like honour where my son's life is concerned, sir. That's for men, not for mothers. And if you can behave without it, then so can I. We're even.'

His eyes were deeply shadowed; she could not tell what impact her fighting words had made upon him, but she was glad to see that he did not find her amusing. 'The lad's life is not in danger, my lady. I've already told you that. The issue is one of access, as you well know, but it was not very bright of you to gamble with that, after the skirmish we had earlier.'

'Well, a man like you *would* think so, wouldn't he? You probably thought I was eager to pay without trying to find another alternative.'

He *did* find that amusing. 'There was a point, I must admit, when I wondered if—'

'Get out!' she snarled. 'And get off my bed. You can stop wondering, sir. There will never be a time when I shall want you within a lance-length of me. Never. And tell your man Joshua to cease from playing games with my son's safety. He is not allowed to use bows and arrows, nor to sit upon a horse by himself. He could have broken his neck on that, too.'

'You can tell Josh yourself tomorrow. As the father of fourteen bairns and grandfather of nine, he'll be interested in your theory. This wee lad has been cooped up like a prize chicken, lady. Never allowed to run wild as lads do. It's time he was let out to see the world. See the smile on his chops? That speaks for itself.'

'That, sir, is because he's here with me.'

Even in shadow, the level gaze of his blue mind-reading eyes made her wish she had not said that. But even as she struggled to form added words of astringency, he leaned towards her like a knight seeing an opening for his sword. 'No one would argue with that, Lady Ebony Moffat, but don't try to get away from me again or it may be some time before you see his smile, sleeping or otherwise. And you may rail all you wish about bargains and honour and such, but don't lose sight of the one we agreed earlier, will you? It's the only one you offered, and I shall keep you to it no matter how many alternatives you can devise. Now, lady,' he stood up, pulling at the short brown tunic that skimmed his buttocks, 'I shall send an escort to take you down to Sir Joseph and to bring you back up here afterwards. He will have orders to lock you in…' he patted the leather pouch at his belt '…and to return the key to me. Your freedom has already begun to shrink a little.' He walked over to the dying fire, picked up a log and tossed it into the embers, pushing at it with his toe as the sparks flew upwards. 'That will help to take the chill out of the air.'

Suddenly enraged by the man's monstrous arrogance, she grabbed at one of the bannocks that lay in the bundle beside her and hurled it at him, wheeling it like a discus across the room.

As if she had meant it as a gift, he caught it with supreme nonchalance, took a bite and returned it exactly to her side in the same manner. *'Au revoir,'* he said, munching. 'Better close the shutters too, Mistress Biddie. There'll be no moon tonight.'

In the silence that followed his departure, Ebony could hear her heart pounding as if she had run upstairs, and when Biddie asked her if she should indeed close the shutters, she could find no virulent gems of abuse to throw after him, only a shake of her head. Picking up the flat breadcake that he had bitten, she studied it abstractedly before putting it back in the linen where it would be needed for their journey tomorrow.

'He's a fine figure of a man, though,' Biddie murmured, finding a return of her natural charity. 'What was it he said about bargains?' She pulled out the truckle-bed from beneath Ebony's and drew it across the rush matting to a place near the fire.

'Nothing that makes any sense.' Ebony rose at last and lay Sam upon the covers, slipping off his muddy shoes. 'Get Sam into here while I go down and take a look at Sir Joseph, Biddie,' she said. 'And I doubt we shall need this any more where we're going.' The knot that tied the bedcurtains to the wall held a sprig of May-blossom that Meg had stuck there that morning and, rather than throw it out of the window, Ebony placed it on the stool where Biddie had been sitting. How useless these old traditions were. If she'd had the slightest interest in remarriage, she certainly wouldn't rely on May-blossom and reflections to help her. 'What are you doing with that?' she asked, staring crossly at Biddie's removal of the little bed. 'Sam's sleeping here with me.'

'Yes, but I'm not,' said Biddie, shaking out the feather mattress. 'I nearly landed on the floor last night.'

Watching his men make preparations for the night, Sir Alex Somers received the congratulations of his friend and second-in-command with his usual wariness. 'Yes, Hugh,' he said. 'As you say, so far so good, but this is only the beginning and the next bit's going to be much trickier. Save the compliments till we're through.'

'And the lady?' Hugh said, predictably. 'She looks like trouble, Alex. Certainly not as carefree as she had us believe earlier, is she? Did you get what you were after?'

Alex was used to such teasing. 'Do I *look* as if I've been mauled by a wildcat, Hugh?'

'Think you can handle her, then?'

There was no bragging affirmation, but Alex's laugh was almost soundless, softening into a smile that needed no words to explain it. He stuck his thumbs into his belt.

'I see,' said Hugh. 'But she's a widow, don't forget. That's something you hadn't bargained for. Hadn't you better be a bit careful?' His eyes strayed to the corner of the shadowy hall where a beautiful black cat crouched on top of a trestle-table, her green eyes blazing at Alex's shaggy deerhound below.

'That, my friend, is a general misconception.'

'What is?'

'That one needs to be especially careful with widows. You're getting confused with virgins.'

'Mark my words,' Hugh said, 'I know about these things. Widows are not like the others, you know, in spite of your superior knowledge. They've had experience, it's true, but when a widow's actually loved her husband, she doesn't find it easy to let him go. It's as if he was still with her. They're funny like that. Loyal creatures, even after death.' When Alex made no comment, Hugh continued, 'That doesn't seem to stop them wanting, mind you, but they don't admit it. Takes ages to convince them that it's all right to start again.'

'Yes, well thank you, Hugh, but I haven't got ages and I'm perfectly aware of the confusion. I'd have to be extremely dim not to be, wouldn't I? And now I think you should go and mind your own damn business and leave me to get on with mine.'

'All right. But you'll be wanting my help before long.'

'Possibly. That's what you're being paid for, so have aid ready.'

Hugh's eyes widened. 'That bad?' He watched the cat stand and arch its back, holding its tail vertically like a flagpole. The deerhound stood motionless, debating the outcome.

'Oh, yes, certainly that bad. Go on, I give you permission to laugh when you see the blood.'

'Whose?'

'Anybody's.'

Left alone, Alex understood only too well the reasons for Hugh's concern, neither of them having anticipated the dire condition of Sir Joseph Moffat that day, nor could they have known the connection between his grandson and the two stunningly beautiful women who had taken their breath away earlier.

They had known that the grandson would be a precious weapon to use against old man Moffat, a sure way of extracting the information they needed, but now the situation had changed and was likely to do so even more, by the look of things, and, try as one might, it would be difficult to keep a cool head with those two ferocious beauties in opposition, one protecting her son and the other her father.

Nevertheless, Hugh's observation had not gone to waste. It was inconceivable that the old man had not already made plans to marry them both off to local lairds or to noblemen, and Alex could not help wondering if she had already been promised to one of them. Not that it made any difference: she had made him an offer and that was a prize not to be rejected for the sake of such niceties. A widow she might be, desolate, loyal and chaste, but he would not deny her the satisfaction of becoming a martyr for the child, since that's what she seemed intent on. The fun would begin when she discovered that it was all quite unnecessary.

The hollow click-clack of the key was the last humiliating blow at the end of an unforgettably harrowing day. Ebony had pleaded to be allowed to stay with Meg in the claustrophobic steward's office that had begun to reek of Sir Joseph's sweaty bulk and the unguents they had plastered over him. But her dour escort had not been open to bribery and she had been obliged to leave before she had had time to fully explain why her plan to escape had gone wrong. Meg had assured her that she understood, but Ebony knew she didn't. How could she? Almost in tears, she hit out at the door, but not so hard as to wake Biddie and Sam.

Biddie's hope of more sleeping-space appeared to have misfired, for now Sam's fair head was on the pillow next to her dark curls, their faces inches from each other in sleep, and Ebony could guess how Biddie had relented after only one small wheedle.

Tiptoeing across to the unshuttered window, she looked out into the darkness, just able to make out the shining black loch below, the black line of forest on the far shore, the ragged outline of mountains against the clear starlit sky. He was wrong about there being no moon, she thought; the silver crescent hung like a fine sickle that the men used to cut the hay. No light, but a slim signal of hope, focussing her thoughts.

In many ways she would find it hard to leave the place that had been her home for three years as a maid and three as a widow, though regret did not accurately describe the fear that she could now admit with no act of bravado to maintain. Sir Joseph had kept her and her child safe from harm and hunger during the terrible years of famine that had affected the whole of Europe. At the time she had paid scant attention to the itinerant merchants' tales of rotting crops and drowned livestock, of starving villagers eating rats and dogs and worse, and of salt costing as much as gold, of the murrain that affected herds of cattle, the shortage of wool, the closure of markets, the ruin of tracks, roads and bridges. She had had her own losses to contend with, a terrified child, her own black despair. Who could lose more than that?

Sir Joseph's stores had not suffered; he had money and a large castle sited well above the flooded glens. His fields were between wooded slopes, well drained and safe enough for his precious herds of pure-bred Galloway ponies. He had contacts in every town and port, and what he lacked he gained by raiding, as others did. His cellars had never been empty of expensive wines.

That, of course, was only part of the story, for to raid consistently and indiscriminately, as he did, one must needs be ruthless to a degree, unprincipled, brutal, and without a shred of compassion. In these traits, no one surpassed Sir Joseph Moffat. His name inspired fear in men, his reputation for hard-dealing was legendary, and Ebony was afraid of what he was doing to his grandson. The only ones who had not feared him were Robbie and Meg and, perhaps, his nephew. Now Sir Joseph was immobilised, and Ebony had exchanged that fear for another kind, though of an equally ruthless nature.

She could have borne her incarceration at Castle Kells with a better grace if Sir Joseph had been less of a tyrant, living only for what he could get and who he could subdue to get it. His conduct was the opposite of that which she wanted Sam to emulate, yet keeping a six-year-old out of his grandparent's way was not easily done, even in a castle of this size, and the child had already begun to absorb the horror stories that Sir Joseph in his wisdom believed would make a man of him. He was never on hand to soothe away Sam's shrieks of terror at night, to take him hot possets and sleeping-draughts, or to show him the gentler intellectual skills. That, he said, was what the women were for.

There had been many times when she had longed to escape from Galloway, from Sir Joseph's crudeness, his swearing and unacceptable bad manners, his rough friends who overstayed their welcome. She had asked to be allowed to go, many times, and had been refused permission. Where would she go to? Sir Joseph had bellowed at her. Who indeed? Lady Jean Nevillestowe, her mother, had disappeared in the same year as Sir Joseph's wife, though her destination had been harder to place. Two years ago, Scottish reivers had broken into her beautiful home in Carlisle, terrorised her servants, stolen everything they could carry and abducted her, too. After which there had been conflicting accounts of Lady Jean's willingness or unwillingness to be abducted, though only the most ungenerous critic could blame her, an extremely attractive and wealthy widow. The fact that no ransom had been demanded for her release suggested that whoever was holding her had no intention of selling her back.

Ebony had worried constantly, but Sir Joseph would not allow her to take Sam to Carlisle, and she dared not go without him. Since 1317 she had had no word of her mother or her whereabouts, and the guilt of not being able to communicate weighed as much as death itself.

Pushing herself away from the cool draughts of night air, she closed the shutters at last, drawing her mind back to more immediate dangers. She had made constant enquiries about who these raiders could be, where they had come from, who had seen them arrive, but the wounded men knew nothing of any consequence apart from agreeing that they certainly knew what they were doing. More non-committal replies came from the household servants who seemed too relieved to venture any curses upon them. Her main concerns, however, were for Meg in a lonely vigil with only her maid and chaplain to aid her. Had she herself not been involved in this foolish talk of escapes, she would have been free to offer her comfort.

As she undressed, thoughts of the day's happenings jostled through her mind, reminding her of the shameful things she had hoped to suppress. She slipped her small dagger under her pillow and, so that she would be able to locate it accurately, she sent her hand several times to seek it in the dark, just in case.

Being deserted by both Biddie and Sam at the same time took some getting used to, and for a long time she lay exhausted but too concerned to sleep as she listened to Biddie's gentle snores, to the hoots of an owl and its mate. There were still nights when she longed for Robbie's arms, yet there was self-reproach too that her yearning ought to have endured longer, been more loyal, more specific. Lately, she had begun to question whether their loving had contained all the ingredients of a lasting passion, and why, if she craved his loving warmth, was she unable to recall the details of his body or remember how she felt at the moment of his release.

At first, he had been before her whether waking or sleeping, always gently adoring. More recently, her need for a man's arms and kisses was so strong that she could scarcely tell whether it was Robbie who called to her or whether it was her own body crying out to be reminded of what it was missing, some of which she had never experienced. No man had held her since her loss, except for today, nor had she wanted one to except in the deepest seclusion of the night when the vibrations came silently to overpower her with a craving that left her trembling, ashamed and weeping.

Her first half-sleep was broken and confused by a blur of remorseless questions without answers, most of them concerning a large and commanding figure that stalked into each jumbled scene, restraining her, taking her offer with a staggering self-assurance. It would mean no more to him than some light relief on his journey, a trophy to flaunt after a successful raid. But vague notions of what this threatened intimacy would mean to her were, in the darkness of her longings, not as clear-cut as she had made them sound at the time of her bargaining, and then there was little more than a token sign of those sacred memories of Robbie as they became alarmingly confused with indecent curiosity.

Barely inside the boundaries of sleep, a warmth spread comfortingly across her back. Was it Sam? Or Biddie? Or Robbie? His knees tucked beneath hers, curving her into his lap and cradling her into a deeper sleep. Later, she turned and felt her head being lifted gently to rest in the crook of his shoulder, pulled closer to his body, enfolded by his warm arms with her naked breasts against his chest, her hair lifted away, her forehead brushed by his lips. As it had so often done, her leg moved over to rest on top of his, and she heard her breathing change to the ragged gasps of craving that invariably left her desolate, alone, and whimpering in her sleep. This time, however, his comfort stayed with her until a peace came to replace the dream without waking her.

Chapter Three

As far as Brother Walter was concerned, it was
never too late to pray for a lost soul. His droning
continued until a discreet cough from Mistress Meg
Moffat brought his lengthy litany to an end and he
rose from his knees at the side of Sir Joseph's peaceful body, closing his book.

Meg gave him a moment to collect himself. 'I'd
better allow the men in to remove Sir Joseph to the
winter hall,' she said. 'They've been waiting for some
time, and we must start the day, brother.'

'Yes, of course, mistress. Let them come.'

The initial shock of Sir Joseph's death just after
midnight had left Meg bewildered with conflicting
thoughts of relief, guilt at her relief, and some trepidation about having the castle overrun by raiders at
this most inconvenient time. Grief was no doubt
somewhere on her list, but so far she had not come
across it, and Janet's sobbing was too soon for Meg's
liking. 'Do stop it, Janet,' she said. 'I know you're
overwrought, but Sir Joseph would not have recovered, you know. Brother Walter warned us of that.
He's at peace now, and so are we.'

Dame Janet sniffed, blinking at the stark truth. She was well padded, white-haired, and wearing a white wimple like a clothes-line in a high wind and a woe-begone expression that reflected a deep sensitivity rather than a general misery. Much of her shyness stemmed from being a middle-aged, physically unattractive spinster in a household of males, the head of whom had delighted in making her the butt of his jests.

Meg would have nothing to do with forced emotions. She flung her long mane of chestnut hair behind her and signalled to the men to come in, the steward, the reeve, the chamberlain, and Sir Joseph's elderly valet, all of them strong enough to bear a corner each of the makeshift stretcher.

'My condolences, Mistress Meg,' the tall stately chamberlain said. 'We'll tak care o'thengs, dinna ye fash yersel. Leave him tae us.'

'Yes, Master Morner, I will, thank you. I don't know what will happen now. Those men are supposed to be leaving today. Did they get whatever it was they came for?'

'Weel, they're combing through the cellars already. I had to gi' 'em the keys. Yesterday they went through the stables like watter through a spoot. He'd not be best pleased if he knew, wouldn't Sir Joseph.'

'Then it's just as well he doesn't, Master Morner. Still, what *are* they after? Lady Ebony tells me they're looking for information.'

'There's enough stuff in the cellars to keep 'em happy for a year or so, but they'll need more pack-ponies than we've got to carry it all away wi' 'em. I expect they'll ask us aboot the trading Sir Joseph does.'

'Is that what they've come for, d'ye think?'

'I wouldna be surprised, mistress.' He took a corner of the stretcher and, with a mighty heave, hauled the large body off the table, manoeuvring him away with grunted directions through the door.

Balefully, Dame Janet watched him go. 'Shall I go and tell Lady Ebony?' she said.

'I believe Sir Alex went up to give her the news just after Father went last night,' Meg said. 'Poor Ebony. Out of the frying pan and into the fire.'

'Into the fire, mistress? How?'

'Well, if they *do* go today, she's supposed to be going too. They want to take Sam, you see.'

Dame Janet's shock was overlooked as a figure from the doorway called an order to the men he had passed in the passageway, and then came further into the room, looking about him with distaste. 'So this is where you've been holed up, is it? My sympathies, Mistress Moffat.'

'Who're you?' Meg looked him up and down, not pleased by a tone that held so little of the sympathy he was offering.

His face pleased her even less, his eyes merrily holding her stare as if he could have asked for nothing better than an argument with her. And when her gesture drew Dame Janet back to her side, she saw how in one glance he was appraising her as he would some special merchandise on offer at a good price. 'Of course, we've not actually met, have we? Hugh of Leyland, mistress. Sir Alex Somers's right-hand man. I'm here to offer my help.'

Meg picked up her skirts and took a step towards the door. 'Come, Janet. I'm in no frame of mind for silly small talk, and there's much to be done. Since when did reivers offer help, for heaven's sake? I've scarce heard anything so ridiculous. They spend all day putting the fear of God into everyone, they take the garrison off to heaven-knows-where, they blunder through the castle storerooms and then we hear that they're about to help.' She almost shrieked the word as she tried to march past him, but he caught her arm and held her back, causing a furious whirlwind of retaliation that made him duck and think again how to detain her.

Dame Janet remonstrated. 'Sir! You've done enough damage here!'

'Shut up, Janet!' Meg snapped. 'This oaf couldn't damage a caged parrot. Keep out of my steward's office, you great lout! There's nothing in here *you* could want. He doesn't keep money in here.'

'Problems already, Hugh?' Sir Alex flattened himself against the doorframe as Meg stalked past him with her chestnut hair swinging down her back. Dame Janet's affronted glare would have soured the milk.

'Whew!' said Hugh. 'Good thing I ducked. Why don't they attack you?'

'Because I don't grab at them. They tend not to like it.'

'Then I should hoist her over my shoulder. Is that the idea?'

'As a last resort.' Sir Alex smiled at the jibe and cast an eye over the room's disarray. There were bowls of reddened water and cloths, pots of salves, a flask of stale brown urine, bloodied bandages, piles of linen and an empty trestle-table ruckled with soiled sheeting. From between the grubby fold of linen, he lifted a strand of black leather upon which hung a small silver key. 'And what might this be about?' he said, holding it up. 'It's been cut from round his neck, by the look o' things, so now we have the job of finding out what it unlocks.' He slipped the key and its thong into his pouch.

'Which may take a few days. Is that what you're thinking?'

'Things have changed with the old man's death, Hugh. There's no reason now why we shouldn't stay till we've found what we're after, especially since we'll get nothing out of him. The hostage threat hardly applies now, does it? Though I've a mind to make it sound as if it's still a possibility. See what I mean?'

'I'll go along with whatever you decide. If you want to hold on to that as a warning in case of trouble, then go ahead. I'll back you… With those two we'll need all the ammunition we can find.'

'Good. Staying on in the owner's place may be a bit unorthodox, but we can easily defend ourselves here, if need be.'

'There'll have to be a funeral, Alex. His cronies will come, and I don't suppose they'll be the cream of society.'

'All the more reason for us to stay a while. Think of those two beauties playing hostess to Moffat's pals, will ye? Doesn't bear thinking about.'

'But ye ken the rules aboot castles and women, Alex. No castle can be held by a woman without her man. She has to be out in a day or two and away to her dower-hoos.'

'That's true enough, especially when there's so much raiding about. So, if we're not entirely wel- come, that rule will be enough to grant us extra time. As long as we're here to protect them, I can see us having time to do our duty to the king on two fronts. Defend the castle *and* find proof of what he suspects.'

'Guid. So I'll tell the men before they start saddling up, shall I?'

'Yes, Hugh. Do that. Then organise the garrison hall. I want this place better organised and prepared for some outside opposition. The odds are shortening. Make a start while I go and tell the new laird's mother. She was asleep last night when I went up.'

Hugh's eyebrows lifted in amusement. 'Now *there*'s a thing. The wee lad will be in his ma's wardship now, won't he? So we can expect a fair few interested parties flocking around to marry the mother and get their hands on the castle and whatever else they can before young Sam comes of age.'

'More than likely, Hugh.'

'And where do you stand in all this, my fine friend?'

'Right at the front.'

'No! Is that so?' Hugh grinned. 'As close as that?'

'Even closer.' He gave Hugh a friendly shove. 'Get going, will you?'

Hugh halted in the doorway. 'Just one more thing. When do we tell them what our business is?'

Leaning his bottom on the table, Alex folded his arms and looked down at them critically. 'I doubt we can keep it from them much longer. They've already noted the differences and by the end of today there'll be too many to hide. Reivers don't make a habit of organising their victims' funerals, do they? Or being present at them. Well, not formally. I'll have to break the news to Lady Ebony very soon. I'll let you tell Mistress Meg.'

'Thank you. Can I borrow your chain-mail?'

'No, I shall need it myself.' Smiling, they headed for the great hall which, for some reason, was apparently known as the summer hall.

Sitting on the edge of her bed, Lady Ebony listened with only half her attention to Sam and Biddie's chatter, the other half riveted upon the upturned pillow beneath which her dagger still lay. Goose bumps had risen along her arms, causing her breath to forget itself and her mind to try to untangle facts from impressions that refused to disappear. The part of the bed next to where she lay *had* been warmer than usual. The pillow *had* shown a distinct dent in it next to hers. The dirk *was* upside-down under the pillow, not as she had placed it; she had almost cut her hand seeking the hilt. She *had* experienced the most vivid dream yet of Robbie's body next to hers, his arms wrapping her, his lips on her forehead. Uncannily, awesomely vivid. She glanced down at her thighs; she had pressed them against his, overlapping him. The feel of his skin, hairy and warm, still tingled. 'God in heaven!' she whispered.

'What, Mama? Are you saying your prayers?' Sam bounced over to her, hobbled round his ankles by his long braies. 'Look, you've still got the May-blossom up there. Shall we be taking it with us?'

Aghast, she looked round the half-drawn bedcurtain to see that the branch of white hawthorn she had removed earlier was back where it had been before. 'Did you put this back up here, Biddie?' she asked.

Biddie pulled Sam's braies up, tucking the shirt inside. 'Time you were doing this yourself, young man. What? May-blossom? Nay, it was on the stool last night. Must have done it yourself without thinking, mistress.'

Ebony knew that she had not. Her scalp prickled, sending thoughts scattering and refusing to settle on the too-awful truth, imposing a ban of silence on the incriminating evidence that might reveal how her dream was not a dream at all. No, she would not—could not—admit that her body had betrayed her by wanting him. She did *not* want him, unless he was Robbie.

She was still tying an old black ribbon around her thick black plait when the door was noisily unlocked. As before, knock and opening came together.

'Sir Alex,' Biddie said, 'my lady has not yet finished her toilette.'

Sam, marginally more welcoming, saw no harm in a gentle contradiction, which he was lately getting the hang of. 'She's only plaiting her hair,' he said, 'but she doesn't allow men in her chamber, sir, except Master Morner the chamberlain. May I ask your business?'

Resisting the smile that would have offended, Sir Alex stood gravely to attention. 'My pardon, Laird of Kells,' he said. 'My business is quite urgent or I'd never have interrupted a lady's privacy. May I speak with Lady Ebony?'

'That's my grandfather's title, not mine,' he said, pleased to be able to correct an adult on so many points.

'Yes, that's what I've come to speak about. May I?'

Biddie took Sam by the hand to draw him away before he became addicted. 'Come,' she said, 'in here.' She took him into the garderobe.

'Laird of Kells?' Ebony said, quietly. 'You have…news…do you?' She stood by the bed, sheathing the dirk that had been the cause of her consternation. 'Is it Sir Joseph?' He looked, she thought, particularly pleased with himself, as if remembering that a smile would be extremely bad form.

'I'm sorry, my lady. He died soon after midnight.'

Another shock. She had not quite expected it. Her hand flew to her midriff and pressed against the faded rose-madder kirtle that was not yet laced down the side. 'Last *night*?' she whispered. 'And you have only just come to tell me…at *dawn*? Did it not occur to you that Mistress Moffat might have needed my comfort, or that I should have been there? *With* her?'

'Yes, it did.' His glance fell upon the bed, then back to her face. 'You were asleep.'

The implication of what he was telling her, even at a time like this, was impossible to disregard, and during the long silence loaded with unspoken accusations and admissions, Ebony resolved that neither on this occasion nor on any other would she give him the satisfaction of admitting that she knew what he also knew. Had there not been another more urgent subject claiming their attention, she might have given way to the urge to examine more closely the bronzed throat that showed at his open shirt-neck, the muscular forearms and wrists below rolled-up sleeves. But no, it was safer to deny that it could ever have happened. To do otherwise would be the first step to disaster.

'I was locked in!' she snapped. 'I only hope Mistress Moffat will be able to forgive my appalling lack of compassion. Perhaps in future—'

'In future, lady,' he interrupted, brusquely, 'there will be different sleeping arrangements, so the need will not arise. Now, if you wish it, I will escort you downstairs to see Mistress Moffat and Sir Joseph, too, later on. He's being laid out in the winter hall. You may wish Master Sam to see him there.'

Her slim dark brows drew together like curlicues. 'Just a minute. Different sleeping arrangements? You are talking about today's journey, I take it?'

'Not exactly. I'm talking about Castle Kells, my lady. We have decided to stay here a while, now that Sir Joseph is no longer here to defend it.' He was quick to explain, as her hostility gave way to disbelief. 'Otherwise you and your household would be obliged to move out immediately. The king doesn't allow his castles to remain undefended, not for more than one day. I'm sure you're already aware of that, as Mistress Moffat will be.'

She was not. The problem of defence had never been discussed. Sir Joseph had believed himself to be immortal. Move out, or have these brigands stay? Something here was not making sense. Reivers never stayed. They damaged, thieved, destroyed and killed, and then they ran, hiding their tracks and their identity for as long as they could.

'No!' she said with a quick glance at the garderobe curtain. 'No, you cannot stay here. You *must* not!' Already her fears were racing ahead, preparing her for what might happen, for what he had assured her *would* happen. Last night he had shown her how easy it would be, but to pay the full price here at Castle Kells she would have to deceive Meg, as well as Biddie and Sam, and that was asking yet more of her, more than she had offered in the first place.

'Why must we not, my lady?' he said, keeping his voice low, as she did. 'You think there's a danger we

may eventually be accepted, our presence…
enjoyed…perhaps?'

'Quite the opposite. I think, sir, that you may find
how two seemingly helpless women guarding one
helpless child may be too uncomfortable for you and
your rabble. I don't know who you pretend to be,
but—' Her breath ran out before she had finished, and
she could have cried with relief as the door opened
and Meg entered, breathless for quite a different reason. They ran to each other, clinging and rocking as
if they had been parted for a year instead of a night,
a night in which the world had changed for each of
them in the most primeval manner imaginable.

Biddie and Sam joined them while the audience of
one, feeling that his presence was redundant, left the
room with the same practised silence he had used
after midnight, his departure too late not to hear
Meg's plaintive cry, 'Ebbie…Ebbie! What's happening to us?'

No matter what crisis might threaten to disrupt the
daily routine of the castle, there were men whose duty
it was to maintain a constant order in the household,
outside on the estate, and all places in between. Sir
Joseph had never kept a large number of retainers; he
was too mean for that. Of the thirty or so men who
had served on guard duty, most were now halfway to
Dumfries, the few wounded under lock and key. His
household servants were under the direct control of
the steward, while the estate steward, the bailiff and
the reeve managed the laird's properties, including the
castle and the village beyond. While he was alive, Sir
Joseph had dealt personally with the various officials:
now this duty must be taken over by Meg and Ebony

between them, for only they could decide how to proceed with the domestic arrangements. It was not new to them.

Ebony's spontaneous objection to having Sir Alex's unwelcome army of almost a hundred men at loose in the castle was revised as soon as its full impact was perceived. For one thing, any delay in their departure would hopefully lessen the threat to both Sam and herself, and even a short delay was better than none at all. Moreover, their departure would mean that poor Meg would have to make shift for herself, forfeit the castle, and set up with Dame Janet and a handful of servants in one of Sir Joseph's remote and uncomfortable properties where the cellars would be nowhere near as well stocked as those at Castle Kells and where her protection would be inadequate. This year might well be the last of the famine years, God willing, but nothing in Scotland was yet back to normal, and Ebony was instantly aware of her own selfishness in thinking first of her dilemma when Meg's predicament would be life-threatening. Suddenly, there was a need for protection.

As she suspected, Meg was only vaguely aware of the rule about the defence of castles; she had never given it much thought. Nor had Sir Joseph made provisions for the event, since he had expected Meg to be married as soon as he could find a wealthy man with more than usual courage to want to call him father-in-law. Not surprisingly, such men were not so thick on the ground, and others who had presented themselves had got short shrift from Meg, whose determination regarding such matters was every bit as great as her father's.

'Then we have little choice, Ebbie,' said Meg. 'Do

we? I don't like this situation at all, but nor do I like the idea of packing my bits and pieces on to a pack-pony and trudging up to some remote croft up the glen. I know my father has several manors here and there, but we've never upped and moved around several times a year as the English do, have we? I think he found it safer to stay put, and we've got to do the same, for Sam's sake as well as our own. Besides, I'll be damned if I'll allow those ruffians to drive us out. Not that we're being given much of a choice,' she added in an undertone. 'Arrogant hooligans!'

Used to Meg's deceptive toughness, Ebony found some comfort in having that decision made for her. In the past, Meg had been her rock, a sister in every sense and far more resilient than her slight frame and delicately freckled features would suggest. Her nut-brown daintiness and gemstone eyes might have lured men into her orbit, but her tongue was as sharp as her dirk, her hand like the flash of a trout, and no man except her brother had held her thoughts for longer than the passing of a butterfly. Capable Meg; shocked by her father's sudden abandonment, but thinking that it was typical of the man to give them so little warning.

'Be sure to claim his signet ring, Meggie, won't you?' Ebony said, sliding a hand through Sam's hair. Standing between her knees, he clung to her, pensive, and suddenly very still.

'I've taken it already,' said Meg. 'It's in my pouch. Here you are. You must have it and keep it safe for Sam. We don't want anyone else putting his seal on things.'

Ebony took it and placed it in the pouch at her

girdle. 'He'd have been hunting on a morning like this, Meg,' she said.

'He would, and we'd have had the hall full of roaring stone-drunk men all night long, too. We're going to change things here, Ebbie. And the first thing I'm going to do is— Oh, dear!'

'What is it?'

'I'm forgetting. You're the mistress here, not me. As the young laird's guardian, it's for you to decide any changes.'

'We'll make joint decisions, Meg. Any changes will be made together. Now, shall we go down and see what's to be done? There's a funeral to arrange, for one.'

The young Laird of Kells spoke softly from her breast. 'I can hear your heart beating, Mama. Does that mean you're alive?'

'Yes, my wee lad. It does. Go and listen to Aunt Meg's and see if she is, too.'

He did, and she was.

The newest turn of events, however, placed a strain on both women, not least because of its uncertainty, and it occurred to both of them at intervals throughout the day that the only constant theme was change itself. Plans could only be short term; orders for provisions and accommodation had to be multiplied; commands issued by Meg and Ebony had to bypass new ones issued by Sir Alex or Master Hugh; men told to do this were taken off to do something else, and when Sam was needed for his usual hour's rest he was nowhere to be found, nor was Biddie. Livid with anger, Ebony went to find him.

There was a wide patch of ground at the far end of

the rambling castle wall that the men used for jousting
and sword-practice. It had been levelled and fenced
off, and had probably seen more young squires learning to ride than six-year-olds. Ebony's anger was not
lessened by the absence of Biddie, by the presence of
Joshua and two assistants, and by Sir Alex himself.
In fact, she saw their involvement with her property
as a personal affront to her authority and would have
said so there and then but for the danger of distracting
Sam's attention. Naturally, she felt that the pony, one
of Sir Joseph's pure-bred Galloways, was too big for
him.

Sam's performance in the saddle, or lack of it, was
all that she could have predicted, had she been consulted, his enthusiasm and pluck being an inadequate
defence against slithering sideways into the turf as the
pony's gait quickened. Her natural reaction was to
rush to him, but her attempt to dive under the fence
was prevented by Sir Alex's arm that came like a tree-
trunk across her, hauling her back. She pushed against
him, twisting furiously, but Sam was up on his feet
and ready for the next undignified tussle before the
restraint was lowered.

'Let me go to him!' she snarled.

'No! Stay out of the way. Stirrups, lad!' he yelled
at Sam.

Ebony winced as the child lurched and bounced yet
again, far more pained than he at the demands they
were making of him, and for his limitations about
which she knew more than these men. 'That's
enough!' she said. 'He's tired. He's had enough now.'

'Leave him. They know what they're doing.'

'They *don't*!'

'Look at him. Look at his face. He's loving it.'

Sam was grinning from ear to ear, his back like a ramrod as he listened to Master Joshua's instructions. 'Hands together. Sit down properly!'

'I am…am doing,' he panted.

'You're not doing. Sit up straight. Don't pull or he'll stop.'

'Yes…yes!'

'And keep your mouth shut. Speak with your hands and heels.'

He stayed in the saddle, dizzy with success, adoring Joshua and completely oblivious to his mother's anxiety. 'I did it!' he yelled, seeing her at last. 'I can do it, can't I, Master Joshua?'

'Bit more practice and we'll get there,' said Josh. 'But don't think you've finished, young man. You have to groom him now. Come on. A good rider looks after his mount.' Winking knowingly at Ebony, he led the pony and rider away towards the stables.

Ebony still had reservations. 'He's getting over-tired,' she said, rounding on Sir Alex. 'And what makes you think it's appropriate to be doing this when his grandfather has just died? Is this the way to teach a child respect?'

The practice ground was deserted, but the angle between the wall and the castle tower provided greater privacy and, without answering her directly, he trapped her arm against his body and drew her, none too gently, into the seclusion of the corner. The wall was at her back, her feet unbalanced, her hands holding him at a distance; her attack turned all at once to defence.

This was not what she had come here for. Once more, her child had been taken beyond her control, nor was his enjoyment at issue. With the best of intentions, she had given this man an inch and he believed he could take a yard, and he had better be stopped before he assumed control of her, too. She fought him with a fury that reflected her desperation at the trap from which escape seemed increasingly impossible.

Her hand almost reached the dagger, but not quite. She bit at his hand, but only succeeded in grazing his knuckle with her teeth. She tried to knee him but he was ready for that, sidestepping into the space between her legs. She saw red. Squealing with rage, and with a violent twist of her body, she bent like a tensioned bow to release herself from his arms. Unable to swing her hand back, she raked at him with her nails and felt the terrible contact of the skin on his neck before her wrist was caught again. Her other hand caused similar damage to his cheek before it was twisted cruelly behind her, putting an end to her brief but violent retaliation.

Before she could avoid him he took possession of her mouth with his own, this time with no softening from either of them as her lips were forced apart to take his invasion. Devising every resistance against his authority, she was still powerless against him, held by her thick plait and the scruff of her neck, made to wait upon his mastery.

Her legs were unprepared for the suddenness of release and, rather than fall, she clung to his sleeve while holding a hand to her mouth, her tears of helpless anger betraying the hurt.

'That, my lady, was a reward,' he said, hoarsely. 'In case you were wondering.'

'For what?' she croaked.

'For protecting your child from danger, even though there was none.'

Her reply scalded him with its contempt. 'I don't *need* a reward for that, you great patronising dolt. It comes as part of motherhood. Rabbits do it. Birds, bitches, even whores do it. Women who sell themselves. Now leave me *alone*!'

'I shall not leave you alone. You know I shall not.' He hesitated, then strode away with a hand to his cheek and not a backward glance.

Round the corner of the armourer's workshop he collided heavily with Hugh of Leyland, who grasped him by the shoulders to steady him, looking closely at the parallel lines of blood on his friend's face and neck. 'Ah! Sent you packing, did she, lad?' he chuckled.

His laugh was cut short with startling speed when he found himself flat on his back on the cobbled yard, holding on to his jaw as though it might fall off. 'What?' he squeaked. 'You gave me permission to laugh when—'

'Well, I've changed my bloody mind!' Sir Alex yelled at him, stalking away. 'And why is there no supper ready? Are we all supposed to be fasting today?'

There was no question of the two factions eating supper together, for although duties must be attended to, a certain restraint must be observed, with Sir Joseph laid out not fifty yards away. Besides, they were enemies.

Anxious to conceal from Meg the effects of her violent clash with their leader, Ebony attempted a positive demeanour as she supervised their private meal of rabbit and mushrooms, cold roast venison and young nettles, boiled. There were hot griddle-cakes with honey, Sam's favourite, but the chastened Biddie had to feed him the last few mouthfuls with his eyes half-closed.

'You see,' Ebony said, 'he's absolutely all-in. I knew he would be. Hours of daylight left and he'll sleep until well before cock-crow and then wake us all up. With a wee rest this afternoon, he could have gone to bed later and slept till a decent time. He'll not do this tomorrow, mind you.'

'The answer is,' said Meg, licking her sticky fingers, 'to let Biddie and Sam sleep by themselves.'

'Not in a separate room,' Ebony said. 'I need him with me in case he has nightmares.'

'Did he have one last night?'

'No.'

'Well, then.' Meg wiped her fingers on the napkin. 'I think you could give it a try and see what happens. You need your sleep as much as he does.' She laid a hand over Ebony's, noting the strain of the last two days in her eyes. 'Come on, love. He's getting to be a big lad. We don't need to be squashed up like rabbits in a place this size, and we don't have to ask Father's permission to breathe, now.'

Biddie agreed, having been kicked out of bed two nights ago. Taking Sam up in her arms, she placed him on Ebony's knees. 'If you hold him a while, I'll go and make that bed up for us in the tower room below yours. It's wider than the truckle-bed we had last night, and you know he's always wanted to sleep in there where the windows look out on to the courtyard.'

'What if he wakes and needs me?'

'If he needs you, he can come up to you, can't he?'

The battle had been half-lost already, and Sam was growing up. There was little point in denying it. 'We'll give it a try,' she said.

'Now,' said Meg as soon as Biddie had gone, 'we have to get another problem sorted out before tomorrow.' She leaned her arms on the table and wiped up a shining dome of honey with a finger. 'Those men are *not* reivers, Ebbie. They're here on some other business and we have to find out what it is. Now. Tonight.'

Ebony hitched Sam further on to her knees and adjusted his sleeping head on her arm. 'I know,' she said. 'It's what I've been thinking all day. Reivers don't bother to teach their victims' children how to ride, for one thing, nor do they ever want to hang about in time for a funeral. They'd be identified.'

'And I don't know any family of the name of Somers. Or Leyland.'

'Leyland is down in Lancashire, but this man's a Lowlander.'

'There's something strange going on, Ebbie. We have to find out who they're working for and what they're after. They've been all through the stables, and they've had men in the pastures herding the Galloways up.'

'What for?'

'That's something else we need to know.'

The Galloways were Sir Joseph's pride. The pure-bred ponies were ideal as both mounts and pack-horses, sure-footed and hardy, very fast and possessed of remarkable stamina. Out in all weathers, they could feed on heather as well as rough pasture; they were dark brown against the rock-strewn hillsides and invisible at night. The Laird of Kells had bred them from his grandsire's herd, eventually owning the largest in the Lowlands of Scotland. Men had tried to steal rather than to buy them and, to Meg and Ebony, the matter seemed clear.

'Horse thieves,' Ebony said. 'They have to be. But what's this information they're after?'

'It's a ruse. I don't believe it. My father sells the Galloways to King Robert for the Scots to use in battle. That's what's made him wealthy. If they take our herd, we're done.'

'But what's to prevent them from giving us some cock-and-bull story about what they're up to? They can admit that they're not reivers and then tell us anything they like. How do we check if it's true? Those two are glib enough to lure a badger out, Meg, and twice as clever as a dog-fox.'

'There are two of us, don't forget, and we're equally as bright, though they'll not have worked that out yet. If we can see through them at this stage, then we can choose what else to believe, can't we? Come on. Here's Biddie. Let's go and arrange that interview, Eb.'

It was not as difficult as they had imagined, Master Hugh of Leyland being alone and near enough to the auditor's office to be herded like a startled bullock into a holding-pen. His first reaction was of a natural delight at being the object of their joint attention until a second look at their determined and decidedly chilly expressions brought his smile to a standstill, then to a retreat. 'Ladies,' he said, backing into the chequered counting-board, 'how may I assist you?'

'The truth will do, for a start,' said Ebony. 'But

don't bother to embroider it, if you please. We are
both accomplished needlewomen and we know how
to unpick what we don't like. Even in the gloaming.'

'The truth…about what?'

The room looked out over the inner courtyard
through a row of square-topped windows against
which a table was piled with ledgers, strong-boxes,
rolls of parchment, bags of coins, ink-horns and
quills; the green and black counting-board held tally-
sticks ready for the next reckoning-day. The two
women stood with their backs to the door, their hands
held threateningly near the dirks at their waists. Hugh
could hardly have missed their intentional animosity.

'The truth about your business, sir. What is it, exactly?' said Meg, icily.

To their amazement, he did not prevaricate. 'We
are on the king's business,' he said. 'We had every
intention of making that clear to you.'

'How thoughtful,' said Ebony. 'After a certain pe-
riod of misunderstanding and chaos, of course. Which
king?'

Hugh's face readjusted itself as he realised his
omission. 'Why, the Scottish king, Robert Bruce,' he
said. 'Surely you didn't think—?'

'Oh, no,' Meg snapped, 'we don't do too much of
that. Women, you see. We leave the clever stuff to
the men. Now, speak slowly and clearly, Master Leyland, and tell us why you had to beat your way into
my father's castle at the very moment of his return.
Don't tell us that it was the best time to take him by
surprise; we can work that out for ourselves. Just tell
us why you couldn't have knocked on the door and
asked politely for entry. Being on the *king's business*.'

They might have interpreted his slight grimace as a silent release of pent-up breath before he spoke, but neither of them could have known of his struggle to keep his mind away from Meg's delectable form, her electrifying eyes, that hair. 'Because, mistress, an element of surprise was essential to the success of our mission. Had Sir Joseph been expecting us, he would have taken the obvious steps to conceal what we are looking for. Or to evade us altogether. Or kill us.'

'And what *are* you looking for?' said Ebony. 'His herd of Galloways? You could have seen those as you came through the village.'

'You think we're thieves. That's natural, I suppose.'

'Answer the question, sir!' she snapped.

Hugh debated which of them was fiercest, the mother or the redhead. 'We're here to discover for the king by what means Sir Joseph sells his ponies to both the English cavalry *and* the Scots, and whether,' he went on quickly as their faces blanched, 'it is true that the horses he steals during his raids are then sold on to whoever pays the highest price, from either side. Serious crimes, ladies.'

The brief silence, as he expected, was merely the calm before the storm, but it was Sir Joseph's daughter who sprang to her lawless father's defence like a she-wolf. 'How…how *dare* you? How dare you break your way in here at this time and accuse my father of being a traitor to his country? *Get out!* And before you leave this place once and for all, sir, put your whiter-than-white money down *there*—' she stabbed a finger on to the chequered board '—and pay me for the food you and your rabble have eaten during your stay. Your story *stinks*, as you do.' The whiteness of her skin held spots of red on each cheek, and her hand trembled over the hilt of her dirk.

Ebony took the hand and held it tightly. 'Don't,' she whispered, knowing what Meg was capable of. 'Let me.'

'You asked for the truth,' said Hugh of Leyland.

Ebony was in a better position than Meg to hear it. 'Before you insult my sister and me with any more of this blather, sir, we want to see your proof. Show me the king's writ.'

Master Leyland's chin went up a notch as he directed a look towards the doorway. 'Over to you, my friend,' he said, quietly.

Sir Alex pushed his shoulder off the stone arch and came further into the room, closing the door behind him, one hand already undoing the laces of his pouch, lifting the flap. He drew out a folded piece of parchment that had seen better days and unfolded it with care, presenting it to Meg. It was written in Latin, the language of officialdom.

Meg handed it to Ebony, who read: 'To whom it may concern, I by the Grace of God, Robert Bruce, King of Scotland, do hereby endow Alex Somers, knight, and Hugh of Leyland, gentleman, with my authority to be about my business in enquiring, apprehending and bringing to justice all those who oppose my sovereignty, controls and laws. And I further state that any demands made by these my servants and officers of the Crown in the furtherance of their duty shall be met without hindrance from all loyal citizens of Scotland. This permit is issued on the seventh day of August in the Year of Our Lord, thirteen hundred and ten.'

Slowly, she lowered the grubby parchment in time

to catch the twitch of an eyebrow from across the room. Clearly, they had not expected her to be able to read and translate so fluently, but nor had she thought to see such a document in the possession of men she had believed to be reivers. She felt Sir Alex's eyes upon her, blue and intensely aware, and she knew he must have heard every word of the previous conversation. What was more, Hugh of Leyland must have known he was there, and yet not by one flicker of an eyelid had he given him away.

Any satisfaction Ebony had felt at being correct in her suspicions was negated by her seething fury at what it implied, at her foolish unnecessary bargain, their threats and duplicity. It was unforgivable. 'If you are indeed the King of Scotland's most trusted officers,' she said as if addressing a couple of slime-covered rodents, 'then I pray we may never have the misfortune to meet with his worst specimens. I cannot believe his Grace would approve of your disgraceful underhand methods.'

'We use whatever methods are appropriate, my lady,' Sir Alex said, straight faced, the red lines scored like ink upon his cheek. 'But there was nothing underhand here. As Hugh has told you, we would have been resisted. Sir Joseph knew of the king's suspicions for some time and chose to disregard them. He knew it was only a matter of time before—'

'Not *underhand*?' Ebony yelped. 'Telling us you were reivers, taking our men, tearing the place apart and throwing it into chaos, and Sir Joseph dying of his wounds in the middle of your rampaging? Not underhand? What *was* it, then?'

'No one told you we were reivers, my lady.'

'No, they didn't, did they? Reivers don't usually announce themselves. But you said—'

'No, I didn't! Think. *You* insisted that we were, and no one bothered to contradict you.'

Meg took Ebony's part. 'Oh, come, sir,' she said, harshly. 'You fully intended to give us all that impression, and you know it. Look at your men, armed to the teeth and clothed like raiders. Not riding ponies like reivers, I grant you, but not blazoning the king's livery either, are you?'

'We wear the king's badges, mistress, but we conceal them when need be. The facts are that we used the occasion of Sir Joseph's return to gain access, and it would have made no difference whether he'd been whole, wounded, or dead. There are times when we cannot be too nice about these details and, whether you choose to believe what Hugh has told you or not, this is the truth. Sir Joseph *has* been selling his valuable Galloways to the English, and stolen horses too. And that, Mistress Moffat, is a treasonable offence for which he cannot now pay with his life. However, no man works alone in these matters, and we need to know who else is involved in his buying-and-selling network. That is what we are here to discover by whatever means it takes. We also need to know which are the stolen horses, who they belong to and, if possible, return them.' He used the stunned silence to add, 'Some of them, you see, belong to abbeys in both Scotland and England. Sir Joseph was not too particular about their provenance as long as they were the best.'

This was too much for Meg, whose eyes held rows of pearls along her lashes that caught the light before they dropped on to the fur edge of her surcoat.

'No...*no!*' she croaked. 'Not today of all days. I cannot...*won't* believe it! He was not a traitor. You cannot prove it.' She fell sobbing into Ebony's arms, unable to accept that the crimes about which she already knew, the raiding and thieving, could be compounded further. His reiving was bad enough, but to aid the enemy was unthinkable. Surely they must be mistaken.

Hating both men, Ebony forced the interview on, determined to make them admit their disgraceful part in the misunderstanding. 'My sister knows her father better than you do, sir,' she said over Meg's shoulder, 'and you have a lot to answer for, forcing your way in here at such a time. You even threatened to take hostages, and now I suppose you will tell us that *that* was a detail you cannot be too nice about.'

Hugh of Leyland had been primed to answer this, though he knew nothing of the real reason. 'That was no idle threat, my lady. It is common enough for the king's men to require hostages against good behaviour, or even to hold them in exchange for information. Whether we stay or leave, the young Laird of Kells will be safe in our hands for the time, but his fate will depend on your co-operation in helping us to find what we're looking for.'

A weaker man would have been temporarily paralysed by the glare that burned in Ebony's eyes around the granite hardness. 'And you had better know, sir, that if you so much as touch a hair of the young laird's head, you will be keeping Sir Joseph closer company than you intended. And that is no idle threat, either. As for *you*, sir...' she turned to Sir Alex, seething hatred from every pore '...you are *despicable!* Do what you have to do and then go. We can manage one more funeral between us, and we can defend the castle alone for as long as need be, despite what you say. Come, Meggie. To spend another moment in such company will turn our stomachs at this time of night.'

'You'd rather we had been reivers, my lady?' said Sir Alex, opening the door.

Ebony turned Meg towards the passageway, supporting her. 'I'd rather you were *gone*, sir. Tonight would not be soon enough.'

Chapter Four

The room at the top of the wooden stairs, recently occupied by Sir Joseph Moffat, was a disgrace. Master Morner, the chamberlain, had never been able to persuade his difficult master against keeping his favourite falcons in there or allowing his hounds to sleep on the bed. Four of them, all as large as heifers.

'This is…disgusting,' said Meg, wrinkling her nose. She had not been in the room since her mother had died. Her tears had dried in the heat of her anger, the latter emotion being more to her taste than weeping, though the revelations of the past hour had shaken her as much as her father's death. As the shocks crowded upon her, one after the other, she turned to Ebony for comfort. 'They've been in here too,' she said, speaking of Sir Alex's men. 'While a man lies dying, they're poking into his strong-boxes and chest. Just look at this mess.'

Parchment rolls and pieces of armour, helmets and discarded clothing were scattered everywhere, but Ebony found it hard not to suspect that the general shabbiness of the solar was of more than two days' making. The falcons and hounds had been removed, but the bedhangings and smelly fur bedcovers were fit only for a bonfire. Now was not the time to say so. She took Meg's hand, holding back her own highly personal reaction to the men's sudden change of identity which, in a way, was worse than her first frenzied assumption.

There was little that she would have disbelieved about her father-in-law's activities, though treason would have been uncharacteristic of a man who proclaimed his Scottishness almost hourly. 'It can't be true,' she said, gently. 'He'd never have put any of us in such danger. I know it.' Hand in hand, they walked over to the window that, like Sam and Biddie's new tower room, overlooked the courtyard as well as the loch. 'I don't have this view,' she said. 'I suppose he didn't want me to see what he was bringing back from his raids.'

'So, with their so-called evidence, the result will be the same as if my father had lived, won't it? He'd have been arrested and imprisoned, and then executed for aiding the enemy, and they'd replace us with men able to defend the castle and provide the king with fighting men. Either way, we can't stay.'

'In theory, Meg. But Sir Joseph has connections, doesn't he? Influential friends. They'd come to our aid, surely? Would they speak up for him?'

'Those who aren't involved, too. Like Sir Alex said, people don't work alone at that kind of thing, do they? Does the king forgive traitors?'

'It does happen. Neither King Edward of England nor Robert of Scotland has so many castles and stalwart men to defend them that either can afford to eliminate anyone who steps out of line occasionally.

Sometimes they're fined and then reinstated. After new promises of loyalty, of course.'

'How do you know all that?'

'Robbie told me.'

'But as things stand, we're in a difficult position, aren't we?'

'Very. Unless we can get Sir Joseph's friends to help us out.' The idea did not appeal to her any more than it did to Meg.

'Huh! You know what kind of help they'd offer us first, don't you? We'll be pestered again to marry into their families, especially you, as Sam's guardian.'

'So the alternative is for us to prove that your father was loyal. He may well have broken every other law, Meg, but surely not that. There must be someone who'd speak up for him.'

'Davy would. He's always been in Father's confidence. They've worked closely together for years. He'd help.'

'Unless he's involved, too.'

'Nonsense, love. Davy doesn't go reiving. He's in the wine business. He'd not know a Galloway from a donkey.'

Ebony smiled at the sarcasm. 'I think he might, Meg.'

Davy Moffat was Sir Joseph's only nephew, a wine merchant by trade. Living in the centre of Dumfries, his connections were with the greatest noble houses of Lowland Scotland, including the abbeys and priories. Anyone able to afford the best wines from Gascony, Castile, Anjou and Portugal relied on Davy Moffat to supply it, irrespective of the high prices due to war and famine. Since Robbie's death, Sir Joseph had taken it for granted that his nephew would be

Ebony's next husband, ignoring all her protests that she had no intention of taking him, or anyone else, to her bed. It would have been highly convenient from a practical point of view, Sir Joseph had told her repeatedly. What better for young Sam than a stepfather he already knew? A man of property, related to one of Scotland's oldest families; a widower who longed for a son of his own; a lusty husband who would give her a new start in life. His inducements were endless and incessant.

He had not needed to explain that Davy would automatically acquire all the Moffat property that Ebony held as a widow, plus the use of all rents and dues from Sam's property inherited from his father, until Sam came of age. If it would be a good match for Ebony, it would be even more advantageous for Davy Moffat.

'It's worth a try, even so,' said Meg. 'I'd rather ask Davy before anyone else. But tell me something, Ebbie. How are we going to explain the presence of all these strangers to the funeral guests? Are they going to pretend to be mourners, or are they going to take themselves off for a few days?'

'Truly, I don't know, love. I can suggest they make themselves scarce, but you know there'll be quite a crowd who'll stay for the feasting and go back home the next morning, or even later. And much as we dislike having the king's men poking their noses into our affairs, those men could be made to earn their bread by keeping order. You know what your father's friends can be like when they're in their cups, and, if we have to act as hosts, we're going to need help.'

Meg's silence was easy to understand. To ask those two-faced ruffians for help would be like turning to the devil himself. 'I don't like it,' she said, leaning against the wall. 'It's true that we shall need help now that our own men have gone, but it might be better to find out what they have in mind before we ask them outright.'

'Finding out what those two have in mind has taken us two whole days, Meggie. We have two more till the funeral. We can but try.'

'And tomorrow, we'll have this place cleaned out completely. We can have straw mattresses brought in, and the men guests can come in here straight from the hall. Don't forget to lock your door, Eb. Did you get your key back?'

'No,' said Ebony. 'But I will.'

Sam and Biddie were snugly asleep on a new feather mattress in the little tower room below hers, their bed curtained all round to make an alcove against the wall, canopied above, sheepskin-rugged below. On top of his pile of neatly folded clothes on the oak chest lay Sam's wooden sword, and Ebony wondered guiltily whether it could be right for him to show such a brief and shallow sorrow at his grandfather's demise or whether these men had done her a favour by taking his mind off the loss.

Further up the winding staircase, she found that the shutters had been closed across her windows, the cressets lit, and the fire crackling in welcome. She could have barricaded herself in as a temporary measure until she could obtain the key, but the idea of young Sam or Biddie not being able to reach her in the middle of the night was enough to change her mind, and the door was left unsecured, though not without some misgivings.

'What is happening to us?' she whispered, echoing Meg's cry.

She opened one shutter wide enough to lean her head against the mullions and to breathe in the sweet-scented night air that wafted across the loch, hoping to find the peace she had often sought in this way. But it was not peace that came. Instead, the concerns that she had suppressed over the last hour stole back even as far as her fingertips, curling them tightly around the stone with an anger as real as pain. He had allowed her to offer herself and to believe it was necessary, selfless, motherly. He had deliberated, questioned her motives, shaming her further. He had accepted and taken part-payment when he could have eased her fears and offered help instead of encouraging her stupidity. The man was a fiend; a deceitful, contemptuous adventurer.

Looking across at the smooth enticing bed, a soft dream encroached like the shimmer of an owl's wing at night, gone in the blink of an eye. On impulse, she padded across to where the May-blossom still hung, removed it, and took it back to the window where, hurled into the blackness, it disappeared as fast as the dream.

Her sleep was fitful, rarely deep enough to evade shadowy recollections of last night. More than once, she sat up to watch the door through a chink in the bedcurtains, almost sure that she heard it open, telling herself as she lay back again that it might have been Biddie or Sam. But the door did not open until the dawn came to disappoint her with its ordinariness, leaving her quite unaware that not once had she dreamed of Robbie.

* * *

Making no offers of a truce to their parasitic guests, nor even the semblance of one, Ebony and Meg went about the business of the day resolved to keep them at a considerable distance to underscore the escalation of hostilities. While Meg gave orders concerning her father's solar with an amazing absence of sentiment, Ebony went to the chapel to speak to Brother Walter about the funeral arrangements, but found that the man she most hoped to avoid had arrived before her to claim the chaplain's attention.

She would have turned away and closed the door behind her, but Sir Alex's legs were long enough to reach her, his hand drawing her back with more authority than his voice, which she would have ignored.

Brother Walter did not catch the frown that crossed her face as she bridled at the knight's gentle curb on her arm. 'Ah, Lady Ebony, 'tis guid that ye came, after what we said at prayers this morning. Sir Alex has teld me that he and his men will be guests at the funeral on Friday, and since we were all mistaken aboot their real purrpose in coming here, I've teld him they'll be welcome.'

The low stone vaulting criss-crossed above their heads and rippled with patterns of reflected light from the water that lapped against one wall, washing across the faces of both men. Sir Alex's hair was dark and sleek as if he had bathed in the loch that morning. Ebony drew her mind back, but was unable to prevent the sharpness of her reply. 'Well, I'm glad he told *somebody*, brother. I would have been more impressed if he had had the good manners to confer with Mistress Moffat or myself first, but make him feel welcome by all means, if that's what you want. I cannot add my voice to it, nor will my sister.'

'Nae, lassie—' Brother Walter looked sorrowfully from her to Sir Alex and back again '—ye mus'na be too dour on the man. He's only doing his job, and we can use a crood o' braw men noo that ours are gone awa'. They'll be no dressed as reivers, ye ken. They've got proper braies and buits to wear, and there'll nae be a steel bonnet in sight, he tells me.'

'Does he indeed, brother? Then we must be thankful he tells one of us something intelligent from time to time. And has he told you whether these uninvited guests are to be friends of Sir Joseph's, or are they supposed to be ours? Some warning on that would be useful so that our little female minds are not confused by all the turning of coats.'

By the gradual warmth that stole across the priest's usually morose face, she knew that, behind her, Sir Alex was laughing and that he had won Brother Walter to his side.

'I'm wasting my time here,' she said, picking up her skirts. 'I'll send the steward and the chamberlain to you to act as interpreters.'

Sir Alex placed his hand against the wide stone pillar to bar her way. 'A moment, my lady, if you please. Our misunderstanding—'

'Your deceit, sir!' she snapped, holding herself away as if her intention had never been to pass him. 'Let us call it by its proper name, shall we?'

'Nae…lassie!' Brother Walter scolded again, gently. 'We have nae time for such as this. Ye have tae accept that it'll be easier to explain Sir Alex's presence here as a captain with his men passing through on their way to the muster at Newcastle. That way, you'll be—'

'Easier for whom, brother?' Ebony said. 'Why

cannot they admit who they are and what they're after. Why confuse the issue with half-truths?'

'Because, my lady,' said Sir Alex, 'it's not a half-truth. Granted, it's not the whole truth either, but we *are* on our way across the Wall to the muster at Newcastle where we expect to meet up with King Robert. He intends to engage the English in battle, you see, to regain Berwick, so there's no lie in saying that that's where we're bound, eventually. But to tell Sir Joseph's friends that we're investigating his activities will be counter-productive, when we hope to find out which of *them* are involved in the same business. In a way, this will save us days of legwork, but they'll not open up to us if they think they'll be incriminating themselves. Whether you're Scottish or English, the truth of this matter must be cleared up for the sake of the laird's family. You'll not be wanting these accusations to hang over your heads indefinitely, will you?'

'And I suppose you're lingering here at Castle Kells for five or six days for a well-earned rest, are you? Is that to be a part of the deceit, too?'

'To buy some of his Galloways and to rest our wounded men. There's no deceit in that, lady.'

'Except that the wounded men are Sir Joseph's, not yours.'

'A small point. They'll not be meeting them, and my men will be helping for a while now that Sir Joseph's have gone on to Newcastle.'

'Another small point? They were sent to Dumfries.'

He shook his head. 'On horseback to Newcastle, my lady. Eighty miles or so. They're well-equipped fighting men,' he said, his blue eyes hardening. 'They can fight legally for their king, for once, instead of illegally for their master, and think themselves fortunate not to be locked up at Dumfries. Hard times we're in. They'll see something of the famine on the way, something they'll not have appreciated from quite the same viewpoint, something that *you'd* have seen if you'd been out of this place oftener.'

That hit a raw nerve. 'And you'd know what you were talking about better, sir, if you'd been locked up in this place oftener, as I and my child have. You think I wanted to stay imprisoned? Not to be free? If it were not for Sam and Meg, I'd—' Suddenly aware of what she was divulging to this stranger, she bit back the rest of her tirade, picked up her skirts again, and strode past them both out of the chapel.

At the slam of the heavy door Brother Walter shook his head sadly and sighed. 'Ah, I ken noo how ye got yer stripes, laddie. She's a fearsome wench is that, but ye need tae have a strong hawking-glove handy, and a huid. They make a braw pair, the raven and the vixen, eh?'

'Yes,' said Sir Alex, 'but both can be tamed, brother.'

'And your lads? Can they be tamed, too?'

The tall bronzed Scot gave a huff of laughter at that. Every one of his men had been hand-picked, each one an expert in his own field, cook, saddler, engineer and armourer, farrier, doctor, linguist and scribe. There was even a harpist and an ordained priest amongst them, though no one would have known one from the other. All were experienced horsemen, dedicated to their leaders, to each other and to their mission. They had to be. Usually dressed in an assortment of leather, wool and padded-linen riding clothes, they were festooned with belts, swords and dirks, scarves around their necks and steel helmets on their heads, and it was no disadvantage for them to be taken for night-raiding reivers, disguise being their speciality. In a matter of moments, they could be a nobleman's household on the move, a marketing expedition, or a laird's servants about escort duty. Physically fit and highly skilled in warfare, they had accompanied Sir Alex to every part of Europe on the King of Scotland's business, most recently to Ireland.

Now, they had been sent to Galloway where an unexpected funeral would be an interesting diversion for them. They would take it in their stride, as usual. 'Oh, I think so, brother,' said Sir Alex. 'They're a versatile bunch. Now, tell me, if you please, who we might expect to meet on Friday. Relatives, for instance. And is it true what Lady Ebony says about her being kept a prisoner here?'

Brother Walter's face sagged like that of a bloodhound. 'Aye,' he said, quietly, lowering his backside carefully on to the altar steps. 'I think if ye want tae save yersel' some muir stripes, laddie, ye'd better know what ye're dealing with. Sit ye doon a while.'

The straw laid along the garden pathway caught on the toes of Ebony's shoes, making her aware—just in time—of a pile of early coleworts cut by the gardener's lad. There was little else ready to harvest at this time of year. She slowed, knowing that she had no good reason to be here when there were so many other tasks claiming her attention, rooms for guests, extra hands to be hired, liveries to be checked, torch-bearers, bell-ringers, food lists. But the sad truth was that she was allowing that man to irritate her and, instead of keeping her head clear for urgent matters, her thoughts were vibrating like harp strings on a tune of their own.

His voice. His scathing words about her supposed indifference to the famine, to others' misery. Was there something in what he said? And *had* she been as imprisoned as she implied? Was that not partly to do with her own wishes to stay inside the castle's confines with Sam? He had criticised her over Sam's few skills, suggesting that it was she who was holding him back, but what did he know about children or about her reasons? Damn him!

The gardener's lad stood up with his armful of green leaves just in time to see Lady Ebony turn and almost crash headlong into the arms of Sir Alex Somers, yelping with fright. Disappointed, the lad was called away before he could witness how she managed to get round him but, when he looked over his shoulder, they were still there like a couple of snarling terriers at a stand-off.

'Nothing more to say, m'lady?' said Sir Alex.

I could say that I hate you. 'Only to ask for the key to my chamber, sir. I cannot feel secure with so many strangers in the castle, and more to come.'

'Your safety will be my prime concern, and I shall have guards put on Mistress Meg's door, too, as long as the funeral guests are here. The key will stay in my pouch.'

'I do not need your protection. I need my key.'

'I know exactly what you need, my lady.'

Already too rattled by their earlier confrontation to find a suitably stinging reply, she looked pointedly beyond him. 'I am busy,' she said. 'Let me pass, if you please. And if you know what I need, perhaps you can pick up the colewort and take it to the kitchen, then find the marshall and tell him—no! No! Put me down!' Squirming had no effect, for she was held hard against him and, in those first chastening moments of utter helplessness, could not even tell in which direction he was carrying her. Worse still, his last enigmatic remark gave rise to her fear that, eventually, she would have to pay without any preamble about permission, convenience, or location. 'No,' she pleaded. 'No…please…not yet!'

He put his back against the door in the garden wall, and she saw the stone arch curve over their heads, felt a different level of sound as he strode easily down the rough path that led to the waterfall. Below them, the lock sparkled under sun and clouds, deep ultramarine, grey and silver, edges of brown like the coats of red deer, the black of forests on the far side. A bench made from slabs of stone was set to one side of the path where she and Meg often sat to comb out their wet hair, and it was here that he put her down and held her while he sat astride it and made her do the same with her back against his chest. Taking her wrists, he held them across her, sealing her into an embrace she had not experienced for so long that it seemed almost new to her, except for a dream two nights ago.

'Please don't,' she said. His mouth was on the side of her head and she could feel him sniffing gently at her hair, sending impulses shuddering into her thighs. 'I have to help Meg. She needs me.'

'So do I,' he said, 'and it may be a wee bit safer for me if we talk like this. Do you think so, wench? Where your sharp tongue and claws can't do much harm?'

The possibility that he knew about the waterfall was now a certainty; his wet hair and the resolute progress through the garden, and now this convenient bench which he must have seen earlier, with the castle wall like a suntrap behind them. 'What is it you need to know?' she said, looking down at his big boots tucked behind her legs. They were bigger than Robbie's, his thighs thicker and longer. Dusted with brown hair, his hands and wrists nestled beneath her breasts, no doubt feeling her warmth through the fine wool of her kirtle.

'Tell me about your father-in-law's friends. Those who'll be coming to his funeral. The ones he does business with.'

'We have no way of knowing who'll be here until they arrive,' she said, coldly. 'We send the news out and then wait to see. Some will come from Stranraer away to the west, some from Dumfries, some from Ayrshire. There'll be the Galloway sheriff and his assistant, the warden of the March and his deputy, the keepers and captains and local barons. Castle Kells is not an easy place to reach at short notice.'

'And the relatives?'

'They'll come, wanting to know what he left them.'

'And what *has* he left them?'

'That's Meg's department, not mine. Ask her.'

'I will.'

Like this? Her back was warm against him, but she told herself how she hated it, hated him, his arms, his disgraceful familiarity.

'And who's this nephew, Davy Moffat?' he asked. 'Does he come top of your list of second husbands, or bottom?' Her struggles made him laugh and tighten his hold on her. 'All right…all right,' he said. 'Question answered.'

'There is no list!' she snapped, twisting. 'I have no intention of—'

'Well, *you* may not have, but the old man certainly did, didn't he? A nephew. All in the family. Wealthy. But a *wine merchant*?' His laugh was buried in her hair. 'I can't see you being married to a—'

'Who I marry has nothing to do with you,' she said, smarting. 'Keep your enquiries to Sir Joseph's affairs and then go. I doubt you'll find what you're looking for.'

'Why do you say that?'

'Because whatever else Sir Joseph might have been, I cannot believe he was a traitor to his country. I had little love for him, if you must know, but no one was more fiercely patriotic than he. Whoever was selling Galloways to my countrymen, it would not be him. He'd have died rather than let an Englishman ride them into battle against the Scots.'

'But they're the only kind of horses they can use over rough ground.'

'Of course they're not! There are English-bred dales and fell ponies. Do your groundwork, man!'

'M…mm. And how often does he visit, this eager suitor of yours?'

'If you mean Master Moffat, he brings wine and—'

'How *often*?'

She shrugged. 'Every few weeks. He stays a few days for the hunting, then he returns home.'

'Loaded with venison, no doubt. Does he take ponies back to Dumfries?'

'Well, he brings pack-ponies to carry the wine, so

I expect he takes them back again. I don't take much interest.'

'Good,' he whispered. 'Does young Sam like him?'

'He's very kind to Sam.'

His hands took her wrists away to rest upon each knee so slowly that a red squirrel foraged busily about their feet. She had never known a man move so silently or so gracefully as this man. Nor, come to think of it, had she ever bothered to question her true feelings about Davy Moffat's intentions as she did now. He had been kind to Sam and to her and perhaps, in time, with her father-in-law's continued persuasion, she might have relented and married him, if only to remove herself and her son from Sir Joseph's bad influence. Yet there was no attraction except in material matters, and the idea of being intimate with him held no appeal.

His wife had died in childbirth four years ago, their baby too, and even Meg could not quite understand Ebony's reluctance to move into a fine house in the town and become the wife of one of its most influential citizens. Meg believed him to be a good catch. Ebony had told them both that she was not yet ready to remarry, though the night-times could have told them a different story.

'And are you going to tell him about your offer to me, my lady? Or would you prefer me to tell him?'

She watched the distant speck of a boat move swiftly across the mirrored loch leaving a fine hairline wake behind it. 'You ought to have been a reiver after all, sir. Malice becomes you as much as deceit does. Tell Master Moffat whatever you like. I cannot be responsible either for your actions or for his feelings. Anyway, one look at you and he'll realise I was desperate.' His quiet laughter shook against her back, and now his hands relaxed and slid gently up her arms, over her elbows, upwards to her shoulder, and she could have leapt away but did not. 'I have a better idea than yours,' she said, turning her face to one of his hands. 'You could forget all about it. The bargain is outdated. Everything has changed. You will not need to take Sam.'

'No,' he whispered in her ear. 'The bargain stands. Anything else?'

When she made no reply, his hands slipped away, leaving her shoulders and back strangely cool, her mind drawn back to the little boat, to its purposeful independence and directness. And when at last she was moved to speak to him about freedom, she found that she was quite alone.

There were too many tasks still to be completed for her to spend time looking either backwards or forwards, which was in some ways a blessing. Far from coming to any harm, Sam had been playing with the bailiff's two lads under Biddie's watchfulness, their wooden ponies on wheels making fewer demands on their balance, their lances converted later on to fishing rods.

An army of villagers had been hired to help with the preparations, using the kitchen courtyard to skin and clean the carcasses of beef and veal, four venison, boars, twenty lambs, dozens of pheasants, ducks and geese, chicken and pigeons, rabbits and herons. Every number called across the yard concerned bushels, barrels, boxes-full and gallons, every oven was working overtime, every pair of hands plucking, cutting, stripping and stuffing. There would be feather pillows for every guest, if the kitchen courtyard was any indication.

'Five *hundred* herrings?' Ebony said. 'Are you sure?'

'Yes, m'lady,' said the second steward, trying not to sneeze. 'And eels, salmon, trout, pike and lamprey. Three hundred manchet loaves baked yesterday, same of pandemain, clapbread and bannocks today. The baker's men have been at it non-stop. I have to go and forage out those boxes of dates, figs and ginger that Master Moffat brought in last time, and see if I can put my hands on some more ground almonds. Cook's nearly blowing his top in there.' He looked towards the kitchen buildings where a lad wheeled a barrowload of logs through the door. 'Best not go in there just now, m'lady. Oh, and Mistress Meg's been asking for you. She's with the laird.'

She found Meg coming away from the winter hall where the laird's body lay in state surrounded by his valet, two squires and a page. 'You should take a rest now,' Ebony said. 'Come, love. It'll soon be suppertime.'

Meg shook her head. 'I must go across to the gatehouse to see that Davy's room is ready. I've sent Janet across. It won't take me long.'

'But why now? They'll not be here till tomorrow.'

Meg's eyelids were heavy and translucent with weariness and emotion. 'Davy's here.' She smiled. 'We should have known he'd be first to arrive.'

'Here…already?'

'In the summer hall with Sir Alex. Shall you go and tend him till his room's ready? Just give me half an hour?'

'I could go and do the room, Meggie.'

If there was a suggestion of a plea, Meg chose not to hear it. 'You know it's you he wants to see most of all. And Sam.'

Ebony placed a hand on Meg's arm. 'Don't let's go into that, love. Please. This is no time to be discussing futures.'

'However much I agree with you, Eb, I doubt if *he* will.'

It had not occurred to either of them that Master Davy Moffat would arrive ahead of his sister and her husband who lived in the same town. It was always safer to travel in numbers. But the uncomfortable flutter of excitement she experienced in the screens passage was not at the sight of him through a chink in the heavy woollen curtain, but at the man to whom he was talking.

Between the lower end of the hall and the service rooms ran a passage that was screened off by high wooden panelling with two openings, each one curtained until mealtimes when the hall servants would carry dishes of food through from the kitchens. A door at each end of the passage gave access to the courtyards, but there were no windows here, only smells and sounds, the feel of cold stone slabs beneath one's feet and whatever sights presented themselves through the narrow gaps, or an open door.

Holding a hurriedly tidied Sam by the hand, she hesitated and then, with a smile at the child, held the curtain aside. The inevitable comparison between the two men was made the instant she stepped into the hall. Reflecting off the white linen on the high table, the pinkish evening light picked up the harsh brightness of Davy's royal blue tunic and made a bold contrast against the neutrals, soft greens and brown leather of Sir Alex's workmanlike gear. Long dagged streamers hung from Davy's sleeves almost to the floor, his black and yellow striped chausses skimming over long legs up to the extremely short scalloped edge of a tunic barely long enough to hide a very conspicuous bulge behind an embroidered flap tied with gold laces. It was obviously meant to be noticed.

The two men stood in easy conversation, Sir Alex topping Master Davy by an inch or two, his wide shoulders and narrow hips putting to shame the other man's gaudy leanness, the long neck that held up a slight head with fair straight hair that, brushed off his forehead, fell tidily on to his collar. But he lacked his cousin's devastating eyes, and his mouth was too red and full-lipped for a man, and Ebony thought he was like a male bird with plumage ready to impress a mate. He was mannered and charming but superficial for all that, and while she could dislike the man by his side with a hearty intensity, she could find no feelings of any kind for Master Davy Moffat. She did, however, feel suddenly dowdy and unkempt.

Master Davy instantly broke off the conversation, coming forward to meet her with hands outstretched and an expression of relief in his round pale eyes. 'Ah, Lady Ebony,' he said. 'What a terrible time this is for you and my cousin. So courageous.' He took her by the shoulders and kissed her on the mouth, a greeting which should have meant nothing singular but somehow always did with Davy, who lingered just a mite too long.

She saw Sir Alex out of the corner of her eye, watching every move. She would have to be careful here, for any suggestion of hostility between them would provoke Davy's unwanted protection and a spate of questions she could well do without. 'Greetings, Master Davy,' she said. 'It was good of you to come so promptly. Sam, make your bow.' She placed a hand on Sam's back, moving him forward.

There had always been a restrained politeness between Sam and Master Davy that neither of them knew how to extend into the kind of easy respect the child had already found in three days with Master Joshua. Their smiles and bows were courteous, but hardly warm. Sam looked to his mother for approval, taking her hand again.

All will be well, now that I'm here, Master Davy's expression said, directing his next observation over Sam's head. 'I swear he's grown since last I saw him,' he said. 'Has he learnt the Latin verse I gave him?'

'No, but he's learnt to ride his pony at last.'

Master Davy's eyes widened in horror. 'Ride? Good heavens, m'lady. Surely that's too dangerous for a wee lad, isn't it? What's the purpose in that?'

Ebony saw the lift of a single eyebrow beyond her, but kept her face straight. 'Why, I suppose to get from one place to the other without wearing his legs out. Sir Joseph gave him the pony, so perhaps that's what he had in mind too.'

'Hmm!' Master Davy turned to the tall silent man behind him as if he suspected some collusion. 'Do you approve of this, Sir Alex?'

'What Lady Moffat allows her son to do should need no approval from either of us, Master Moffat. Sam will always be safe in his mother's care.'

Lacking the support he had hoped for, he allowed the subject to drop as Ebony swung the conversation towards Meg and her late father, the funeral and the pity of it all. Hugh of Leyland joined them for an introduction, forcing yet another comparison between the king's officers and the vintner, not only in looks but in manners also. She plied them with wines, which Master Davy could not resist telling them were from his warehouse. Expensive, exclusive; they were fortunate to be sampling it, he told them, missing the almost imperceptible wink exchanged behind his head.

On this occasion, eating alone was out of the question, Meg having agreed with Ebony that their smouldering resentment of the two men's tactics must be hidden from the guests who would otherwise be unlikely to co-operate in any enquiries. But neither of them was a good actress. Living in a household of brutally plain-speaking men, their diplomatic skills had rarely been stretched further than hiding their disgust of Sir Joseph's habits and their dislike of his friends, which had usually meant keeping out of their way. Now, this would not be possible, and they would have to try harder.

The supper in the summer hall, though not the main meal of the day, was still a formal affair in which the two women's attention was required for their guests' comfort. Without appearing to notice, it was also directed towards their manners, having assumed for no very good reason that those of the two captains would have deteriorated along with those of their men. It was soon revealed how wrong their assumption was, both captains and men practising every courtesy as if they had lived their lives in a noble household. Nor did they tax Ebony and Meg by overplaying a friendship that did not exist, and Master Davy was apparently taken in by the display of mild affability that accompanied the meal, though he was perplexed by the men's knowledge of wines, at which he had expected to triumph.

He took Meg aside after the tables had been dismantled and, against a background of mournful bagpipes and tabors, put his queries to her. 'Where did you say these men were from, Meg?'

She had had to share Master Leyland's trencher, and the effort of keeping a civil tongue in her head was beginning to show. 'They're not from anywhere in particular,' she said. 'If you promise to keep your face straight, I'll tell you why they're here.'

'They're not just passing through, then?'

'Not exactly. But you mustn't discuss this with the other guests or my father's name will never be cleared. They'll refuse to co-operate.'

'What are you talking about? Cleared of *what*?'

'I told you to keep your face straight, Davy.'

He pulled it back, not entirely successfully. 'Cleared,' he said, 'of what?'

'They have orders from the king to investigate the sale of the Galloways to the English.'

'That's illegal!'

'I *know* it is. That's what it's all about. They need to know who else is in the business with him. You should be able to help us in that.'

Davy had paled. 'Well, I'm not sure who his contacts are, Meg.'

'The point is,' Meg growled, 'he's *innocent*, Davy. He doesn't *have* any dealings in treachery of that kind. You know how he feels about traitors, and you *do* know who his contacts are. You know more about what my father does than anyone. You and he spend…*spent* hours talking about his business.'

'God…this is serious, Meg.'

'You don't need to tell me that. We need your help. Ebony and I may lose the castle if they can prove what they think they already know.'

'They've discussed it with you?'

'Briefly. Last night. Ebony too. They've been through all his papers. Everything.'

'God almighty! And the stores, too?'

'Yes, though I don't know what they expected to find there.'

Davy groaned, unable to keep his eyes from straying to the two strangers in conversation with Brother Walter. 'Where's his key, Meg?' he said. 'Did you remove it from around his neck?'

Meg stared at him. 'I don't know anything about a key round his neck…oh…wait! Was it on a piece of leather?'

'Yes.'

A hand went to her forehead. 'I had to cut it to get at his wounds. It'll have gone, Davy. I gave orders to burn the stuff he was lying in. It was so—'

'Yes…never mind it. I can force the box open, I suppose.'

'What box?'

'Er…oh, his most private documents. Don't worry, they'll not have found it. Where's his signet ring?'

'Ebony has it.'

'She'd better let me have it. I'll keep it safe.'

'It *is* safe. No one can use it now except Sam.'

'And Ebony, as his guardian.'

'Well, we shall have everything inventoried, once this is all over. The lawyers will be here next week, so we'll sort it out then.'

There was no reply from Davy, and no one but he

could tell how shallow his breathing had become, and how unquiet the beating in his chest.

His next target was Ebony, who had never seen any reason to foster Davy's interest in her and saw none now. Yet she was able to show an appreciation of his concern. 'That's very kind of you,' she said to his sympathetic approach. 'So Meg's explained the situation?'

'She has,' he said, scooping his streaming sleeves up off the rushes and settling them neatly over his knees. 'It's a very grave situation, my lady. Very grave indeed.'

She could have wished he'd chosen a more sensitive adjective. 'Yes,' she said. 'Meg and I hoped you'd be able to help sort it all out.'

'I don't know. I *may* be able to.' He pursed his lips and looked away.

That was not quite the positive tone she had expected of him, he who had so eagerly broadcast his admiration of his uncle's affairs and connections. Even Sir Joseph's reiving was accepted by him as a fact of life, as indeed it was by other lairds and homeowners. '*May* be able to?' she said. 'You surely don't believe he could have been so disloyal, do you?'

'Well, no…er…no, of course I don't. But these are difficult times, my lady, and if these men have strong evidence, it will be very difficult to prove otherwise.'

Someone else had only recently reminded her of hard times. 'I would not have thought a man of your calibre would find it impossible to clear his uncle's name,' she said, demurely, 'when so much is at stake. He would have expected you to take the reins at a time like this, I think.'

As soon as his eyes fixed on hers in a kind of slow

dawning, she realised that she had phrased it clumsily and that, because of the mutual desires of uncle and nephew concerning herself, his thoughts had gone quite naturally askew. It was the last thing she wanted, but it was already too late.

Sitting suddenly upright, he placed a warm hand over hers before she could sense what was coming. 'My *dear* lady, he would! I'm so glad you've come round to our way of thinking at last. Perhaps we might find the time to discuss the matter in private tomorrow?'

She removed his hand and replaced it carefully on his knee. 'Master Davy, I think you may have—' The wailing bagpipes roared to a crescendo of sound that no voice could penetrate and, when she looked up to search for a way out of her dilemma, she found the steely blue of Sir Alex's eyes reaching her from half-way down the hall as if he had heard every word.

He bore down upon them like an eagle from a crag. 'I wonder if I may speak with you, Master Moffat?' he said, ignoring Ebony's obvious relief. 'Hugh and I have been having an argument about the origin of Malmsey. You're the only one who can put us right.'

It was a challenge Master Davy could not ignore, even at a time like that.

The usual night-time sounds of castle life were becoming less strident as Ebony said goodnight to Sam. Once again, he was almost too tired to hear the end of his bedtime story; turning his head on the pillow, he was asleep even before her hand left his forehead. 'Another night without bad dreams?' she whispered to Biddie.

Folding his clothes, the maid nodded. 'Aye,' she

said. 'I don't quite know why his grandpa's death should have made such a difference to him, mistress, but there was nae sound from him for the last two nights. You all right on your own up there?'

'Well enough. I shall sleep soundly tonight, Biddie.'

Ebony's forecast was reasonably accurate, such was her exhaustion. With the fire little more than a glow of burnt-out logs, there were no lights for her to watch dancing over the rafters before her eyes closed. Her thoughts slowed to a walk before their headlong release into a memory she had tried hard all day to keep out, the strength of warm arms holding her, the lips close to her hair that sent a tingle of messages down to her knees. Cool on her skin, the linen sheets were like the May dew in which she and Meg had rolled, and though she tried to close the door of her mind, it opened stealthily again. Her last thoughts chastised her for Master Davy's misunderstanding, which, if she had had her wits about her, would not have happened. Now, she would have to find a way of reversing his new-found encouragement. A large man came striding across the hall to rescue her, and she was overtaken by wicked sensations again.

Lethargic with sleep, she felt Robbie's arms enfold her, his warmth settling at her back, spooning her into him. His hand came round to find her breast, but even as her hand covered his approvingly, she fell back into the dark soundless void. The fire had died altogether when one of her drowsy senses warned her that there was something more to her dream than mere illusion, for sound had never played a part as it did now. She listened to the gentle regular breathing behind her head and knew that it was not hers. At the same time, her hand moved over the one cupping her breast, instantly recognising by touch alone that it was not Robbie's. Beyond that, she dared not give it a name.

The rhythm of the breathing changed as the hand moved tenderly across her, slowly caressing, stroking, allowing her hand to rest on its wrist as if to control it. She caught her breath, holding it as the hand moved down over her ribcage like a tangible shadow so softly that, if it had not been for the downy-soft hair along the arm and the firm muscular undulations beneath the skin, she might have closed her eyes and told herself to go back to sleep. But wasn't this what she had wanted last night, when he had not come?

Gradually, cautiously, the hand slid over the satin of her hip, slipping into her groin, taking time to caress before covering her stomach in one giant span. She gasped, moaning and arching herself against him, feeling the response in his body as he took control, knowing exactly what she needed. As he had said. Without words to break the dream, she bathed in his slowly sweeping caresses, wantonly spreading herself under his hands, wrapping her legs over his, delighting in the rasp of his hairiness upon her soft skin as a harp vibrates under the skilled fingers of the harpist.

Trembling, her body begged for more of the sensations denied to it for three barren colourless years and, as if this harpist knew the exact melody, his hands willingly played upon her, though her needs were reawakened rather than put to rest. Intensified, not satisfied. Abandoning all inhibitions, allowing no thoughts, she asked herself no questions and sought no answers from him, but gave herself up entirely to the darkness and to the bliss of his expertise. Avidly, she searched for his lips, holding his head to hers with both arms to savour every exquisite taste and to plot with her mouth the contours of the face to which she had recently been so unkind. It did not matter now. That had been in another world; this was for the darkness.

Strangely, there were no thoughts of what else lay beyond, for what she had here was of an intensity she had never experienced before. All her previous loving had been hurried, routine and confined to three obvious parts of her anatomy; this man was showing her something too sublime to end in anything but tears for what she had missed and found. This belonged to some forbidden time without name, without explanation, guilt or shame. A time that would disappear with the dawn.

His fingers, large and tender, caressed her back in long slow sweeps, his voice hushing her with wordless sounds of a deeper timbre than Robbie's, more musical and soothing. She let herself be rocked and held, comforted and still echoing with chords, stirred by his magic, wanting more but suddenly afraid. At last, she slept again with her mouth against his chest and, as dawn crept through her eyelids, a small naked body materialised alongside her where the larger one had been.

'Mama!' he called. 'It's daytime and I had no bad dreams again.'

Chapter Five

Sir Joseph Moffat's chamber, which Meg had made habitable for her male guests was not, after all, being used as she had intended, a reversal guaranteed to infuriate her. She slammed the heavy studded door with some difficulty, not so much embarrassed by the sight of so many men in varying stages of undress as angered that her plans had been disregarded.

'Where is Sir Alex Somers?' she yelled across the hall.

The sight and sound of Mistress Moffat at the top of the wooden staircase on the wall behind the dais stopped most of the hall servants in their tracks until a man strode through the screens at the far end to settle the problem. 'Will I do, mistress?' called Hugh of Leyland, failing to register an acceptable degree of alarm on his handsome face.

'No, sir, you won't!' Meg replied, tripping briskly down the stairs. 'I need to get that chamber cleared of bodies, and you seem to be incapable of doing anything remotely useful.'

Hugh bit back the smile. 'I thought bodies is what

you intended it for,' he said. His facetiousness was ill timed.

'Leave the thinking on household matters to me, if you please,' she called to him. 'That chamber was Sir Joseph's and I will say who's to use it. Get those men out of there at once. They can sleep in the hall and stables like the other men.' Meg was flushed with anger, but now the drained and faded image of the last three days was replaced by a new vitality that a good night's sleep, a bath, and a change of clothes had brought. The blue kirtle and cream linen surcoat fitted her curvaceous figure snugly, her sleeves clung as far as her knuckles and the wide neckline revealed a length of white neck above which her red-brown hair coiled over her ears like plaited buns. Fine gold nets dotted with seed-pearls covered them, and a golden filet sat over her brow, for Meg had no intention of being seen as the dowdy Moffat woman amongst her father's acquaintances. Besides, she revelled in the management of numbers and today she would need her wits about her.

'You're probably right,' said Hugh. 'They *can* sleep almost anywhere, but since the hall will be full of noisy guests till the early hours, it seems sensible to have the men where they can be on hand to control things, should some…er…restraint be necessary.' He watched her approach, wondering why Alex should have thought the two of them would need help. They could, he thought, probably manage single-handed.

She stopped at an arm's length from him, spitting with indignation. 'Believe it or not, Master Leyland,' she said, 'I *am* quite capable of understanding the reasoning behind that, but Lady Moffat and myself are still the joint keepers of Castle Kells until we are removed, and we are the ones who make decisions about accommodation. In future, perhaps you will have the courtesy to discuss things with us before you do any more reorganising.'

'Certainly, mistress. I'll pass your message on to Sir Alex. And where would you like *me* to sleep?' By his look, he had no doubts about the answer he would like to have heard.

Meg's reply, however, was less hospitable. 'In the loch!' she said, walking away.

Following her, he caught a medley of mock-sour faces and knowing grins from servants who had overheard the exchange. Dame Janet, he thought, had done an excellent job with the hair, but he would give much to be allowed to undo her handiwork. 'If I may be allowed to explain?' he said.

'You've explained, after your fashion. Now I have to go and find somewhere else for the guests.' She swept through the curtain into the screens-passage, meeting her cousin coming from the opposite direction and looking, he told her, for Sir Alex. 'You'll not find him,' Meg said, loudly. 'You'll have to make do with Master Leyland, like the rest of us. He seems to have organised us all into batches.'

'Meg...don't go!' Master Davy said. 'I can't get into Sir Joseph's room. It's full of men. What's the idea?'

'Ask *him*,' she said, tipping her head.

Hugh forestalled him. 'Is there a problem, Master Moffat?' he said. 'Did you want to sleep there too?' His grey eyes could see in the gloom as well as in the light of the hall, and Master Davy's heightened colour was not, he thought, due to physical exertion alone.

'No, sir. But my uncle's documents are there and I need to retrieve them.'

'Then you *will* have to speak to Sir Alex,' Hugh said. 'We have already removed some of them.'

Master Davy's mouth slackened, wobbling his lips, and for a very uneasy moment he was unable to speak, though his face spoke volumes. Aghast, he looked from Hugh to Meg, then into the darkness of the passage. 'But that's *too* bad, Master Leyland. Those are private documents.'

'Yes, I know,' Hugh said, watching Davy's flush disappear. 'That's why we've moved them for safe-keeping. We'd not want anyone poking into Sir Joseph's affairs, would we? And the ones that are left are safe enough with the men.'

'Well…er…no, of course not. But…'

Meg's irritation resurfaced. 'What's the matter, Davy? They were only bills of sale and agreements, surely? I don't like it either, but it's to prove to them that everything is as it should be. My father had nothing to hide, as you well know.'

'Do you agree, Master Moffat?' said Hugh.

'About what?'

'That Sir Joseph had nothing to hide.'

'Well, yes, as far as I know.'

His guarded qualification goaded Meg to a furious defence of her father that she had never had to exercise before. 'As far as you *know*? What *are* you saying, Davy? Of course you know. How could you not? You're the one who helped him with his business dealings. You know exactly what he did. It's no secret that he went reiving, but this is about betrayal, and my father would never have…look…' she grabbed at his sleeve '…*tell* him, will you?'

Angrily, he shook Meg off. 'I *have* said so, Meg. You heard me say so. But there are things in there that I *need*!' His last word was almost a yelp as he marched off in the direction he had come, and the crash of the stableyard door added another dimension to his dramatically odd behaviour.

'Is he usually so excitable?' Hugh said to the astonished Meg.

She swung her head away so as not to look at him. 'No,' she said. 'He's not excitable at all.'

'So what's all that about, do you think?'

'That's what I'd like to know. Perhaps I could tell you more if my sister and I were allowed to see what you've removed. We've lost the key to one of his boxes.'

'Oh? Which box?'

'I don't know which one. Davy said…'

He waited. 'Yes? Davy said?'

'Nothing. I must get a move on.' She took her skirts in her hand and then paused, refusing to lift her eyes further than the buckle on his belt. 'Where *have* you been sleeping, as a matter of interest?'

'Here. In the hall. With the men,' he said, airily.

'Well, there's a chamber at the top of those stairs.' She pointed to the well of a spiral staircase in the corner of the dark passageway. 'It's a guest room over the buttery and pantry with two beds in it, and a garderobe, and a good lock on the door. It should do well enough for you and Sir Alex, and it's near the hall. I'll have the beds made up for you.'

'Thank you, mistress,' he said. 'May I ask where your chamber is?'

She was away before his question was complete. 'No, you may not,' she said coolly, over her shoulder.

But his voice caught her up before she reached the door. 'I need to know.'

'You need to know too much!' she called, and was gone.

Hugh returned to the hall, still laughing.

'What's amusing you, lad?' said Sir Alex. 'One of the Valkyries, was it?'

'The little red squirrel. What a cracker. One of these days...'

'One of these days, Hugh, you'll get caught. Permanently. Come with me.' He led the way to a bench away from the centre where the open hearth was built on a platform of large stone slabs. A pile of white wood-ash was being tidied ready for the evening and, to one side, several men hauled on a pulley to lower the giant cartwheel candle-holder down from the rafters. Even under the eye of the pantler with his bucket, old candle-ends were being sneaked into pouches.

Hugh was still grinning. 'Yes,' he said. 'I might even like it. I've just bumped into our vintner friend, and he's mighty upset that we've taken some of Sir Joseph's documents, and apparently they both knew that his key is missing. I wondered whether to tell Mistress Meg that we've opened the box, but decided not to.'

'Best to wait and see what happens. As far as I can see, we've got the proof about the laird, but I think there may be more to it than that, Hugh.'

'You mean his contacts?'

'No, I mean Master Moffat himself. He's putting on some kind of act, I'm sure of it. And he's about to corner the lady too, if I read the signs correctly.'

Hugh didn't agree. 'She'll not be caught by the likes of him.'

'Well, people do strange things when they feel threatened, don't they?'

Uncertain of the exact direction of his friend's thoughts, Hugh stole a glance sideways. 'All right, so we'll watch him. He may still try to retrieve the box, even with the men there. The good news is that we've been given our own room.'

'That's a step forward. Well done, Hugh.'

'So where did *you* sleep last night?'

Even coming from Hugh, that was a signal for Alex to change the subject. 'I've posted three men on the tower where Lady Ebony sleeps,' he said. 'The bairn and his maid are in the chamber below. The guard is to be changed every six hours night and day. Same for Mistress Meg, Hugh. Right?'

'Right. A step forward at last, my friend. Eh?'

'No, not quite. You were right about widows being different.'

'Ah,' said Hugh. 'Denials then, is it? Is that what the fight was about?'

'And contradictions. Quite a challenge. Come on,' he said, rising to his feet. 'Checking to be done. Guests arriving today, I expect.'

'Just one thing,' said Hugh. 'Exactly where *is* Mistress Meg's room?'

Alex stopped and turned a look of fatherly reproach upon his friend's expectant face. 'Tch!' he said. 'You mean to say that we're four whole days in and you haven't discovered *that* yet? Good grief, lad, I was wrong. You'll not get caught at all at this rate, and certainly not permanently.' He threw a punch at Hugh's shoulder and strode off before Hugh could retaliate.

* * *

They had not been idle since their arrival at Castle
Kells. To establish proof of Sir Joseph's treachery,
they had examined every one of his horses and ponies
for brand marks on rump or shoulder. Their discoveries tied in neatly with the Castle Kells brand on
English ponies that had been captured after raids and
skirmishes, but they had not expected to find, hidden
away in the food stores, crates full of the best armour
and weaponry that money could buy, imported from
Italy and Spain. While there was no law against buy-
ing the best armour, the question of why Sir Joseph
was storing so much made them wonder who it was
intended for, his own countrymen, or the highest bid-
der? And who had helped him to import it, in the first
place?

The other commodity found in vast quantities in
the Castle Kells storerooms was the one for which the
whole country had been crying out since the floods
of 1315. Grain. Sir Joseph had enough in his stores
to feed the whole of Scotland for a year and more,
while men fought for a day's supply, starved for the
lack of it, or paid prices a hundred times its former
value. There were many questions to be asked and
answered here at the castle, one of which would be
about the exact involvement of Master Davy Moffat
and the two women who appeared to be protesting
innocence with ominous regularity.

In matters of dress, Meg and Ebony both had similar reasons to make more effort than usual, though
in Ebony's case there were other reasons of a more
complex nature to confuse the issue. Biddie thought
that all this indecision was a mite unnecessary, the
result, she thought, of the last few days' turmoil. She

sighed and unfolded once more the plum-coloured silken kirtle shot with violet and laid it on the bed. 'Now,' she said, patiently, 'which surcoat is it to be, the wine, the mist, or the rose-dawn?'

Ebony's thoughts were off on a wild good chase of their own. 'Mist,' she said, glancing across at the selection, but choosing the name rather than the colour. If only the mist would thicken and hide what she was sure had taken place over there in that bed, then she would be able to keep her resolution not to allow dreams into her daytime, the two being so obviously irreconcilable. 'It doesn't make any sense,' she whispered, fingering a white silk wimple.

Biddie lowered the grey silk she had just picked up. 'You said…'

'No, I don't mean the surcoat.'

'What, then?' said Biddie, mystified.

'Thoughts.'

She would have been more reconciled if it had all been his doing, but it had been hers too, from the little she could recall. She had welcomed him and demanded far more than she dared to admit, and it was herself she must blame for using him more than he had used her, in spite of his threats. But why?

'What thoughts?' said Biddie, kindly. She came across to where Ebony was standing by the window, looking out on to the stretch of shimmering water lined with moving ripples, sparkling, changing. 'Ye're not having bad dreams, are ye, now that Sam and me's not with ye? We can always come back.'

'No, Biddie. Not bad dreams. Just vivid ones.' It would have been so easy to accept the offer, to say, yes, come back, I cannot sleep well without you. But the vivid dreams were ahead of her, taunting her to recall the exact route of his hands in places where Robbie's had never ventured to caress. They were so clear that the breath in her lungs waited upon the memory of his hard body against hers, his possessive arms and understanding silence that had not needed to hear what it was that she wanted. He had disappeared before she woke, and that was what she had wanted, too. Like her, he would give no sign of what he knew had happened, nor would he promise to leave her in peace, of that she was certain. Yet it could not be allowed to continue or resolve itself in consummation; she must not let it happen again; she must consider alternatives, having that very moment rejected the most obvious one.

'Do my hair, love,' she said, holding up the wimple to cover her throat and neck. 'I want everything concealed today. I can do without Master Davy's eyes wandering all over me.' Would Biddie know that it was not *his* eyes that concerned her, but the other pair of steel blue that never missed a detail? He would read her guilt and panic and see the binding of hair and the covering of bare skin as futile attempts at rejection, and he would come again if only to prove to her that, after three years, her heart was ready to be mended. Then he would leave without a backward glance, and her heart would stay in a perpetual winter.

Avoidance soon became a secondary issue as the business of the day quickened, calling for Ebony's managerial skills before the guests' arrival. In the linen room, she piled twelve tunics of clean livery for the pages into the outstretched arms of Biddie and Sam, giving instructions for them to be delivered to the dormitory over the bakehouse.

Waiting his turn after the interruption, Master Morner, the chamberlain, continued with the checklist. 'The yeomans' chamber with three beds, m'lady?' he said.

'That'll do for the sheriff and his deputy and two men. Put an extra mattress on the floor.'

'And Baron Cardale?'

'Top of the east tower with his men.'

'He has bad knees, m'lady.'

'They're not too bad to go whoring, Master Morner.' She saw the man's wry expression and relented. 'Oh, well, he can have the chamber next to the muniment room. Put Mistress Cairns and her husband up in the east tower instead.'

The chamberlain's expression warmed as they shared the jest concerning the distance the pair would have to walk to the great hall. 'Yes, m'lady. And now there's only the warden and his assistant, and Captain Wishart, and—' He broke off, noting how Lady Ebony's attention had suddenly wavered and then ebbed altogether at the sight of someone behind him.

'Don't give my room away, Master Morner, if you please,' said Sir Alex. 'I should hate to lose it before I've had a chance to sleep in it myself.'

Deciding it was time to make an exit, the chamberlain bowed. 'Indeed I won't, sir. Excuse me, m'lady,' he said.

Sir Alex's presence was the last thing Ebony wanted, busy or not, and she had no intention of letting him think otherwise. By the same token, to scamper away like a scared mouse would give him the wrong impression. 'What is it, sir? I must be on hand to receive our guests at any moment.'

'Before dinner?' he said, looking around him at the folded piles of linen, blankets and furs, the shelves of coverlets and curtains, cushions, liveries and rolls of woollen cloth.

'Yes, before dinner. Some will be here before mid-day if they've rested overnight on the way. Please, excuse me.' In one quick glance, she saw that his plain soldierly dress had now been exchanged for an elegant attire that would not have seemed out of place in any courtly society. Fortunately, unlike Master Davy's flamboyancy, Sir Alex's tunic and chausses were of various tones of woad-blue that, though not an expensive colour, had been cut with such precision that the pleated, piped and dagged woollen cloth clung to his imposing figure with hardly a wrinkle. A creamy-white linen chainse showed in a long V from neck to waist, and the extravagantly long sleeves of his short pleated surcoat had been tied in loose knots to keep them off the floor.

Before she could pass him to reach the door, his hand came to rest on the latch, barring her way. 'It's all right,' he said. 'No reason to panic. I need to speak with you, that's all.'

She backed away, refusing to look into his eyes, but knowing how they sought out the details of her revised outfit as she had done in a more cursory fash-ion with his. 'What is it?' she asked again, hearing her repetition like that of a foolish maid. 'I trust you'll make it brief.' His scrutiny unnerved her, and she found herself trembling, dreading that he would speak of that which must remain unspoken between them.

'The Mistress Cairns you mentioned just now,' he said. 'Who is this lady?'

'She's Master Davy's sister. She and her husband live near him in Dumfries. He's a lawyer.' Her feet had taken her slowly backwards to the far wall of the linen-room where a shelf touched her shoulder-blades.

'You didn't tell me he had a sister.'

'You didn't ask.'

'And they're close, are they, apart from living nearby?'

'They're family. Of course they're close.'

'And Master Davy Moffat lives alone?'

'Why ask *me* about him?' she snapped. 'Ask him. He likes to talk.'

He smiled at that as if she had said more about herself than she had intended. 'I probably will. But let me tell you something before he finishes saying to you what he almost said last night.'

'I don't know what you're referring to. He said all kinds—'

'I think you do, my lady, so hear me out. If and when he proposes that you should marry him, which I'm sure he will, you will not accept him. Is that understood?' He continued, in spite of her attempt to interrupt. 'I know you've said that you don't intend to remarry, but things are changing daily, and I want it to be quite clear to him that he will not be the temporary Laird of Kells. I want to see how he reacts when he's thwarted.'

Now she turned the full force of her ice-bound flint eyes upon his and saw them glint as if they had been duelling with swords instead of words. 'It is quite clear, sir, that you have taken leave of your senses since we last spoke. When I wish to accept a proposal of marriage, I shall do so without anyone's advice or permission and in my own good time for my own reasons. I am a widow, sir, not a maid, and no one will ever have control of my life again. The last control has just gone and I'm in no hurry to accept another, I thank you.'

Though unsmiling, his eyes registered admiration. 'I see. Just the same, my lady, bear in mind what I've said. I shall do my best to rescue you if he makes a nuisance of himself, but I cannot be everywhere at once.'

'Then it's plain to see how little you know about women, Sir Alex, or you'd be aware of the devices we keep in our sleeves for men who make nuisances of themselves. You have recently discovered one of them. Remember?' But even as she searched for the tell-tale stripes on his cheek and neck, she realised that they had disappeared and, as he slowly approached, felt the emptiness of her words. She would never have done it again, for in her half-dreams she recalled how her mouth and lips had comforted his wounds. The taste of his skin was still with her.

As if to test her threat, he advanced until there was little space between them, touching her only with his eyes. 'Are you still fighting me, or yourself, my lady? Eh? Full of fears and conflicts. Rejecting what your mind wants, and wanting what your body spurns. Hating anything that reminds you of how it should be. And you think that's being disloyal, do you?'

Unable to face him again and fearful of what he might do next, she turned her back on him with a sob of anguish, the sense of his words flying straight to her heart, hurting her with their accuracy. She covered her face with her hands so as not to look at him, though the body he had set alight last night still quivered with desire. 'Leave me,' she said through her fingers. 'You have no right to do this. Make your enquiries and then leave.' Resting her head against the shelf, she felt his warmth seep into her back and his hand take her by the shoulder, felt the fine linen cloth being lifted off her neck and the softness of his lips upon her skin, beginning at the neckline and moving slowly upwards along her spine. Breathless, spellbound, she stood under his tender assault as he explored from side to side, tilting her head to aid his access to her neck, still refusing to look but unable to move away.

Finally, he lowered the wimple and rearranged its folds. 'Hush, my beauty,' he whispered. 'You're like a bird that's gone back to the wild that needs gentling again. Methinks you're starting to remember what it feels like, aren't you? There's no disloyalty in that, wee lass. 'Tis a natural reaction.'

Softened and enfeebled by his magic, she told herself angrily how wrong he was yet again. From her Robbie, there had been nothing like that to remember, for though he had been kind and careful, he had never bestowed such simple and persuasive caresses upon the back of her neck nor had she ever known how it could cause her to ache with emptiness and yearn to be filled. She had loved him, but now she found herself responding with frightening spontaneity to a man with neither qualms nor conscience, a man who had already shown himself to be utterly ruthless.

Preparing to contradict his theory, she turned, but saw only Sam and Biddie returning for their next task. Of Sir Alex there was no sign.

'Why, what is it, mistress?' said Biddie, all concern. 'Is it…' she glanced at the door '…is it that man?' She took Sam by the hand and led him towards a shelf. 'Sam love, be a good lad and count out twenty of those blankets for me, will you? Then set them upon the chest.' She returned to Ebony and drew her like a mother to the small cushioned window-seat. 'Now, what's it all about?' she said. 'I've seen him looking at ye. Is he upsetting ye, m'lady?'

Explanations were impossible, even at this stage. 'He's telling me that I must not accept a proposal of marriage from Master Davy in case it interferes with his enquiries,' Ebony said. 'I've never heard of such impertinence.'

Biddie's large eyes widened and blinked like an owl. 'Well? And did ye *want* to marry him?'

'No.'

'Oh, right.' The eyes blinked again and grew darkly perplexed. 'It sounds to me as if Sir Whatsit needs his mind taking off you and putting on somebody else,' she said, more or less hitting the nail on the head. 'So what if we were to introduce him quite quickly to Mistress You-know-who? How would that be?'

'To Jennie, you mean? Biddie, you're a marvel. If *she* can't turn his head, then nobody can. I'll make sure he sits next to her at dinner.'

Privately, Biddie believed that her mistress already held that trophy, for the wounds on the aforementioned head had not gone unnoticed by any of them, herself included. Mistress Jennie Cairns might think of herself as God's gift to man, kind or otherwise, but she could not hold a candle to Lady Ebony's dark disturbing beauty that took men's minds off their tasks, and there were few of them who had not laid money on the result of Sir Alex's presence at the castle. They would not take kindly to losing it, but Biddie had a duty to please her mistress at all costs.

'Mark my words,' Biddie said, 'she won't need any

encouragement once she claps eyes on these men. They're a far better-looking crowd than the laird's, and twice as fit. She'll think she's in heaven.'

As usual, Biddie's inherited Scottish canniness was borne out within minutes of the noisy arrival of Master Richard Cairns and his pretty wife Jennie, née Moffat, who saw any gathering as a chance to make sexual conquests rather than to socialise generally. To her, a funeral was no different in this respect than a wedding: even as she was lifted down from her palfrey, her prominent pale-blue Moffat eyes were assessing the undoubted virility of Sir Alex's men, many of whom had undergone the same transformation as their two captains.

By the time Meg reached her, the heavy eyelids had drooped demurely just long enough to convey a proper sympathy for her cousin so suddenly bereft of a father. Their embrace was cordial, but they had never been as close as Ebony had suggested only an hour ago, for Meg would have nothing to do with the kind of perpetual pretence that was as real as life itself to Jennie. Shallow, was what Meg had called her in a moment of uncharity.

'*Dear* Meg,' Jennie said. 'And poor *dear* Uncle Joseph! Tell me what happened.'

'Yes, later,' Meg replied. 'I will, but first you must—'

'And dear Ebony. *Still* not remarried? How can you *bear* it?'

'Perfectly well, thank you,' Ebony said, ritually kissing the air past each fair cheek. 'You're looking well, too.'

Jennie simpered, her glance bouncing off the husband who, at forty-five, was over twice her age. 'You should find one like my Richard,' she whispered. 'He's *such* a sweetie! He lets me do as I please and never says no to me.'

There was a strong signal from Meg warning Ebony not to indulge in the obvious response. 'Good,' Ebony said. 'Sam, make your courtesies.'

'Oh!' Jennie squealed. '*What* a little poppet! How he's grown. And I swear he looks more like his poor dear papa every time I see him. The Moffat hair, too.' She patted him as he came up from his bow and laughed as he dodged away from the next impending caress, her gaze already moving on past the women to her brother. 'Davy! Why could you not have waited for us?' She launched herself upon him in a flurry of sea-green and blue and a flash of sapphires from the gold net that enclosed her bundle of fair hair.

Losing track of Sam's escape, Ebony scanned the busy courtyard, shading her eyes against the bright sun for a small dab of red on a palette of blues, greys and browns. To her complete amazement, she saw him across on the far side beyond the packhorses, sitting happily upon the arm of his hero, Sir Alex, a little arm hooked about his neck and an expression of pride and contentment on his shining face as he watched the busy scene from six feet above ground. The two captains stood side by side, their attention fixed upon the noisy greeting of the two adult siblings, the lift of an eyebrow, a half-smile and a low comment convincing Ebony that something in the scene had pleased them.

She herself was less pleased, not knowing quite what to make of Sam's expanding affection for the man against whom she had such an overwhelming grievance. Fear flitted across her mind and disappeared like a bat in the darkness. Her eyes had already begun to slide away when his glance caught and held them, level and unflinching. He spoke to Sam, who turned to her and waved, blowing her a kiss, and she was obliged to return one of her own that inevitably fell upon both of them at once. There was, she thought, the faintest smile of triumph on his lips before she turned away to speak to Meg.

It would have been a source of great regret to Sir Joseph that he was unable to be present at the splendid midday dinner over which the two women and their efficient household had laboured for days to prepare. Though more guests were arriving continually, the meal itself was memorable for its incongruous jollity, for Ebony's irritation at Jennie Cairns's flirtatious ways with the man who had been placed next to her, and for Master Davy's complete monopolisation of his lawyer brother-in-law to the exclusion of common civility. It seemed that their discussion could not wait for a more private moment.

As Meg approached, Ebony thought that, by the concern in her eyes, this was perhaps what she was about to mention. But she was wrong. 'Ebbie, come over here. You *must* speak to Davy,' she said, drawing her to the end of the dais and glancing into the almoner's platter on its way to the kitchen.

Ebony sat on the edge of the platform. 'That might be tricky,' she said. 'He and Richard have hardly stopped talking long enough to eat.' She noted Meg's refusal to smile, her eyes glaring across at her cousin Jennie.

'He's not being nearly eager enough to follow up

these accusations against my father,' said Meg, searching out the peacock colours in the sunlit hall. 'He's humming and hawing as if he believes it might be true, insisting that he needs to get at my father's box and signet ring rather than sitting down with Sir Alex to confront the problem head on. I really can't make out whether he's playing for time or whether he's not sure how to go about it. Could *you* have a word with him? You know his feelings for you, Eb.'

'Yes, if you think it will help. What d'ye want me to say to him, that I'll give him the ring? I can't see how that will do much good.'

'Promise him anything. Make him a bit keener to help, that's all. He doesn't want to tell me why he needs my father's box that's hidden away somewhere, but you'll be able to persuade him that we need help urgently. It may not make any difference to whether we're allowed to stay here, but it'll certainly affect Sam's inheritance if the king decides to believe what those two will tell him.' She did not need to dwell on her own anguish at the thought of having her father branded as a traitor to his country. Instead, her eyes led Ebony's towards the figures of the two captains whose attention was centred upon her flirtatious cousin Jennie at that moment. 'My God!' she growled. 'Will ye look at her, Eb—did ye ever see anything as shameless as that? Would ye not think she'd come to a wedding more than a funeral? The *hussy*!'

Angered for the same secret reasons as Meg, Ebony looked away. 'I'll speak to him. Don't worry about it. Sir Joseph's name *must* be cleared. Leave it to me.'

With all that had yet to be done, there was no time to seek Master Davy out before supper, after which there was no need, for it was he who came to her with the request for a moment of her time while the tables were being folded and cleared away. If it had not been for Meg's quick nod of the head from across the hall she might have reminded him of her duty to the guests, but the musicians were making an ear-splitting entry, young Sam was with Josh and Biddie, and uppermost in Ebony's mind was Meg's plea for help.

'Of course,' she said, wincing at the din. 'Can you lip-read?'

Master Davy mimed a negative and pointed to the door at one side of the high table. The passage leading towards the steward's office was not where she would have chosen to linger with recent agonising memories still so fresh in her mind but, as the door closed upon the clamour, Davy kept her waiting for the point of his invitation. 'My dear Lady Ebony,' he said, 'will you sit a while? Here, on this window-seat?' He sat next to her and leaned an arm along the sill, his fingers just touching her shoulder. 'You're looking strained. This must have been a terrible time for you. Have you not been sleeping well?'

She thought that a curious remark for him to have made, but she could not answer it truthfully. 'It's been worse for Meg than for me,' she said. 'She's very concerned about her father, you know. These men seem quite convinced of his guilt. Have you come up with any evidence that could clear him? Bills of sale? That kind of thing?'

He sighed and looked down at his pointed toes. 'If only they'd not got here first,' he said. 'They're making it very difficult for me to prove anything to the contrary, Lady Ebony. They've removed some of his most important effects, the key to his box has been lost, and I cannot reach the box itself because it's in his room where Sir Alex's men are billeted. And I'm not going to rummage in there to show them where it is or they'll take that, too. And then there's his signet ring, which I believe you hold. If I'm to finalise the pending bills of sale, they have to be signed and sealed with his seal.'

Ebony frowned. 'But I don't see how anyone can use his seal now, after his death. If the sale of ponies is not finalised by now, it will have to wait. Surely you were not thinking of forging his signature, were you?'

Master Davy leaned forward, his smile intended to allay her fears. 'Of *course* not,' he said. 'All I want to do is to make sure that if there *is* anything incriminating, I can either remove it or change English sales to Scottish ones.' His voice was irritatingly soothing, as if explaining to a child.

But Ebony's frown did not clear. 'If there *is* anything incriminating, Master Davy? What in God's name are you saying? That you believe he was making sales to my countrymen? Is that what you truly believe?'

There was an explosion of breath which Ebony thought sounded like the beginning of a very inappropriate laugh. 'Lady Ebony,' he said, looking at her thighs instead of her face, 'have you given any thought to how it must look to these men, an English woman living in a Scottish household, daughter-in-law to an influential laird whose dealings with his English neighbours are under suspicion? Do you not think it will surely have occurred to them that your

English connections would have been an advantage to my uncle in his…well, frankly…injudicious sales to men on the other side of the border? Sir Joseph was never one to ignore a connection when he saw the benefits to the Moffat family, was he? Why else do you believe he was keen for his only son to marry into an English rather than a Scottish family? And *you* have benefited from it quite considerably, haven't you, while others around you have been left wanting?'

'If you call having my husband murdered a *benefit*, Master Davy,' she whispered, coldly, 'then, yes, I was fortunate. And to have been cared for to such a degree that I've no idea where my mother is, nor did Sir Joseph ever make any enquiries on my behalf. Call those benefits, if you like. But if you think he made use of my English connections, then think again, sir. He did not.'

'Can you be so sure of that, my lady?'

'Can *you* be sure of your accusations?'

'Yes, I can. I assisted him in his business matters, remember, and if only I had access to his documents and his seal, then I could show you exactly what he was doing.'

'So you are implicated too, I take it?'

'Not so. I merely did his bidding as his most trusted clerk. I asked no questions, and all I wish to do now is to provide Meg with proof of his innocence, which I can probably manage to do if you will help me. And if I may say so, my lady, you may find it in your own interest to assist me in this, as an Englishwoman.'

Could there be something in what he said? Would Sir Joseph have flaunted his connections with the ancient English Nevillestowe family to foster trust in his business dealings with English buyers? Would he have implicated his own daughter-in-law in illegal activities, and had Robbie been involved too, for all his denials? Had their marriage been one more string to his bow? And, yes, she had been well cared for, for would she now have to untangle herself from this mess and pay even more dearly for it?

She found that she was breathless, as if the walls had begun to press in upon her. 'What is it you want me to do?' she said. 'Give you his ring? Obtain the box for you? I can manage to do that, I think.'

'Thank you. But there's more than that, dear lady. Last night, you suggested that I should be taking the lead in these matters and I assured you that I would. My brother-in-law has promised his expertise too.' His fingers touched her shoulder to lift a corner of the fine white wimple for a peep at the bare neck beneath. 'You must know how I've longed to hear you say that. It was Sir Joseph's dearest wish that I should be the one to care for you and young Sam, you know, and I think there has never been a time when you needed a husband with some influence more urgently than you do now. Marriage to me will give you the security you're going to need while Sir Joseph's affairs are being investigated in the courts. Of course, I would see that Cousin Meg is offered security too until a husband can be found for her, that goes without saying, but what young Sam needs most of all is a firm hand, a tutor, and a secure home life instead of this godforsaken place. And you, my dear lady, need…a man…in your bed.' His fingers had begun a warm journey along her neck, drawing her towards his moist waiting mouth, his eyes already closing in anticipation.

Frantically computing all the reasons why and why not, she tried to hold him away, but found an iron resistance under her hands. The stone windowsill at her back pressed hard, reminding her how poorly she had timed her response to his persuasive talk about security and how, had he but known it, her predicament was more complicated than he supposed. Once she had fulfilled her bargain with Sir Alex, she might quite possibly have another life to provide for as well as herself and Sam, and then she might be glad of this offer of protection, though the deceit and pain of it would be very great. A bastard child born to a widow would do little for her claim to be faithful to her late husband's memory, but would she have the gall to pass it off as Davy Moffat's, if she were to accept him? She had promised to help Meg, but then there was Sir Alex's warning to complicate matters even more, pulling the argument this way and that in the wake of her genuine aversion to remarriage.

His hot breath was upon her face, his hand already fumbling near her knee. She twisted and pushed away, ready to demand more time, to prevaricate. Anything but this. 'Wait!' she said, using all her strength. 'No, sir! This is *not* what I meant. You are mistaken, Master Davy. I *don't* need a man in my bed.' Using all her efforts, she placed a forearm across him and levered herself upright, away from his groping hand. Pulling her skirts down, she felt more cheapened by this assault than she had by Sir Alex's response, for this man showed less control and had less reason to assume that she was willing.

'What?' he said, falling back as if waking from a dream. 'Not what you meant? Oh, come, my lady. Of *course* that's what you…'

'Permit me to know my own mind, sir!' she yelped, angrily. 'If you misunderstood me, that's your own affair. I said nothing about marriage to you, and if you'd listened properly you'd *know* that.'

For once she had managed to silence him, so that now he sat like one who'd been delivered a nasty blow to the head, blinking himself back to reality. 'Would I?' he said, plaintively. 'Oh, then what *did* you say?'

'I said that you should be able to take the reins, by which I meant to sort out Meg's problems concerning her father. She's your cousin, you know, and it's no use telling me how much *I'll* benefit by marrying you when the boot's on the other foot, Master Davy. If you can prove Sir Joseph's innocence then you'll be in a better position to ask for a reward, won't you? No man takes his prize before he's completed the task, sir. A fact you seem to have forgotten.'

Greedily, his eyes wandered over her as with one hand he tried to remould the lower half of his face. 'You've got someone else in mind,' he said.

Without hesitation, she answered, 'No. In spite of what you think, Sam and I will do very well as we are. It's Meg who needs help, and I have no mind to indulge in marriage talk while she's up to her neck in accusations of treason. I'm surprised you can think otherwise. Shame on you, Master Davy.'

Her message found its target. 'You mean,' he said, crestfallen but not defeated, 'that you'll consider my proposal once this business has been sorted out? Really?'

'If the outcome is as we know it should be, then I *will* consider it. I could hardly do otherwise, could I? But please don't take that as an acceptance.'

'There *is* someone else, isn't there?' he insisted.

This time she hesitated while her mind clung to a precious dream that had come lately to comfort her lonely nights and drift away with the dawn. She was tempted to lie and say that there was Robbie, but there was a better reason for the truth. 'Yes, there is my mother. Now that Sir Joseph can no longer prevent me from going to Carlisle, I intend to find out what's happened to her. Until my mind is settled on that subject also, the issue of remarriage will have to wait. I'm sorry, but we were close. I have to find her.'

'I can help you with that, if you'll allow it,' Master Davy said, standing up and pulling his clothes into line, placing his heel on the end of one long sleeve as he did so. 'I can make enquiries. I do some business over the border, you know.' His smugness suffered as he yanked at the sleeve and brushed the dust off the end.

Ebony could have asked why he had never offered before, but assumed that he had been influenced by Sir Joseph, as they all had. 'Thank you,' she said. 'I shall need all the help I can get. Now, I must return to my guests.'

'And the seal? The box? Could you—?'

Ahead of them, the door to the hall opened with a sudden burst of sound, yelps and cries of excitement and a propulsion of bodies, the upper half of Sam just visible between two enormous grey wolfhounds, their pink tongues lolling and tails lashing in enjoyment. With a hand on the ring of each studded collar, he was being dragged along as fast as his legs would carry him, accompanied by the breathless Biddie and Dame Janet.

Ebony had been about to delve into her pouch, but

the sight of her child being pulled off his feet by two
monstrous hounds overcame every other consideration, for it was clear to her that the cries of the two
women were being interpreted by the hounds as encouragement when their commands had always been
boomed by deep-voiced males. She caught at a wide
leather collar as it passed, waist-high, but it was too
wide and the hounds too strong to be stopped, and
Master Davy's orders to Sam to let go were unheard
in the peals of laughter. But a loud bellow from the
doorway of the steward's office brought them all to
an immediate standstill, the two hounds flattening
themselves to the floor so suddenly that Sam went
down with them with a muffled thud, his little fingers
slipping numbly from the rings. He was speechless
with laughter, and Ebony's heart ached at the sight of
him.

Sir Alex Somers appeared in the doorway of the
steward's room almost within touching distance of
Ebony, his words reaching only her over the pile of
furry bodies. 'A firm hand he needs, is it? Not much
wrong with the ones he's got, I'd have thought.' He
bent to Sam and heaved him up into the air like a
puppet, settling him into Biddie's arms. 'Come on up,
my lad!' he said. 'Master Moffat, would you be good
enough to escort these gentle people back to the hall
and give them a beaker of your best Rhenish wine, if
you can find a cask somewhere? Ah, Josh!' he called
as Master Joshua appeared with the well-mannered
deerhounds. 'Take these two animals away, will
you?' He trusted Joshua to understand the message.

Master Davy's reluctance to leave Lady Ebony
with this man was understandable, for he had failed
to bring the conversation to a satisfactory conclusion.

Though he preferred not to argue the case, his look of extreme annoyance could not have been missed, even by the hounds. 'Lady Ebony?' he said. 'You'll come too?'

Her mouth opened to reply, but Sir Alex's answer was already prepared. 'Lady Ebony will stay here with me a while,' he said firmly and without elaboration, and Master Moffat had no option but to go.

'You *heard*,' Ebony scolded as soon as the door had closed. 'You were in there all the time and you heard everything. *Didn't* you? Did you arrange that little farce as well, sir, by some sixth sense?'

'The timing was perfect, wasn't it?' he said. 'I'd like to claim credit for it, but no, it was sheer coincidence. However, I would not have allowed you to hand over the signet ring, my lady. That would have been very foolish.'

'The ring is mine to do with as I wish, for the time being. And you find it excusable to eavesdrop on a private conversation, apparently.'

The corners of his mouth dimpled and straightened again. 'A very touching, intimate and interesting conversation, my lady. Most enjoyable. You did well to hold him off.' He leaned a shoulder against the wall. 'But before you go off in an indignant rage, stop to ask yourself *why* he wants it. He can't possibly use it.'

'He said he could help Meg and that's all I'm concerned about.' Against her will, her eyes feasted on the shape of him, his casual grace, the brown hair as thick as a bear's pelt, the sturdy column of his neck, the square jaw and firm contours of his mouth scored by fine lines. His blue eyes caught the last of the evening light like distant lamps. More than any other man she had met, this man was her match, though the knowledge was neither comfortable nor frightening. She made as if to leave him, but his hand caught her wrist and held her arm taut like an anchor-chain.

'Tch, tch! Here's a woman who acts first and thinks later,' he whispered. 'Impulsive woman! Impetuous. What else are you going to give away before you're stopped? You'd have given yourself to that idiot if I'd not warned you against it, and even then you gave him hope for no good reason. Bargaining to keep your child, to help your kin.' He swung her hand. 'Too generous, lass. What you offer is irresistible. People will take advantage.'

'You can tell me *that*?' she said, looking at his hand on her wrist.

'Yes. I can tell you that. I'm the only one who will.'

'Don't say any more,' she whispered, turning her head away.

Unspoken words wove themselves between moments of silence before he said, 'One thing more. Whatever Master Moffat tells you he has done for you or his cousin, you must give him nothing, not the seal or the box, if you know where to look for it. You must put him off a while longer, and don't be concerned; we're watching him closely. He's not quite Sir Joseph's innocent clerk he wants you to believe.'

'You mean he's involved somehow?'

'More than likely. Best if you keep that to yourself. Understand?'

'Yes, but that's all very well. He's promised to help me find my mother, and he'll not exert himself over that unless I offer something in return.'

'Offer him something by all means as long as it's

not the something you've already offered me. That will be mine until I choose to relinquish it, my lady.'

She pulled her hand free. 'Then I suggest you take what Mistress Cairns has to offer instead, sir. We all know that *her* interest reaches little further than a man's braies.'

'Easy, my beauty,' he laughed, softly. 'You keep Master Moffat at a distance and I'll do the same with his sister. How will that do?'

'Keep her where you like!' she snapped, walking away with the sound of his laughter wrapping her like a shadow.

Chapter Six

But for one redeeming feature, the day of the funeral was best dismissed as an event to be endured with as good a grace as possible, though the effort took Ebony and Meg almost to the end of their tethers. It was not only the weirdness of seeing one's larger-than-life father being lowered into the dark family vault in the village church. That was bad enough. But the pall of respectful sympathy that had accompanied the body to its resting place was so quickly put aside on the return to the castle that Ebony and Meg wondered what it would take to stir their guests' hearts for longer than an hour or two. Telling themselves that Sir Joseph would certainly have displayed the same eagerness for food and wine, particularly the latter, if he had been there, was little comfort. Death was a frequent visitor, and the departed one must be given a merry send-off which he could boast about to his ancestors, even if Sir Joseph's friends took merriness to a different level of meaning.

A quiet service in the castle chapel had started the proceedings, the midday meal had passed without incident, and the arrival of even more guests, residential and local, appeared to fulfil all Meg's predictions that every mouth in Galloway would take this chance to feed at the old laird's table while he was looking the other way. Both hostesses made them welcome. At the feast after the funeral, however, some of Sir Joseph's closest friends took it upon themselves to behave as if *they* were the hosts instead of Meg and Ebony, ordering the hall servants to bring yet more dishes, the butler to broach more casks of wine, boxing the server's ears for being too slow, the page's ears for dithering. Seeing the situation worsen, Ebony sent Biddie and Sam up to bed.

The noise and rowdiness intensified, Master Davy's attempts at control were either disregarded or derided and he had no means of enforcing his wishes without creating an incident of even greater seriousness. Stories concerning Sir Joseph's raiding exploits led to the reopening of old rivalries, to quarrelling and foul language, to insults, counterinsults and challenges falling just short of physical violence, which many of the guests found entertaining enough to encourage. Ebony could see that this was what Sir Alex and Master Leyland found most informative and that, while they appeared to be enjoying the spectacle of grown men abandoning their manners, the two men were in fact taking careful note of who was condemning whom, even asking questions that the loud-mouthed ones were eager to answer. Most of all, she saw how they persisted in their pretence at ignorance even after Master Davy tried his hardest to silence the boasts about Sir Joseph's affairs. For the king's men, it must have been the most effortless enquiry they had ever conducted, and probably one of the noisiest.

It was well past midnight when Ebony and Meg

left the high table to confer, sure that their guests were
not ready to be moved for quite some time.

'Leave them to it,' Meg said, tight-lipped and white
with fatigue. 'It's going to get worse before it gets
better, and I'm damned if I'll ask Sir Alex to inter-
vene.'

'Meg, there's going to be a riot any moment now,'
said Ebony. 'Just look at them. They'll be drinking
all night long if we don't stop them and the place will
be wrecked. Brother Walter's sloped off to bed, so
there's no help from him. We said we'd make some
changes and I have a mind to start now. I've had
enough of this.'

'And I've had enough of that damned woman.
She's actually egging them on.'

'Who…Jennie?'

She had no need to ask, having kept a close but
unwilling eye on Mistress Cairns's blatant attempts to
claim the attention of the male guests, particularly Sir
Alex and Master Leyland. Her kirtle and cote-hardie
had obviously been chosen to reveal an expanse of
bare shoulder and, whenever she leaned forward, a
provocative view of the deep cleft between her
breasts. Needless to say, she had spent much of the
evening leaning forward, and twelve hours of the
woman's posturing had begun to irritate both Ebony
and Meg more than usual for reasons neither of them
could name.

'I wouldn't want to get on the wrong side of her
yet, Meg. Not till we've had the help we need from
Davy and Master Richard. You know what a vindic-
tive little piece she can be.'

She had told Meg of last night's conversation with
Master Davy, of his promise to help, with the bait of

her consideration hanging over it like a carrot before a donkey. Her modified version of the ending had not been too well received by Meg, who needed a quick solution to the issue of her father's misdeeds and saw no reason for complications. That Sir Alex should have overheard what had been said sounded to Meg more like carelessness than accident, and to have her fragile plans thwarted again by the two interfering strangers was quite unacceptable. She had almost wept with anger at the failure, increasing Ebony's chagrin so much so that, after looking in on her sleeping child, she had barricaded her door with a chest and two stools. In spite of the guards posted at the base of the stairwell, there was one who would be allowed to pass through them. Her night had been anything but seamless with her own foolish mention of Mistress Cairns ringing in her ears to the accompaniment of his delighted laughter.

Their mutual concern about Cousin Jennie's provocation, however, was immediately put aside as, in a distant corner of the hall, they noticed Dame Janet's white wimple surface and submerge again behind the bald head and bulky shoulders of Baron Cardale, her yelp of distress reaching them above the din like a child's cry to its mother. In the narrow space between the side of the dais and the doorway, the two struggling bodies had remained unnoticed by others nearby who were behaving almost as badly, or were too merry to care. But Dame Janet had never been accorded her due respect by her kinsman, Sir Joseph, a state of affairs that his friends now saw fit to perpetuate in his absence. She had passed too close to the lascivious baron on leaving the table, and her virtue was close to being forfeited.

Like a pair of vengeful parents, Ebony and Meg tore along the side of the hall behind the long benches of less noble diners, reaching the ill-matched couple in time to drag the baron's hand out of the screeching dame's surcoat. They yanked him backwards with such ferocity that he fell into the rushes with half the points of his chausses undone, his stomach exposed to view like a new pig's bladder. Dame Janet, who until then had never seen quite so much of a man, gave a choked shriek and slid down the tapestried wall to the floor before they could catch her, signalling to the inebriated guests that here was something they mustn't miss. The scene came alive with both rescuers and cheering supporters who would like to have seen more.

But Meg, who had borne the brunt of the day's emotions, had had more than enough. She turned on them like a wildcat. 'Get out, all of you!' she screamed. 'Go on, get out of my hall and to your rooms. This is how you repay our hospitality, by assaulting our household and forgetting every courtesy due to myself and my sister. If this is how you can best offer your help to the Moffat family, then we can do without you.' She picked up a three-legged stool and hurled it into the crowd of gawping men, hitting several of them at once. 'You may have been my father's friends,' she yelled at them, 'but ye're none of ours. Call yourselves civilised? Go on...*go*!' Her voice had worn to a screech, and she did not see who it was that came to present a wide shoulder and two strong arms to hold her.

Ebony did. Hugh of Leyland and Sir Alex appeared as if from nowhere to usher the guests away, crunching food, platters and knives underfoot, stepping over upturned benches, comatose bodies and pools of wine and ale that poured off the dais into a mash of soggy rushes. She pulled Dame Janet's clothes back into place before she came round and allowed two of Sir Alex's men to lift her on to a bench. Nevertheless, as she held a glass of wine to Dame Janet's lips, she could not miss the signs of surprise, envy and contempt on the faces of the male guests at the sight of Meg in Master Leyland's arms, and at the efficiency of the king's men, every one of them stone cold sober, who swarmed like worker bees to carry out Meg's orders to the letter.

Ebony turned to Sir Alex, her tone reflecting Meg's recent fury. 'A few moments sooner, sir, and this could have been avoided,' she said. 'I thought we might have relied on you to prevent this kind of thing happening to us, but you were too busy collecting evidence, of course. You must feel quite satisfied by the way things have gone for you, and to hell with the needs of those whose hospitality you've abused in the process.'

He stood with his hands on hips, feet apart, his eyes hard and unmoved to pity or repentance. 'The situation was always under control,' he replied, harshly, 'and none of us has abused your hospitality, my lady. Tomorrow you'll be able to see how we've brought things to a close more effectively than either you or Mistress Moffat could have done on your own. They'd have taken little notice of you. There's no real harm done.'

'Then tell that to Dame Janet and Mistress Meg,' Ebony snapped. 'And just *look* at this place! No real harm done?'

'I'll get some of the women to escort Dame Janet

to her chamber. She's only frightened. She'll recover soon enough. And as for Mistress Moffat, well…' he turned to observe the amazing progress of his friend '…I think she's being taken good care of.' Indeed, as Dame Janet was being made ready to leave, her mistress was being carried across the hall in Hugh of Leyland's arms, his eyes carefully avoiding those of Master Davy.

The latter was clearly vexed by the sight. 'What's going on?' he yelled, pushing his way towards Sir Alex. 'Where's that cocky young thing taking my cousin Meg? Has everyone taken leave of their senses? Tell me what she was so upset about, Lady Ebony, if you please. Is *this* man about to cart *you* off like Master Leyland?' Like everyone else, he had drunk more than his share.

To get into an argument of this sort after all that had happened was beyond Ebony, and though she was not as distraught as Meg, the effort of caring about Master Davy's hurt pride was too much. 'Get off to bed, Davy,' she said, quietly. 'It's late and I prefer sleep to arguments about relationships.'

'Sleep? With *him*?' Davy said, brushing a lock of limp blond hair out of his eyes.

Goaded, Ebony would have retaliated, but Sir Alex got there first. 'Yes, with me, man. Who d'ye think? Now get out of here and let's get the place fit for the night, what's left of it.'

Master Davy tried to glare the man down, but found that the effort was too painful. Next, he tried to focus on Ebony's feet. 'I see,' he said. 'Then I was right. There *is* somebody else. As I suspected. Well, now I know where I stand. I bid you both a very goodnight.' Unsteadily, he barged his way across the debris on the hall floor and through the crowds that drifted out, singing discordantly, into the night.

Appalled at the speed with which her efforts at appeasement had been undone, Ebony found a new lease of energy to berate Sir Alex as much for Meg's sake as her own. 'Have you *any* idea,' she scolded, 'of the damage you've just done by that *stupid* remark? You may have intended it to sound frivolous, sir, but we've all passed that point at this late hour, and now he believes that Meg and I are conspiring with you, if not worse. We were relying on his help, Sir Alex, not his enmity, as you well know. Tomorrow, you must tell him you were speaking in jest.'

But Sir Alex's manner had not softened, nor did he show the smallest trace of regret. 'We'll worry about Master Moffat's damaged hopes in due course, my lady,' he said, taking her arm in a firm grip. 'Tonight we'll concern ourselves with what matters. Now, you will be escorted to your room while we sort things out down here. Go on,' he said, noting her reluctance. 'It's been a long day. Go to bed.'

It was not how she had wanted the day to end, with matters growing ever more unsettled, but tiredness was overtaking her and she had no will to prolong events with useless reprimands. Even so, she had reckoned without Mistress Cairns, who came mincing over from the far side of the hall, too late to hear the heated exchanges but having caught sight of Master Leyland and Meg leaving the hall together. She reached Ebony, swivelling her glassy eyes towards the screens-passage and easing her kirtle a little further off her shoulders.

'I must say,' she whispered, 'Cousin Meg didn't waste much time, did she? And you look exhausted,

Ebony dear. Why don't you go up to your bed now? I can manage the hall servants, you know. We'll have this place cleared up in no time at all.' The quick flicker of her eyes in Sir Alex's direction showed the unmistakable drift of her intentions.

If the hall steward had needed help in directing his staff, Ebony would have held back her exhaustion and stayed, but she knew him better than that. Yet one more misunderstanding, and she was torn between stopping to explain what had happened to Meg or leaving the mischievous Jennie to find out for herself that the relationship was not the way it appeared. Meg couldn't stand the man, but it would do little good to say so with that look in her cousin's eye. 'Yes,' Ebony said. 'You do that, Mistress Jennie. Goodnight. Sleep well.'

She was never to know how she managed to keep her voice so even with a hard ball of pain at the base of her throat. She had never felt it before, but knew that it had something to do with that wretched woman, with the man who could speak so flippantly about her virtue before others, and with the contradictory advantages of not needing to barricade her door. There would be no vivid dreams tonight.

Calling in to take a peep at Sam on the way up to her tower room, she stood by his bedside with the ache of mother love and pride tugging at her heartstrings, entranced by his cherubic features. He had told her how he had sat in Sir Alex's arms again before the funeral service to tell him many of the guests' names, and she had realised with anger how the man was taking advantage of the child's innocent information, just as he would use her, eventually. Earlier, in the courtyard, she had been struck by the facial

similarities that would have deceived some into thinking that they were father and son, and prayed that
Sam would find courage when the time came for the
king's men to leave.

Biddie had no hesitation in confirming the success
of their earlier plan to place Mistress Jennie Cairns in
Sir Alex's path. She was in her shift, mending Sam's
tunic by the light of a candle. 'It worked, didn't it?'
she said, sucking hard at her finger with a frown. 'He
seemed quite taken with her. In fact, both men did. I
dare say Master Richard will be sleeping on his own
till dawn.' She watched another red bead appear, then
sucked again. 'Pleased?' she said, looking up at last.

'Delighted,' said Ebony.

'Shall I come up and undo you?'

'No, love. I can manage alone. Go to bed now.
Goodnight.'

'Goodnight, mistress.' Biddie lay the tunic down,
thinking that for one who was delighted, the expression was decidedly at odds.

For all her extreme tiredness, the images of the
dreadful day and the web of problems that snared her
were more than enough to keep sleep away. There
had been many times when she had wished Sir Joseph
out of her life, but now his removal had taken with
it the security she had come to rely on, and this, tied
to the emotional quagmire of her own making, gave
her none of the peace she had hoped for. For Davy
Moffat's hopes and his uncle's corruption and death
she could not be held responsible, but why these ag-
gravations should all have come together instead of
in manageable pieces was one of life's mysteries. If
it was some cleverly devised test of her courage, she
could have wished for some notice of it.

* * *

Turning restlessly for the twentieth time, her mind still picking like a carrion crow at the scraps of the day, her hand came to rest upon her hip where another hand had been lying in wait for precisely such a moment. She realised then that she *had* slept and that the dream had returned to share in her loneliness, that she had no idea how long it had been with her, and that, if she asked no questions of it, there would be nothing to explain after its departure. In some distant brightly lit time, a part of her sang with joy before the darkness enfolded her, drawing her senses towards the hand on its slow and languorous journey over smooth hip and satin breast.

The body that had been curbed and controlled for so long came instantly alive, quivering with yearnings, aching with emptiness and the demands of grief. He was there, vital and eager, pressing against her and pulling her under him, and she was ready and willing to be possessed and drowned in his loving, to take in all of him in a frenzy of release that blinded all objections with its suddenness. The restraints of the day fell apart, and she clung to him for support.

As if it had anticipated her reaction and prepared for it, the dream was a match for her in every sense. His mouth, locked on hers, drew forth her cries of desire and followed the path of her lips as they foraged for his breath, for the attention that would banish the turmoil in her mind. She set the pace, and he responded by taking control, slipping a thick arm beneath her back to swing her off the pillows, lifting her beautiful breasts towards his waiting mouth. Like a greedy infant, he tugged at her nipples with his lips and tongue.

One ecstatic cry signalled her urgency, and there

was no more delay before her legs parted and he was between them, entering her easily as if he had been doing so nightly for years, yet with the heartstopping excitement of a first time. Her cry took on another meaning as her hand caught at his wrist where he guided himself into her, too late to stop the entry but firm enough to convey her apprehension. This was the first time for her in over three years, the dream must realise. Was it something one could forget how to do?

He waited, allowing himself to be held back. 'It's all right,' he whispered, breaking the rule of silence. 'I know…I know. It's all right.' His wrist brought her hand away as he eased himself further inside, slowly dilating her and sending a shudder of bliss through the perfect body that must now relearn how to give and receive. Again, he waited, seeking her lips with his to complete a circuit of sensations that linked mind and body, cleverly, masterly, magically. His kiss held and softened her, steadying her lungs, and he began to move gently, rhythmically, reminding her of the tender beat of a man's loins and the breathtaking rippling invasion that brought new life throbbing into her emptiness.

She tried to remember and to compare, to assure herself that this was how it had been before, yet each slow and powerful thrust told her that it was not and never had been like this, that she was comparing a boy to a man, an apprentice to a magician. A moan of realisation escaped her and she was lost, caught up in the voluptuous moment that she had never thought could be so sweet.

If she had had any intentions at all, they would perhaps have focussed on making this last while her body was captivated by his rugged weight, not so heavy as to oppress but strong enough to hold her when she writhed against him, tossing in a sea of hair. But she was not in control that night, and the writhing was against a tide too powerful for her, a surging overwhelming torrent that he knew to expect but which she did not. She cried out as it engulfed her again and again under the pace of his relentless plunging, not knowing what it could be and helpless to think, aware only that she was suddenly and wildly ablaze before submitting to a rapturous quenching that made her gasp and shake with wonder.

Utterly amazed by the experience, sated but confused, she lay sprawled across him, held close by his arm, her attempts to cling to the dream failing with each sweep of her hand over his magnificent body. Now, not even exhaustion and half-sleep could help her to pretend that this great virile male could be her gentle Robbie, or that what she had just learned could have been taught by him. They had never made love like that. She had never achieved a climax before, as he had done. What she had discovered was a revelation and addictive and had come from a man who was nameless at night but who by day must remain her enemy.

Smoothing and exploring, her fingers wandered over the fuzz of soft hair on his deep chest and down over the steep slope to his stomach. Robbie had been hairless here; this man had more of everything. And, in spite of his determination to keep her to their outrageous bargain, it was now she who was using him to feed her longings and to return her to full womanhood at the end of her mourning. To her relief, he had not taken her as she had been sure he would, forcibly, uncaring and demanding. He had waited with patience and then led her, step by step, controlling the timing as if she had been a virgin.

An experienced virgin. She smiled at the contradiction. 'Again,' she whispered, on impulse. 'I want it again.' She was unprepared for the quick bunching of his muscles and his warm breath of silent laughter on her face as he flipped her over on to her back, or the weight of his head upon her hair that stifled his chuckles. Too late, she recalled her horror when, at that first meeting in the passageway, he had increased his demands from once to as many times as he wished. And here *she* was, demanding more in the pretend anonymity of darkness where rules were being abandoned by the minute.

The shame of capitulation tensed her body like a bowstring, bracing her arms against his shoulders and drawing up her knees to toss him aside, poor devices that stood no chance of success against the lightning-fast clamp of his body over hers, the iron grip of his hands over her wrists.

It was the only suggestion of force he needed to redirect her mind away from their enmity, for now his lips knew best how to seduce in ways which were quite new to her, and there was no pretence that could conceal her intense pleasure at every touch. This time it was he who set the pace, slowing each intimate caress into light years of melting torment that took her far beyond thought into warm seas of rapture. His hands and lips searched every crevice and plane to find what made her cry out with most poignancy, and when she could bear it no longer, she begged him again to take her, knowing but not caring how that was secretly what he had been waiting to hear.

Too soon, the final phase came like a roaring inferno to engulf them with a terrifying speed, drawing their cries into a duet after the first few vigorous thrusts that took them too far too fast. They fused and floated in a melting-hot tide that bore them away as softly as a cocoon of silk, closing Ebony's mind in sleep without another word being spoken.

The sound of a distant cock-crow made him smile as he stood at the open window, looking out over the loch. The air was cool and fragrant, the water like a dark mirror cut by the fine wake of a boat and a hint of pink at the eastern end, a sign of bad weather to come. He clasped his hands behind his head, breathing deeply and taking the coolness upon his bare chest, his mind sneaking back to the woman in the bed behind him in spite of his efforts to move it forward into the new day. Could anyone have prophesied such a spate of coincidences? The old man out of action and his cronies ready to shout about his affairs like washerwomen: the nephew talking himself into a corner, and two beautiful women, both of them single. And this one?

He turned to glance at her slender form beneath the fur covers. Was there ever such a woman? Beautiful, fierce and loyal, intelligent, sensitive, impulsive and proud. How long would it be before she would let go of her guilt at discovering that she wanted him? Yes, she wanted him, and had done so from the beginning or she'd never have offered herself, subconsciously or otherwise.

Yet there was now more to his original opportunism, he had to admit it, than a basic desire to take advantage of her, to strike a bargain and leave, as he'd done with so many others. This one was different, unique. A rare prize worth keeping. He leaned his elbows on the stone sill and cupped his chin, glad that he'd waited for her these last few nights: to have rushed things would have achieved nothing. Even now he had better expect a rough ride, for she would do her best to pretend that it had not happened or, if it had, that she had been unwilling. Which was a lie, of course: never had a woman been more eager than she, more responsive, or more untutored. Whatever her late husband had taught her, it had not been the art of making love, for although she had natural talent, it had never been awakened until last night when she'd confirmed not only that she wanted him but that she could experience the same natural conclusions as a man. She had wanted more. After all that, she had pleaded for more. His smile broadened. But then, so had he.

Equally encouraging was the knowledge that both women had been glowering at him and Hugh most of the evening as the lawyer's woman pursued them, flirting relentlessly. Lady Ebony had spoken of her in an unguarded moment, thus revealing a first streak of jealousy that she was not even aware of. That had amused him. Well, the lawyer's strumpet wife would probably be a little more subdued today, for last night, after Hugh's return to the hall, they had escorted her up to Moffat's chamber where a certain young knight had been more than willing to oblige her for as long as she wished it, after which she would probably return to her own room well satisfied.

A slight sound from the door made him reach for the dirk that lay on top of his pile of clothes. With his men guarding the stairway, there had been no need to lock the door, though perhaps he should have done.

It opened just wide enough for a little naked figure to sidle into the room and close it silently behind him. 'Sam!' Sir Alex whispered, placing a forefinger to his lips. 'Shh!'

As naturally as to his father, Sam tiptoed across the rushes and into Sir Alex's arms, and, with a grin as wide as a sickle, was lifted high up to view the room from a more interesting level, all thoughts of his mother relegated in favour of his hero. Finding an intimate warmth from the contact, his arms went round the sturdy neck, his legs astride one lean hip with an arm to support him. Sam was in heaven.

'Where's Mama?' he whispered into the nearest ear.

'Over there, asleep.'

Briefly, Sam checked. 'Did you sleep in here?'

'Yes, she was a bit upset about the noisy guests.'

'She always is. It would have been worse with Grandpa here.'

'Would it?'

'Oh, yes.' Sam fondled the receptive ear, marvelling at its size. The little hand moved on to examine the texture of the chest hair. 'I'm glad you're here, even if Mama isn't.'

Sir Alex smiled at the incongruity that apparently meant nothing much to the child. 'Well, you know,' he said, 'we chaps have a lot to learn about our mamas, don't we? They're not always as cross as they make out. Sometimes they use crossness to hide what they really feel.'

'Why do they do that?'

'Because what they really feel is a bit mixed up inside. Like you sometimes, eh?'

'Is that why Mama tells me to sort myself out?'

'Exactly. Except that grownups usually have a fair bit more to sort out because they're bigger. Now, see that boat out there?'

Immediately diverted, Sam nodded. 'Yes, that'll be Geordie.'

'And who's Geordie?'

'Grandpa's woodsman. He takes things to the other side of the loch for Grandpa every weekend. He'll be on his way back to the castle.'

'Who does he meet? D'ye know?'

Sam shook his head. 'Too far to see,' he said, reasonably.

'I'd better get dressed and go down, I suppose. Shall you…?' He turned towards the bed as he spoke, his heart leaping at the sight.

Ebony was now sitting upright against the pillows, hugging her knees, her hair falling over one shoulder like a black silken cloak, an expression of harrowing sadness in her eyes. She stretched out her arms as her child was carried across to her. 'Sam Moffat,' she said, glaring beyond the little fair head at the man's comely face, 'what *are* you doing?'

'Talking man's talk, Mama,' he said, snuggling down.

Like Ebony, Meg had believed that once the funeral was over and done with, matters must improve or, at least, get no worse. They were both wrong. Without saying more than the briefest of farewells, Davy Moffat, his sister Jennie Cairns and her husband Richard had made an early departure from the castle even before the day had fully begun and were now on their way to Dumfries, leaving their hosts astounded by their incivility. Unfortunately there was worse to come, the mischievous siblings having made sure, before they went, to spread the word via one or two gossipy acquaintances that Mistress Meg's anger at her guests' behaviour was not so great as to prevent her from accepting Master Leyland's advances. Yes, he had carried her up to her chamber. They had been seen. And Sir Alex had been heard to say that *he* would be sleeping with Lady Ebony. So much for the grieving Castle Kells women.

'Is it true, Ebbie?' said Meg. 'Did Sir Alex actually say that?'

'I'm afraid,' Ebony said, passing Sam an apple from the bowl, 'that he's taken leave of his senses as everyone else seems to have done. He did say that, I believe, but for heaven's sake don't take any—'

'He *did* sleep with Mama,' Sam chirped, trying to cut the apple with his wooden sword.

'Don't be ridiculous, Sam!' Meg snapped. 'And put that thing down while you're eating.'

'…any notice,' Ebony finished, lamely. There must, she thought, be a way of extricating oneself from this nightmare, if only someone could tell her how to do it. This was neither the time nor the place to explain to Meg what had been happening, and perhaps Sam had better be given the warning, after all, that she had earlier decided was not fair to the child. One should not deceive one's children and expect them not to deceive in return, so her mother had once said. If only she were here.

With all the agility of a wrestler, she turned the subject over. 'But Master Leyland did carry you up to your chamber,' she said. 'That bit was quite true. I expect they thought he'd been—'

'What, Eb? *What* would they think he'd been?'

'Invited?'

'Is that what *you* think?'

'Course it isn't. I saw what happened. I was there. Look, love, this won't do. We're starting to bite each other now. We can't allow those pests to make us lose trust in each other when we both know there's nothing to explain. Come and have something to eat.'

With a sigh, Meg lowered herself on to a bench at the table. Men moved quietly about the hall from which all signs of disturbance had been removed except for the cloying smell of unwashed bodies, wine, candle smoke and the stale food ground into the rushes. 'Then why did they leave like that?' she said. 'I don't see how my behaviour could be construed as in any way worse than Jennie's. Perhaps she quarrelled with Davy and Richard. The problem now is that we've lost whatever help we'd expected from them, which may not have been much if Davy's pathetic whining was anything to go by. We're no further into proving Father's innocence than we were to start with. Thank you, Janet,' she said, accepting a piece of pigeon pie.

It may have been the inappropriate use of the word 'innocence' that struck Ebony at that moment: how the remaining Moffats were thrashing about like fish in a net cast by these two men. Over herself particularly the net had dropped with deadly aim, catching more than the prize she had offered in the first place. And it was herself she had to blame for that.

Suddenly overcome with the gravity of her own problem rather than with Meg's, she dropped her head into her hands and held it there. She was no coward, and she would no doubt find a way of dealing with the dream that had begun to grow and escape the boundaries of the night, but to deceive Meg, Sam and Biddie was not her style. She had never been good at deception. 'I'm sorry,' she mumbled. 'Forgive me.' From a distance, it seemed to her that Robbie was listening.

Meg's voice was closer at hand. 'Are you not feeling well, Ebbie? Did ye not sleep too well?'

If only she knew. Ebony forced a smile and sat up. 'Sorry,' she said. 'I'm all right. These rushes stink.'

'You go up and take a wee rest. I'll have this place swept out and the rushes changed. We can go through Father's things later on.'

Ebony went to her room, but moments later she was slipping through the garden door down the path to the waterfall. By the water's edge, the small wooden boat was tied up to a tree root and, a little higher up, the sheltered pool gave her the seclusion she sought, without Meg for the first time in years.

Undressing slowly, she examined herself for telltale signs of their fierce coupling, which she knew with a terrifying certainty had changed her life for ever. The admission was like a pain in her heart, the delights of that man's arms like a wound to Robbie's memory. Each touch of her hands in places he had kissed were like the twist of the dagger, and each memory of her pleasure betrayed the love of the man who had fathered her son.

Vigorously, she scrubbed at her body with handfuls of soapwort, splashing the cool water over her head and watching the fleecy bubbles flow over the stones into the loch. But Sam's little face was there in every watery surface, his eyes glowing with pride, his arms hugging the man to whom she had sold herself with such fervour, forgetting her scruples. No matter how she sullied the water, the image haunted her, daring her to tell Sam not to trust the one he had begun to idolise.

She hauled herself out and twisted her hair into a rope, unable to stem the tide of sweet memories, so recent and sharp. He had dressed without haste, aware that his body must be a source of interest to both her and Sam, though she had tried not to be seen looking. His limbs were lean and knotted with muscle, the torso caught in the pale light, so unlike the lightweight Robbie whose loving had been comforting, at most. Neither of them had spoken, and only Sam had bidden him farewell as he left the chamber with a promise to see him later. But for Ebony, there had been a look that said far more than words, a look that stayed with her as she made her way back to the kitchen garden, telling her quite plainly that that would not be the end of the matter.

Chapter Seven

Master Davy Moffat and his sister were not the only ones that morning to make an unusually premature departure. By the time Ebony reached the castle after her bathe, the stable courtyard was teeming with packhorses, palfreys, wagons and mules whose owners had made vague excuses about the worsening weather and duties at home. They had been expected to hang on until well after the weekend.

Meg was receiving her guests' farewells, but there was no sign of Sir Alex or Master Leyland. Brother Walter stood by her side, blowing his nose and polishing it, his mournful features sagging more than ever from the affliction that he was quite unaware had been exacerbated by the change of rushes and the strewing-herbs on the hall floor. Dame Janet suffered in quite a different way, for Baron Cardale was not amongst those who were leaving.

'I can't understand it,' Meg said to Ebony, smiling and waving to the party of riders who clopped away. 'Especially after *their* behaviour.'

Ebony waved, passing her wet linen towel to Biddie and twisting her rope of hair behind her neck.

'Don't grumble,' she said out of the side of her mouth. 'It's what we wanted, isn't it? Who's staying on?'

'About ten of the men. They want to hunt.'

'Ah, so it takes more than the king's men and Davy's aspersions to put them off their hunting.'

There was little doubt that this exodus was what Sir Alex had in mind when he spoke last night of bringing things to a close, yet Ebony would have been just as relieved to see the king's men leaving with the others, in spite of the problem of the castle's defence, for their so-called help had not come cheap, after all. 'It's time we got rid of the lot of them, if you ask me,' she murmured, ambiguously.

Meg turned away as the last riders followed a rumbling wagon out of the gates. 'That was what we wanted, I know,' she said, 'but I'd rather not have done it with so much bad feeling. You should have seen some of the looks that lot gave me just now. You'd think I'd physically abused them.'

Ebony chuckled. 'You *did* throw a stool at them, love,' she said.

'Did I?' Meg's hand flew to her mouth. 'Did I *really*? Oh…my lord! I hope my aim was good. Was it?'

'Excellent. Perhaps we should throw some at those two next. They've put us in a very difficult position after last night, Meg, and it was not the way we wanted things to end. Thanks to them, we now have reputations to defend.' Ahead of them, Brother Walter, Dame Janet and Biddie ambled away up the stone steps that led to the first floor hall. 'Meg, what does Geordie Boyd take to the other end of the loch by boat each weekend?' she said.

Meg paused. 'He doesn't take anything. Why?'

'So what *does* he do?'

'He goes to collect Father's money from sales and dues and whatever else he has to have. He always said it was safer by water than by road. No robbers to ambush him.'

'Where does he collect it from?'

'From a collecting-point at one of his tenant's cottages. But why all the questions about Geordie?'

'So who would have sent him this morning?'

'Well, no one. Why, Eb?'

'Because he was out on the loch early, coming back to the castle.'

Meg came to a halt. 'I didn't send him.'

'Who did, then?'

With a faraway look in her eyes, and a shrug, Meg chewed on her lip before replying. 'Where will he be, d'ye think? In the woodyard?'

They found Master Geordie Boyd stripped to the waist, swinging a great axe through the air and bringing it down with a crack on to the cut end of a log. The two halves fell apart as he looked up, his face darkly unshaven but still attractive, his massive shoulders bulging under smooth brown skin. He was in his early twenties. Unable to hide his fancy for Meg and smiling at the interruption, he propped the axe carefully against the tree-trunk anvil. 'My lady?' he said. 'Mistress Meg?'

Meg came straight to the point. 'Geordie, who sent you out on the loch this morning early?'

He blinked, his eyes quickly warming with amusement. 'Why, mistress. You're the second one tae want to know me whereaboots. Is there something afoot, then?'

Ebony had good reason to shoot her question. 'Who else wanted to know, Geordie?' she said.

'Master Leyland,' said Geordie. 'I told him I'd stayed overnight with my lass and I was coming back early.'

'And that was not true?'

'Not exactly,' he smiled. 'Master Moffat dinna want me to say where I'd been.' Geordie was not practised in the art of subterfuge.

Meg's tone was less brisk, more honeyed. 'But you'll tell us, Geordie, I know, because you were loyal to my father. It was Master Moffat, was it, who sent you to collect Sir Joseph's money?'

'No, mistress. He said he'd do that himself on his way home today. I was to *take* stuff this time, not fetch it.'

'What stuff?'

'Oh, a whole load, mistress. Armour. Sacks of grain. It nearly sank the boat.'

'*Armour?* You're sure?'

'Aye, I'm sure. It was wrapped, but I know the feel of armour and weapons, even through sacking. He keeps it in the grain store. I have to take another load tomorrow.'

'Grain too?'

'Aye. Master Moffat'll get a guid price fer it, mistress. It fetches ten times what it used to, ye ken? I kept a sack for me ma. She'll be having loaves for supper toneet.' He winked at them, laughing at his craftiness.

'Who has the keys to the grain store now, Geordie?' said Ebony.

'The estate steward, m'lady. He has orders to unlock it for me in the morning early, so I can take another boatload.'

'I see. And is anyone else helping you in this be-sides the steward?'

'Ach, no!' he said, proudly. 'I dinna need anyone else, m'lady. I can carry it all, and row it there. I brought most of it here myself in the first place.'

'Just a moment,' said Ebony. 'You're losing me, Geordie. *You* brought it here? Where from?'

'Ach!' The strapping lad shook his bare arms with a laugh. 'I reckon I can tell ye now that Sir Joseph's gone. It was armour and weapons that Master Moffat brought in on ships from Italy and Spain, ye see. He gets it taken to the end o' the loch and leaves it at Ray the Boatmaker's hoose, and I pick it up from there and bring it to the castle to be stored, secret like. And Sir Joseph sells it to his contacts, and then sometimes Master Moffat will take the sold pieces in his wagon to pass on, on his way home.'

Ebony frowned, glancing at Meg. 'So it comes from Dumfries to Castle Kells and then gets taken part of the way back again. So why doesn't Master Moffat keep it in his own cellars, I wonder?'

'Weel, a reckon he hadna enough room there with his wine and all, m'lady. Besides, he said it was better here at the castle because it was Sir Joseph who selled it, him being a fighting man.'

'Do you know who he selled…sold it to?' said Meg.

Geordie's face changed to blankness in one second. 'Nah!' he said, shaking his head. 'It was my job to take and collect, nothing else. Master Moffat would bring wine and grain, too. I had to carry most of it.'

'But grain's been as scarce as gold these last few

years,' said Meg. 'Where did he get that from, I wonder?'

'He shipped it in from abroad where they had no floods, then they kept it in Sir Joseph's store to wait while the prices went up and up. Then he selled it to them who could afford it.' He grinned, all innocence. 'A canny man was your father.'

'And I,' Meg said, 'didn't bother to find out how much we had, or to ask where it was coming from and going to. I should have done.'

'That's the estate steward's job, mistress. He keeps those accounts.'

'So he and Master Moffat would do them together, I suppose.'

'Weel,' said Geordie, hoping to lighten the tone, 'a dinna ken that yer father'd have much to do wi' it when it came to words and figures, did he? He could no more read or write than you or me. That's why he left it to Master Moffat.'

'What?' Ebony breathed the word.

To Meg, this was no revelation, though she had kept it successfully from Ebony until now and had no wish to discuss her father's shortcomings in front of his woodsman. 'Thank you, Geordie. I'm glad you were coming back from your lass's house this morning.' She smiled sweetly at him. 'And I hope your ma enjoys the bread. I'll see she gets some more.'

'Thank ye, mistress.' He touched his forelock and picked up the axe, swinging it without effort to make the next chop, not watching to see them leave.

On the warm kitchen wall next to the woodyard they stopped, full of questions opened up by the interview with Geordie. 'All right,' said Meg, retying the end of her long plait, 'I know it must be a shock

to you, but he didn't want anyone to know. It's why
he never wanted a tutor for Sam, just like he didn't
have one for Robbie or me. He said he didn't think
it was important, but he would like to have been able
to read, I think.'

'It doesn't matter, Meg. Lots of men can't read or
write. What matters is that this sheds a different light
on Davy's involvement, because he's been preparing
your father's bills of sale, I expect. We have to find
his documents and go through them. It strikes me that
your father probably didn't have a clue about what he
was putting his seal to, and that would have laid him
wide open to forgery. Davy could have implicated
him in all kinds of sales, legal and illegal. Where did
you say that box is?'

'It's still in his room, where the men are sleeping.'

'Then we have to get them out and take a look.'

That, however, was going to be easier said than
done; the twenty-four men on night watch slept at
intervals during the day, and neither of the women
was inclined to tip them out of bed, stark naked, to
wait upon their search. Anxious to redeem herself in
Meg's eyes after her failure to obtain Davy's co-
operation, Ebony took the bull by the horns and went
in search of Master Leyland, without success.

She took a flight of stone steps spiralling upwards
to the castle ramparts in the hope of a bird's-eye view,
emerging from a small doorway to the wide pavement
on top of the wall that looked out over the loch on
one side and landwards to the other. Below her in one
courtyard were the thatched roofs of the workshops,
the farrier and the blacksmith and, next to them, the

armourer. A large deerhound waited patiently outside, its tail gently swinging.

Pressing herself back against the battlemented wall, she watched as Sir Alex came out with the armourer, a sword in his hand, his brown head bent to examine it, obviously discussing its weight and balance. He swung it in mighty arcs, making the deerhound dodge well out of range while several of the men in the courtyard stopped to watch, admiring. He disappeared again beneath the thatch, his hand on the armourer's shoulder, and Ebony groped with one hand on the wall to find one of the crenellations where she might sit unseen until her legs found their strength and her heart its normal beat.

It was the first time she had seen him use a weapon and now, in some peculiar alloy of reality and dream, she saw the vigour of the man who had come to her bed last night combined with the naked pagan god who had strolled across her chamber holding her child in his arms, tearing her heart with sadness. In all his aspects he was a superb creature, physically perfect, and an amazing lover. But he was their enemy still, a man who would take advantage of a woman's worst fears without compunction, who had already done so, having discovered the chink in her armour. He was there to blacken her family name in the king's eyes and to dispossess herself and Meg, to threaten Sam's safety. She could not afford to listen to the sound of her heart as it began a slow thaw.

Forgetting her mission, she took her ivory comb from her pouch and began the task of untangling her damp hair, only half-hearing the clang of hammers, the shouts of men and the distant neigh of a horse. Sam was with the bailiff's lads this morning; they would be watching the men go off to hunt, and the castle would be quiet again until evening. She hardly noticed when a large hairy head came to sniff at her hand, staring a greeting with baleful eyes.

Her first impulse was to walk away as Sir Alex stepped through the low doorway on to the ramparts. She had decided earlier to keep well out of his way at all costs, though now she saw that he would be able to help in the matter of the box, failing Master Leyland. In the circumstances, a flight across the ramparts in full view of the courtyard would be cause for gossip. So she went on with her combing, ignoring her sudden breathlessness.

'I heard you were looking for Hugh,' he said, leaning his arms across the top of the wall. 'A fine view from up here. A touch of rain in the air, too.' His hair ruffled in the breeze.

'And privacy would be a fine thing,' she retorted. 'Leave me be, sir.'

He swung round to study her, his eyes laughing at the blush roused by her snapping words. 'Privacy?' he whispered. 'Is that what you wanted? That's not the impression I got.'

She had hoped, and been reasonably certain, that he would make no reference to their fragile alliance, for he had appeared until now to understand the nature of it. His misplaced comment both infuriated and disappointed her more than she could say and, in one bound, her mind was changed. She leapt away from him and made for the small door of the tower on the next angle of the wall, running like a doe through the forest, too fast even for him. Slamming the door behind her, she took the widest part of the steps and spiralled downwards at breakneck speed to the next level, through the small arch and across the wooden floor of the next chamber, down steps, along a passage and up more steps, flattening Brother Walter against the chapel door.

'My lady…?' he called after her. 'Atchoo!'

Moments later, Sir Alex did exactly the same thing. 'Which way?' he said.

'Aargh-ah-shoo!' said the chaplain, pointing to the steps.

The steps led out into the garden where once Biddie had hidden provisions for their escape. On the path, Meg and the gardener were in conversation until the flying figure of Ebony almost knocked them into each other as she passed. Recovering herself, Meg called out, 'Ebbie! Where are you going?' But Ebony didn't stop to explain, and all Meg saw as Ebony disappeared round the corner was her hair billowing behind her like a black sail.

At Sir Alex's appearance, Meg began to understand. She would join in. Two against one. Sisters in arms. She followed, but was immediately intercepted by a large body whose arms caught her, swinging her up into the air out of Sir Alex's path. 'Let me go, ye great…half-wit!' she screamed, wriggling like an eel. 'Let me down!'

Master Hugh Leyland kept a firm hold and marched away with her, neatly side-stepping as Sir Alex passed and calling over his shoulder, 'Down to the waterfall, man. Go!'

For Ebony, the choices were limited, the shallow pool being surrounded by steep sides hung with ferns and dripping with water. With nowhere to go on land, she took three giant leaps on to the boulders at the edge of the loch, her fourth leap taking her into the little boat still tied to the tree root. The sudden shock of her impulsion tipped and rocked it dangerously, sending her keeling over the nearest seat-board to land with a crash in the bottom, her feet propped indecorously and helplessly in the air. Wetness seeped through her kirtle while fury, shock, panic and the offence of his certain presence swamped her mind and body.

He loomed over the side of the boat, watching her struggles, then stopped to untie the rope, stepped into the middle and sat with her feet on the seat beside him, pushing away from the bank and fixing the oars as the water carried them out. Ebony felt the pulling and rocking beneath her, heard the rattle and squeak of the oars, the swish of the water, saw his massive thighs, his wide shoulders leaning forward and back, his arms bent in an easy movement, and his profile as he looked sideways to swing them round and away. He was good at this too, it seemed.

'Go away!' she yelled at him. 'Go…leave me in peace, damn you!' The confines of the boat and his bulk made it impossible for her to scramble up but he took no notice, pulling on the oars as if she had not been there and speeding the boat away from the shore, his buttocks jamming her feet against the side to prevent her from righting herself.

Humiliated by her undignified failure and without anyone else to overhear her, she launched a verbal attack on every single aspect of his physical appearance, character, intentions, deeds and misdeeds, known and imagined, his abilities and his inabilities in every department, which, to say the least, became more and more confused as their distance from the castle increased. Had anyone else offered him a fraction of the abuse that Ebony hurled at him while she lay helpless at his feet, he would probably have killed them, but she was in no position to care. And he, having understood at last how fine a line she was walking between grief and rehabilitation, allowed the harangue to continue until her voice gave out. By which time they were well into the middle of the loch with the castle no more than a brooding pink against a thunderous sky, and an animal of sorts waiting for his master's return.

Laying the oars to rest, Sir Alex helped her slowly to right herself, pulling her up out of the puddle and sitting her wetly on the seat opposite him. He removed his serviceable leather doublet and placed it around her shoulders, ignoring her vitriolic opinions as to its smell, its texture, its unsavoury provenance, but noting the huskiness of her voice worn down by the ravages of intense emotion.

'I hate you!' she snarled with what little breath she had left, but feeling the searing hurt of new yearnings that, until now, had found no place in her unfulfilled existence. She took some moments to recover.

Leaning his arms across his knees, he gave her all his attention as she poured out her injuries concerning her failure to help Meg, his interference with Davy Moffat's proposals, saying nothing until she accused him of using Sam as an innocent source of information. Then, he defended himself.

'Oh, no,' he said, making her jump at the sound of his voice. 'Oh, no, my lass. You need not drag the wee bairn into this. He's not suffered in the least by answering a couple of harmless questions. He's perfectly happy to tell me who people are and to correct me when I get them wrong.'

'What do *you* know of how a six-year-old thinks?' she croaked. 'What do you know of *any* child? Do you see any of the bairns you've sired?'

The question was meant to be rhetorical, but appeared to catch him unawares. 'No,' he said, 'not often.' He looked away over the darkening water patched with ripples. 'Not often enough.'

'Then don't use my child as a pawn in your grown-up games. He's not too young to understand that a naked man in my room is—' Too awful to be spoken, the rest was held back by her hands, and she knew that she was saddling him with the responsibility that was just as much hers, and that he was allowing her to, to ease her misplaced guilt. 'You have maligned me not only in Sam's eyes but in the eyes of our guests too,' she whispered. 'I asked you to explain to Master Davy that you spoke in jest last night, and now he's spread the word that I'm unchaste. And Meg, too. How d'ye think we'll be able to clear Sir Joseph's name without his help? And how d'ye suppose he'll help in finding my mother as he said he would? All hope of that is gone, sir, thanks to you.' From a new source, anguish racked her with sorrow and regret that she had not been able to search for her mother as any daughter would have done.

'Tell me about her,' he said. 'What happened?'

Haltingly, the story emerged. It was still hard for Ebony to believe in her mother's death after two years of total silence, and the not knowing was as difficult to accept as death itself. Lady Jean had visited Ebony only once since her marriage into the Moffat family, a brief attendance at the birth and christening. Since then there had been many letters, shawls for the new baby, a silver rattle, a walking-frame for his first steps, but then nothing more after the news of the raid and her disappearance. Her last letter had been full of sorrow for her daughter's loss, telling her that she would visit as soon as she could. She never appeared.

'And what do you feel about her disappearance?' he asked softly. 'Do you believe she could be alive somewhere?'

Ebony nodded, her eyes searching into the silent depths of water. 'Held by someone? Injured, perhaps? Still alive, though. She *must* still be alive. I'm sure I'd know if she was—'

'Hush, wee lass. Enough. I'll take you back.' He opened the leather pouch at his belt and drew something out, handing it to her. 'Here you are. It's yours. Put it in your pouch.'

'What is it?'

He laid the key to her chamber door on her outstretched palm. 'Use it as you wish. The bargain has been met now.'

Like a hammer, she felt the thud in her chest at the enigmatic message in his piercing blue eyes. 'You mean…?'

'Yes, you're quite free, and safe. You've no more to fear.'

'And Sam?'

'He'll not be taken from you. I don't need a hostage.'

Trying to read his eyes was not easy, his most intimate messages until now having been silent and unseen; others had been unmistakably angry, formal, or veiled behind teasing. But here was a new expression she couldn't fathom, which may have been pity or tenderness, but which could equally have meant an end to his interest in her, like the return of the key.

She shivered and placed the key in her pouch, now puzzled after so many previous confident assertions that her obligations would not be brief. So he had changed his mind. Once *was* enough, after all. 'Thank you. It will remain private? A secret? I'd rather Meg didn't know,' she said, looking away.

The tenderness, if that's what it was, had already disappeared as he took up the oars again. 'That's between you and her,' he said. 'The men who guard your stairway are not blind or deaf. They know who comes and goes, and young Sam—'

'Yes,' she said, grabbing at the bulwarks to keep her balance against the boat's sudden lurch. 'All right. You need say no more. All I was asking is that you'd not boast of it, but I realise that may be asking too much of you. Your conquests must be one of your chief sources of amusement.'

The flash of his white teeth seemed to confirm her fears that this episode was for him only one of many and that already the novelty had worn off. Perhaps it was a sign that soon they would move on to Newcastle as they had said they would.

'The next chief source of amusement, my lady, will be an attack on the castle,' he said, cheerfully, pulling hard at the oars. 'It will probably come in the next few days, so if you were planning a trip to Carlisle I'd postpone it for a while, if I were you. You'll be safer behind walls than on the road.'

'An attack? Are you serious?'

'Couldn't be more so.'

'Who from?'

'Oh,' he grinned again. 'I think we have a fair idea who'll be behind it. We're preparing. Don't be too concerned. You'll be quite safe if you stay inside the castle.'

'So your enquiries are finished, are they?'

'We certainly have a clearer picture than we had two days ago. When we get back, perhaps you and your sister-in-law would join us for a look through the documents in the box. You may be able to shed some light on a few grey areas.'

'You forget, sir, that we are trying to prove one thing while you are trying to prove the opposite. In what way will a meeting help *us*?'

'You're jumping to conclusions again, lass. That's one of your weaknesses. I'd not have dismissed Master Moffat so fast if I'd thought he'd be the slightest use to you. I knew full well he had no such intentions. Quite the opposite. I sent men to search Master Moffat's house in Dumfries while he was away. They'll have taken a wee look into his cellars. It'll be interesting to hear what they find, but it will be equally interesting to see what *he* does when he finds out.' His easy pull on the oars did not falter, nor did he want for breath as he talked. 'We are, in fact, both trying to discover the truth, are we not? I don't get paid more for proving a man to be a traitor than for proving that he isn't.'

Though fascinated by his physical prowess, she was beginning to see a new side to the man who had been so briefly close to her, and it was this display of cool efficiency and resilience that cast a shadow of regret over the concentrated abuse she had thrown his way. He had called her impetuous, and now identified another weakness, but had he not also jumped to some conclusions of his own?

His great leather-booted feet on either side of hers

were braced hard against the ribs of the boat, drawing her thoughts unwillingly back to a softer and warmer location where their legs had not been so opposed as they were now, but where he had steered and controlled her, silently and skilfully.

Slowly, not wanting him to see, her eyes travelled upwards over knees to crotch where a bulge strained against the fabric of his chausses, and for the space of two seconds she felt again the hard thrust of him against her. On the wooden seat of the boat, she tightened against the quick shudder of bliss.

Looking up at last, she found his eyes upon her, reading her mind. Yet when she tried to read his she knew herself to be out of practice, and for the rest of the journey nothing was said to distort the parallel course of their thoughts. At last, as they neared the bank, she broke the silence. 'How did you know I was up there?' she said. 'Did someone tell you?'

He shipped the oars and leaned towards her, speaking slowly. 'I don't close my eyes when I'm wielding my sword, wee lass,' he said. 'I need to see what I'm about.' His reply made perfect sense, yet she retained the impression that he may have been referring to something other than what had happened an hour ago outside the armourer's workshop.

There was more to Meg's furious commands than being prevented from helping Ebony escape Sir Alex's company; there was also fear. Fortunately, her sister-in-law would be unable to witness this attempt by Master Leyland to get close to her, any more than she had witnessed his kiss last night at the door of her chamber. But whereas that lapse had, in a sense, been excusable, given her distress, her conversation with Ebony in the hall that morning had reiterated how important it was that their behaviour should be blameless at this time: not only *be* blameless, but *seen* to be. Any suggestion of warmth or capitulation would be taken as a betrayal of their determination to prove Sir Joseph's loyalty; one could not do that by fraternising with the enemy. That would be why Ebony was running away from Sir Alex. Ebony wouldn't dream of lowering her guard, and nor must she.

The tightness of his grip and the confidence of his stride fuelled Meg's fear that the innocence she had protested only an hour ago was about to be put to the test. She fought silently, employing all her strength against a man who, had she but known it, had never before needed to insist on a woman's co-operation. But all her weapons were ineffective, and she would not scream for help like a laundry maid. With arms, legs and hair flailing, she was tipped on to a flat patch of grass against the outer castle wall where yellow gorse bushes made a shelter as prickly as she.

Her fears increased as, for the first time, she felt the weight of a man over her and the iron strength of his legs as he held her together. Screwing her eyes tightly shut, she tried to keep out his threatening closeness. 'Master Leyland,' she panted, 'this is unworthy of you and…and an insult to me. You wouldn't be taking advantage of me if my father were still alive.' Her arms were pinned under his, but one of her hands held on to his wrist, her fingers too short to enclose it completely. 'I know you must think…after last night…that I am willing…but I'm *not*. I was upset. I was glad of your help. But your kiss meant nothing to me. Please…let me go!' When her eyes opened, she discovered that his face was deadly serious.

'Easy, little vixen,' said Hugh. 'I don't think anything of the sort. This is not meant to insult you any more than that wee kiss last night, but I know by now how to tell when a woman's warming to me.'

Her voice rose in panic. Warming to him was the very last impression she wanted to give. 'I'm not warming to you or anyone,' she said. 'You think I have nothing more to concern me when I've just lost my father? You are arrogant...and everything I *hate* about a man, sir.'

'And what do you like most about a man, mistress?'

'His distance. In your case, several miles. Get *off* me!'

'I will—' he smiled '—for a price.'

She turned her head away to avoid his eyes that might, for all she knew, be able to tell when a woman lied as well as when she was warming. Never would she let him know how she had lain awake half the night, berating herself for a fool to allow the cocky Hugh of Leyland to kiss her with so little resistance. No resistance at all, in fact. Not for the world would she have warned him to return to her Cousin Jennie at his peril, nor dare she pretend to herself that she had taken his fancy any more than half the beddable women in Scotland. She was sure this would not be the first time he had held a woman so for the price of a kiss.

She stared at her fingers on his wrist. 'Master Leyland,' she said, 'this is doubtless a fine game to you. But I am chaste, and to me it is no game to dole out my favours as freely as you do, or as my Cousin Jennie does. I despise her behaviour.'

'So do I, mistress.'

She was sure he was laughing at her, and her hurt was the greater while her heart was so untrustworthy. 'Yes, I'm sure you do. Now let me go, *please.*'

'Remind me to tell you why she went off like a horsefly to a cow-clap this morning. Meanwhile, I'd rather talk about someone closer to me. And this is not just a fine game to me. It's not a game at all, Meg.'

'Then place your hand over your heart and tell me you've never demanded a kiss from a maid before.'

'Let go my hand, then.'

'There.'

'Hand on heart, I've never demanded a kiss from a maid before. I've exchanged kisses, and never been refused. But I've never asked, till now.'

'Then why me? Because I'm a laird's daughter?'

'Because it's the only way I'm going to get one unless I carry you weeping up to your chamber again. And I don't see that happening two nights in a row, and I can't wait a moment longer. And because you're the most beautiful, opal-eyed, bossy, sharp-tongued, spitting-mad little vixen I've ever seen in my life and I'm smitten, Meg Moffat. Smitten. Ask anyone if they've ever seen me smitten before. Enchanted for a while. Occupied, temporarily. But never smitten. And no, I don't intend to rape you. All I ask is a kiss to keep me sane, that's all.'

'And you think this is the best way to go about it, do you?'

'The only way, lass. Would you have stood still for me?'

'No, I would not!'

'There you are, then. I knew it. So.'

'So what?'

'So now you can allow me to continue where we left off last night.'

'Master Leyland, you are here only because you're on the king's business, and I am not your friend and you are not mine, nor will you ever be. In a day or two you will be gone for ever, smitten or not, and the only thing I'm willing to give you for doubting my father's loyalty to King Robert is basic hospitality while you're about it. Which is more than you deserve and more than you'd have got if he'd been here in person. If you want to steal a kiss I cannot stop you, but don't expect that I'll fall at your feet and beg for more, because I won't. Now, if that's the only way you're going to let me go about my business, be quick and get on with it or I shall have some very awkward questions to answer.'

'Cruel virgin.'

'Leave my virginity out of it, if you please.'

'That will be difficult, but I'll try.'

His merry grey-eyed smile almost melted her knees, but she saw little more of it before her eyes closed, quite against her intentions. His kiss last night had been her first from an admirer, though a handful of her father's friends usually lingered over a greeting or farewell in the hope of commending themselves. Hugh of Leyland's mouth, however, was different from the rest; it was wide and well-formed, firm and masculine, and the pity of last night's experience was that her anger had prevented her from enjoying its audacity. What a waste, she had thought later. Would he try again?

This time, his kiss was like a glimpse of heaven that one holds with the lips to keep it there. Tenderly alive, it knew where to seek, how to coax a response, any response, even a hesitant and stumbling one. Meg had expected that their noses might collide or that she might have to hold her breath, but found that her breathing was forgotten in the long exchange that made something quiver deep inside her far away from her lips, prompting her arms to lift and cling, testing the exciting pressure of him. It was not the quick price she had expected to pay, for the first kiss ran ahead into the next without a join, and she was not inclined to balk at its extraordinary length when it was costing her so little.

His hand captured her face, and she did not resist as long as his lips held hers, but then his hand moved downwards over her throat, lower, and lower still. In a sudden awakening, she caught at his wrist, her heart leaping out of control, her eyes coming awake to another innate fear. 'No!' she gasped, feeling the warmth spread through her kirtle. 'That's not...' Her voice trembled.

'No,' he said, softly. 'That's not what we agreed, is it? A pity.' His mouth played tenderly with hers. 'Is that a tear I can taste? Shh. I'll not do thee any harm, sweet Meg. D'ye want me to stop?'

Knuckling the tear away, she nodded.

'And my hand, too?'

She felt the instant coolness return, with the guilt. 'Let me up, Master Leyland. I must get back,' she said, then fell unusually silent for one who was never at a loss for words. And while she was helped to find her feet with far greater courtesy than she had been helped to lose them, she could not look at the man who, more than any other male, had got her to part with so much, and who knew it. So she could only guess how transparently his triumph was reflected in his face.

She dreaded that he would chatter and gloat, or tease her, but to her relief he did not, and she was allowed to leave in a contemplative silence that completely banished her curiosity about what had happened to Cousin Jennie. 'I don't want Lady Ebony or *anyone* to know about this,' Meg said, watching the little boat now far out on the loch. 'She'd be furious with me.'

'You're sure of that, mistress?'

'Quite certain. My brother's widow is much stronger than me.'

'Then she shall not hear of it from my lips, I promise you.'

'Thank you.' Brushing the grass off her skirt, she left him to his own devices, thinking that it was no wonder Ebony felt so bereft if that was what she had been missing since Robbie's death.

For their own private reasons, neither Ebony nor Meg felt able to meet the two men to discuss the contents of the box until after supper when their tear-stained faces had been restored to normal. Meg explained hers as a result of finding that one of the cygnets had been taken by an otter, but she had been shocked by Ebony's appearance and ashamed of her own deceit.

'What happened?' she said, closing the door of the chamber behind Biddie and Sam. 'Did he make a nuisance of himself?'

'No, of course not,' Ebony said, trying to laugh it

off. 'Not in a boat, Meg. Nothing happened. He wanted to talk, and I didn't, that's all.'

'So you didn't talk to him.'

'Yes, I did, but it upset me. I hate the man. I wish they'd go.'

Thoroughly perplexed, but not wanting to press for information in case Ebony should do the same to her, Meg let the matter drop, but their later meeting with the two offending men was so decidedly half-hearted, in spite of the astonishing discoveries, that what should have been a reason for celebration became a reason to make their exits as fast as possible to seek the quiet of Meg's chamber.

Once safely inside, they hugged, fighting back tears of relief. 'It's Davy,' Meg said. 'The damned, sneaking, dishonest little toad. How could he do that to my father, take advantage of his ignorance, forge his signature and make free with his seal like that? How could he do it? And to think I wanted you to accept him, Eb. I'm so sorry, love. Thank heaven you didn't.'

Unwilling to explain how close she had come, Ebony patted her and drew her towards the waning light where raindrops had begun to spatter against the greenish glass windows. Once Meg had explained to them that Sir Joseph could not sign his own name, that he could not read what his nephew was setting the Moffat seal to, the picture had become clear, as did Davy's need to repossess the seal that Ebony held without which he could not tie up the incomplete sales. And whereas the men's investigations had been primarily concerned with the valuable Galloway ponies, they had discovered accounts for precious grain, armour and weapons that Davy, not Sir Joseph, was selling to anyone who could pay, Scottish and English. Between them, he and the estate steward were reaping the payments that Sir Joseph thought were going to him from sales to help the king's wars.

One of the questions still to be answered concerned the origin of the goods that lay in the Castle Kells storeroom. Davy Moffat had a licence to trade in wine, not in other commodities, and he owned no merchant ships as Geordie Boyd had believed. Had there been smuggling? Or piracy? Sir Joseph had been greedy and merciless, too trusting of his nephew, too naïve to realise that his storerooms were being used to keep suspicion away from Davy, too incompetent to discover that some of his ponies were being sold to the wrong side. But he was no traitor. He had, however, been raiding over the border and bringing back horses, some of which had originally been taken from his neighbours by the English. Instead of returning them to their rightful Scottish owners, Sir Joseph had demanded full payment, adding insult to injury. It was this aspect of his unneighbourly behaviour that had most incensed the so-called friends who, at the feast, had made their displeasure known and was behind Sir Alex's announcement that he and his men would be staying a while longer at the castle. Sir Joseph, he said, could not now be punished, but these horses must be restored to their owners for use against the enemy, and Davy Moffat's misdeeds must be pursued to a conclusion. He was quite sure there was more to be discovered.

With the relationships worsening, neither of the women cared to think how they would bear an extension of the men's stay. Against this imposition, they agreed that the threat of losing tenancy of the castle seemed less important.

Later still, when all was dark and quiet, Ebony sat watching Sam's sleeping form while revising Davy Moffat's real reasons for so desperately wanting her to marry him, not to mention his fury that she would not be doing so. Sir Alex's words to her that morning about an expected raid began to make sense; Davy Moffat, he seemed to be saying, was not as new to raiding as he made out to be.

Nodding to the guards on the stairway, she entered her room and rattled the key as if to lock the door, a deceit made for Sam's sake. Even if other issues had been raised that day, one major problem had been removed, though the relief of it had left her both empty and puzzled that his interest should have cooled so quickly.

Was it to do with her desire to keep her dreams secret, to continue a pretence that he was anonymous or worse, that he was Robbie, when quite clearly he was neither? She had tried, but it had not worked, and could never work. He obviously believed that such pretence was both foolish and unnecessary, otherwise he would not have stayed till dawn and risked being seen. Gently teasing, he had tried to speak of it and, like a madwoman, she had pursued the dream, ridden by guilt. Or was it pride?

'Robbie?' she whispered, smoothing a hand over the coverlet. But there was no reply, only the sound of the rain lashing the shutters and the memory of her cries as her body responded to a storm of sweet ca-resses. How could she pretend that Robbie had a part in this when the comparison was so far removed? And how could she now go to Sir Alex and give herself to him when he had decided that enough was enough? Apart from that, he would eventually take his men and go, and to risk a pregnancy in such conditions would be utter madness, and irresponsible. Yet in the lonely night, there were pockets of wakeful longing that made her wonder whether madness might not be preferable to another lifetime of unbearable emptiness of a kind that made her love for Robbie pale into insignificance.

Chapter Eight

The guest chamber over the buttery had now become the headquarters of the king's men where plans could be made in comfort and privacy as a change from a moorland boulder or the forest floor. Fully dressed except for his boots, Sir Alex lay on his bed, staring at the vaulted ceiling, his hands clasped beneath his head, giving his friend and confidante no indication of having heard the last five minutes of unwanted advice concerning his love life. It had been an eventful day.

'Have you heard a word of what I've said?' Hugh asked, uncrossing and recrossing his long legs upon his fur coverlet.

'Most of it,' said Alex. 'How is it that you know so much about widows, anyway?'

'Never mind that. The point is, you can't expect her to make rational decisions at this stage. Why else do you think she was in such a hurry to get away from you this morning? Because she can't explain how she feels.'

'I've told you why she was evading me, Hugh, if only you'd listen,' said Alex with a trace of irritation.

'It's not that she didn't want to talk, it's because I mentioned last night, and quite clearly she can't bring herself to admit what's happening.'

'So then why *did* you mention it, imbecile?'

'Because I thought she might at last, after…'

Hugh waited. 'After she gave herself to you?'

'Yes.'

'And did she talk in the boat?'

'Not of that. As long as she can see me she'll not let me near her. She won't even warm to me. It's as if he's still there, watching, holding her back.'

'Guilt,' said Hugh, knowledgeably.

'Argh! For pity's sake, man. It's been three years. There's more to it than that, I'm sure. It's this place. She's been here since it happened. Memories everywhere. People to remind her. It's time she got away. She needs another bairn.'

Unseen, Hugh's eyebrows lifted. 'Well, she's getting help with that, anyway,' he said.

'Problem is, Hugh, she's not going to want *my* bairn unless I can persuade her to let go of the past. In the dark she'll accept me, but by day I represent a threat. As we all do.'

'Even now, when we've exposed the culprit?'

'She's deceiving her sister-in-law. She doesn't believe Mistress Meg will approve of what she's allowed herself to do. They're a close couple with totally false ideas about each other, those two, and Lady Ebony fears to be seen liking a man who's about to tip them out of their home in the king's name. You know as well as I do that he'll not allow an English woman to hold this place, not even when she's the guardian of the young laird. She believes he might allow her to stay, but he won't. Far too risky. Not unless she married another Scot.'

'And that's where you come in?'

Alex was silent for so long that Hugh thought he'd fallen asleep. 'Alex?' he said, at last.

'I'm here.'

'Marriage?' Hugh prompted.

The reply emerged obliquely. 'I held that wee lad this morning, Hugh, as close as I'd held her, and it set me thinking.'

'Of Nicholas?'

'Aye. He'll be about the same age now. It's time I saw him again.'

'Ye can see him on the way to Newcastle.'

'More than that. He needs a mother and I need a wife.' Like a spring, his body jack-knifed upwards, swinging his legs over the side of the bed like a crane. He sat with his head buried in his hands, muffling his outburst. 'I need her,' he whispered, huskily. 'I want her. God, how I *want* her, Hugh.'

Slowly, Hugh came to sit upright too, wondering at this most unusual sight. 'Ye're in love,' he said. 'By all the saints, man, ye're in love. Well, that makes two of us. Caught at last. Serves us right, I suppose.'

'You too?'

Hugh nodded. 'Hooked. But this is serious. You've got to take action. There's more to this than the state of your heart, you know. If she refuses to accept you by day, you have to go along with it until she can. You'll have to tread carefully, won't you? These things take time, Alex, but we can't stay here for ever.'

'I was going to wait for her to make the next move.'

Hugh groaned. 'Use your sense, will you? We don't have years to wait for that. She's proud. She's mixed up and she's afraid, and now she's taken a step that could land her with a bairn born out of wedlock. And you're waiting for her to come running to you. Forget it, my friend. She'll not do that in a thousand years if she can't admit her feelings for you. You have to keep showing her that you understand, even if you don't, and that you care for her. See?'

'Yeah. You're right.'

'So what *did* she talk about in the boat?'

Smiling sheepishly, Alex sat up and wiped a hand around his face as if waking from a dream. 'It was not complimentary, my friend. Oh, and she's upset about her mother. We may have to go and look for her.'

'That's all we needed.' Hugh went to the window and braced his arms against the sill, his keen eyes searching the darkening courtyard. 'So before we go haring off to find missing parents, what happens here at Castle Kells? The raid won't be tonight, I take it?'

'Not till all the guests have gone. Perhaps tomorrow. I took a good look at the shoreline while I was out on the loch this morning, and I noticed an inlet that you can't see from up here. It leads into the rockface that I went to investigate later and found that *that's* how the stuff gets in and out of the storerooms under the great hall. There's a tunnel, Hugh.'

'Wow! So that's where they'll raid to get the rest of the armour out. The sooner the better.'

'Right. But we can't get the key off the estate steward until young Geordie Boyd has removed his load in the morning, otherwise he'll know that we know about it. So at first light we send half a dozen of the lads up to the end of the loch to the boatmaker's cottage and, as soon as Boyd begins his return trip, they can reclaim the armour and bring it back here. Then we take Richie MacNairn, the steward, and lock him up and at dusk we fill the storeroom with the lads to catch anyone who comes through the tunnel.'

'Good,' said Hugh. 'We'll have the rest of them on the loch side by the inlet to catch the rest, one third on guard duty. About two to one, I think. Yes?'

'Yes. I wouldn't be surprised if that rat-faced Moffat had something to do with his uncle's demise, you know. I can't believe that a man of Sir Joseph's experience would enter a burning building. There's something very odd about that.'

'You think Moffat wants to take over this place?'

'Marry the new laird's guardian, have the use of all his dues and fees from the tenants, as well as the mother's property. He'd be a very wealthy man.'

'Until Sam comes of age.'

'*If* Sam comes of age.'

Hugh started. 'You fear for his life, then?'

'If Moffat were allowed to get his clutches on him, yes, I do.' In an uneasy silence, thoughts circled and moved on. 'Don't forget to single out those two mares that belong to the baron, Hugh. He can take them back with him in the morning.'

'Right. And tonight?'

'Tonight we're on alert. Why, what did you have in mind?'

Hugh's smile broadened. 'Something a little more cosy.'

Alex flopped backwards. 'Without the prickly gorse, I take it?'

The smile vanished as Hugh became suddenly attentive. 'You *saw*?'

'Course I saw, man. I was on the loch facing the shore, wasn't I? So I take it that Mistress Meg is as anxious not to be discovered as Lady Ebony. What a pair they make.'

'Yes,' Hugh moaned. 'Thought I'm not likely to make your kind of progress.'

No, Alex thought. Nor were you offered the kind of bargain I was offered to begin with. 'By the way,' he said, 'young Sam is no longer a potential hostage.'

'Oh? Is that to do with our recent discoveries in the box?'

'Partly. It may help to foster good relations, too.'

'Oh, by all means let us foster good relations, my friend,' Hugh said, allowing a note of pomposity to colour his reply. 'You might continue by bearing in mind what I said to you a few moments ago, too.'

'About what?' He rolled off the bed very quickly to avoid his second-in-command's fists, but the floor was no protection and the wrestling that followed was only interrupted by the entry of Master Joshua, whose observation made them feel more like his grandchildren than his commanding officers.

'Is that all you two can find to do?' he said. 'I thought we were supposed to be preparing for a raid.'

The next morning was Sunday, and thoughts of how to extricate herself from this newest phase of her life had to take second place in Ebony's affairs when there were patients who needed her attention. Brother Walter's affliction, which he thought was a summer head-cold, had made him almost speechless in chapel that morning, and Ebony felt a responsibility to find him a more effective cure than infusions of goldenrod. Then there was Dame Janet, who had worked herself up into a tizzy following the embarrassing episode at the funeral feast, for now Baron Cardale had apologised to her with such abject sincerity that she didn't quite know what to think, and neither Ebony nor Meg wanted to put ideas into her head until they had more to go on. A sedative was needed here.

In the east tower, the handful of wounded men were making good progress, some of them fit enough to return to duties under strict supervision. But as Brother Walter was too unwell to attend them, Ebony had taken on the task, which none of the men grumbled about. It was from these patients that she first heard the shocking tale of what had happened to Mistress Jennie Cairns on the night of the funeral feast, and of how she had been frogmarched back to the east tower by her irate husband who, it seemed, had been warned of her exact whereabouts by Master Hugh Leyland. A certain amount of female screeching and male accusations had floated down the spiral steps that night, followed by a noisy departure only two hours later. As to who had initiated Mistress Cairns's energetic interlude, the answer was exactly what Ebony might have expected.

She went straight to tell Meg, now able to explain the new heights of the Moffats' dudgeon for which, presumably, the two of them would never be forgiven. Their connivance would be taken for granted and some form of retribution would surely follow. Meg agreed. Though withholding any sympathy for Cousin Jennie's comeuppance, they felt that the typical male method of solving her problem showed a frightening ruthlessness on the part of the two men who apparently saw no difficulty in swinging between perfect courtesy and coarseness. The women decided to keep their new knowledge to themselves, using it to maintain and fuel their usual frostiness throughout the day.

As for young Sam, Ebony decided that he must be spoken to, if only to avoid another chance remark like that made yesterday, which Meg had mercifully dismissed as childish nonsense. Her rebuke had puzzled him, the art of lying being something he had never needed to learn.

'I wasn't being ridik-lious, was I, Mama?' he said when Ebony broached the delicate subject of the absence of fathers. He had complained to her that the bailiff's two young sons had teased him about his one-parent status, and he had not been able to answer them.

Ebony's heart lurched, ringing alarm bells. 'You didn't tell them that Sir Alex was...was with me...in my room, did you?' she said.

'No, I forgot,' he said, artlessly. 'Should I have done?'

'Absolutely not!' She took him to the window-seat and cuddled him to her with his head against her breast. 'Some things,' she said, 'are very private and not to be shared with others. It's not that they're wrong things, but we have to choose what we want people to know about what we do. So sometimes we tell them, and sometimes we decide not to. If it's none of their business, we don't. See?'

'Yes, I think so. But I don't know what to tell Barney and Tom when they say I have no papa. I *did* have one, didn't I?'

'You did, sweetheart. He was a dear good man who loved us very much, and we loved him. But he wouldn't have wanted you to be without a father all your life, and I don't suppose—' She halted, suddenly aware of what she was about to say, and think, for the first time.

'Suppose what, Mama?'

'I don't suppose he'd have wanted me to be without a husband, either,' she said carefully. 'Women who live in castles, unless they're very noble indeed, have to have husbands, you see. So when Tom and Barney tease you again, you can tell them that it won't always be like that, and as soon as I can find a nice one for you, we'll be a complete family again, as we used to be. And then they'd better behave if the want to work at the castle.' She hugged him tightly as his little face beamed with delight.

'Will he be like Sir Alex?' he said, breathlessly. 'I wish *he* could be my father.'

'Well, that I doubt, sweetheart. He has a special duty to the king, you see, so he doesn't live in any one place. I don't suppose he or Master Hugh will want to settle down and have a family for a while.'

'Is that why he came up to comfort you after Grandpa's funeral? Because he hasn't got a wife of his own to comfort?'

This was, Ebony thought, rather like walking on eggshells. 'Yes,' she said. 'That's probably the reason.'

'So is that what Master Hugh was doing with Aunt Meg yesterday? Comforting her?'

'What?' Ebony looked down at the top of his head where the fair hair spiralled round, like his father's. She traced it with one finger. 'What are you talking about, Sam Moffat?'

He sprung up and knelt on the cushion, tiring of the cuddles. 'Down there,' he said, craning his neck.

'Don't put your head through!'

'No, I won't. But they were there on the grass, down by the wall. Tom and Barney and me ran after you when we saw you running, but you were out on the loch by the time we reached the garden gate. But we saw Master Hugh lying on top of Aunt Meg and we thought we'd better not disturb them. So we crept back.'

'Oh, Sam love!' Ebony whispered, frowning. 'It couldn't possibly have been Aunt Meg with him. They aren't particularly good friends.'

'They were yesterday, Mama. And it *was* Aunt Meg 'cos I saw her pretty red shoes. I'm not being ridik-lious again,' he assured her. 'Tom and Barney said it was too.'

She had to take several slow and deep breaths before she could get her voice to work at its usual pitch, rather like an organ. 'Listen, love. That's going to be one of those times when you must keep quiet about what you know. We don't always understand the reason for these things, so we say nothing because it's really none of our business. You know I'll explain things to you as far as I can, but it really wouldn't be fair to Aunt Meg if she felt she couldn't do anything without everyone knowing, would it? So I'm not going to try to explain what she might have been doing, because I don't know. Let's just leave it at that and keep it to ourselves, eh?'

'Yes, Mama. I don't suppose Tom and Barney will speak of it. They said they've seen men and maids kissing lots of times.' He climbed down, his interest already on the wane.

Ebony's interest was not. 'Not to ask Master Hugh about it either,' she warned.

'No, Mama. I wouldn't ask any of the king's men. They've told me never to chatter about what they do.'

'I'm very relieved to hear it, love.'

'Can I go down now? Master Josh is going to show me how to skin a deer.'

Wishing that Master Josh could instruct her adored six-year-old in some more edifying matter, Ebony swallowed her disapproval and tried to applaud his enthusiasm, for who could tell when it might be useful to him? 'Will Biddie be there?' she said, forecasting the negative response, the smile.

'Yes,' Sam called from the door. 'She's always there when I'm with Master Josh. They like each other.'

Good grief, she thought, watching the door close. What on earth is happening to everyone in the space of one week? Is it spring?

She stayed on the window-seat for quite some time after Sam had left, her mind frantically occupied with the startling revelation that could not be explained away as childish imagination. The three boys could hardly have been mistaken, for Meg's pretty red shoes were a source of teasing from all sides, and she *had* been on the path as Ebony ran past. There had been signs of tears on Meg's face, a certain restraint, an inability to look at Master Hugh instead of the more usual asperity. Yet she had not confided in anyone.

Had she, Ebony, not just delivered a lecture to Sam on the virtues of minding one's own business, she might have made some instant but discreet investigations of her own, but second thoughts decided against it. When Meg wanted her to know, she would tell her.

On the morning of the next day, Ebony's new knowledge about the state of Meg's heart was enhanced, this time at first hand. As the last guests clattered noisily out of the stableyard loaded with casks of wine and carcasses of venison, no one seemed quite sure why Dame Janet was quietly weeping, whether for sadness or relief, no one had the courage to ask for fear of the unexpected. Meg's immediate concern about Baron Cardale was that he was taking away two of Sir Joseph's mares, and that no one had consulted her about their removal. Ebony thought that Meg's indignation was far in excess of her usual uninterest about which horses came and went, but supposed that she was finding some kind of relief in her semi-public chastisement of Master Hugh. It was loud, shrill, and heads were turning.

Master Hugh withstood the first assault, but then appeared suddenly to tire of it, taking her arm and marching her away indoors with nothing like the protest one might have expected.

'Where's he taking her?' Ebony said, her eyes wide with concern. She made a move to follow them, but her arm was held by Sir Alex in an unrelenting grip that he refused to relax, even when she shook it. 'Let go!'

'No. Leave them alone. He knows what he's doing.'

'He doesn't! And she's my sister. She's not—'

'She'll come to no harm, and they'll not thank you for chasing after them like a mother hen. Come away.' His grip slackened, but she knew he would catch her if she moved.

'You *know* something,' she challenged him. 'Don't you?'

Amused by this turn of events, his blue eyes were like windows into his mind, clear enough this time for her to see through. 'Just leave them,' he said.

But she knew that he knew. 'And why is Baron Cardale taking those mares away? Who gave him permission?'

'Hugh did,' he said. 'They belong to the baron. They have his brand on their rumps.'

'So why are they here?' She knew the answer to that: Sam's pony had an L branded on its flank, even though it had come originally from the Castle Kells herd. Others were watching. She dared not say any more. She moved away, calling to Sam and Biddie to join her.

Sam was reluctant, hoping for rescue from Sir Alex. 'Where are we going?' he said, shuffling his feet through a puddle.

'To see the swans and cygnets,' she said.

'But Sir Alex said I could have my pony shod this morning.'

The hero intervened. 'Go with your lady mother, Sam,' he said. 'I'll come to find you when the farrier's ready for the pony.'

By the time their eyes met and held, all amusement had disappeared, and now his expression was that of a parent sharing the joys of a child's admiration which, for the life of her, Ebony could not deliberately quench with scathing words. She had seen them stark naked and whispering together, confiding. Last night had been as empty and as haunted by memories as the one before, and now her body was raw with longing for the lover who came in the darkness. She knew confusion in all its guises. 'I'm sorry,' she whispered.

His eyes widened, fractionally. 'For what?' he said.

'For the abuse yesterday. I was…' She cast her eyes around for a suitable word but could find none.

'Capsized?' he offered. 'It was nothing, my lady. Forgotten.'

'Thank you. Biddie will bring Sam to you. No need to come looking.'

His nod was curt, but he remained watching as the three walked across the stable yard. No, two walked, one skipped.

Having assured herself that the swan family was intact, Ebony could not resist prying into Meg's affairs, even after all she had said to Sam on the subject, hoping to find out what had happened after her overreaction in the stableyard. She might as well have spared herself the effort, for Meg would say nothing.

'Nothing,' she said brightly. 'Nothing at all. He didn't want everyone to hear, that's all.'

'Hear what?'

'That the horses belonged to Baron Cardale.'

'But they apparently knew that. Didn't they?'

'Oh…' Meg shrugged '…I don't know. I shall be glad when those men have left, then we can both be mistresses in our own home again.' She picked up a jar of salve to check its label. 'There's a woman down in the village with a dreadful rash, but I can't go and visit her because we've been told to stay in the castle. I shall have to find one of the men to take it.'

And that seemed to be all she had to say. Seemed to be, though her outward show of nonchalance was a cover for the inner turmoil she had no idea how to combat. Master Leyland had been angry with her attempt to tear strips off him in public and had handled her more roughly than she had ever been handled before. According to her, his self-defence was no excuse. Then, to show her who had the upper hand, he had kissed her again in the dark stone passageway, none too gently. It had been his hands as much as his kiss, for he had a way of holding a woman that kept her thrillingly helpless, as when he'd carried her upstairs after the feast. He was experienced and far too sure of himself, and he was not the kind of man her father would have approved of. So she told herself repeatedly.

Nevertheless, as she and Ebony sat together with their sewing by the last light of day, Meg was remarkably thoughtful, so much so that more than one of Ebony's remarks went unanswered. And when she asked what day it would be tomorrow, Meg had answered, 'Yes, love.'

Since, Meg, Biddie and Sam slept in rooms that faced inwards to the large courtyard, it was they who came to Ebony's chamber early next morning with the news that there had been a raid on the castle and that they had been awake all night with the noise. Which was not strictly true, but added a touch of drama to an otherwise invisible event.

Throwing a woollen coverlet around her, Ebony accommodated not only Sam on her bed but Biddie, Meg and Dame Janet, too, leaving no room for Master Morner the chamberlain, who talked as he arranged the lady's room. 'Well planned,' he said, replacing the burnt wicks in the cresset. 'They were well prepared. You have to hand it to those chaps. They know what they're doing.'

'Any injuries?' asked Meg. 'Prisoners? Who were they? Locals?'

'A handful killed,' he said, without emotion. 'Reivers, not Sir Alex's men. Several caught. No damage. A few wounds, naturally.'

'Well-planned wounds,' said Ebony, quietly.

'Plenty of noise, though,' said Dame Janet.

'They'll not be local,' said the chamberlain, 'but they knew exactly what they were after and how to get at it.'

'The armour?' said Ebony.

'Armour and weaponry, my lady. They went back empty-handed as fast as they could row.'

'They came in from the loch, did they?'

'By boat. It looks as if Richie MacNairn's been doing a bit o' thieving on the side. They've got him locked up too.'

'The estate steward?' said Dame Janet. 'Oh, he's *such* a nice man.'

She was prevented from saying any more in the steward's favour by Meg's frown, but when the subject had been fully discussed, Ebony was left to Sam's unceasing questions. He had slept through the noise from the courtyard and could not understand how, after three years of nightmares, he could have missed such an earth-shattering milestone in his young life, especially when there was so little to show for it.

'Sir Alex stopped them, didn't he, Mama? Didn't he, Biddie?'

'Come on down,' said Biddie, 'and put some clothes on if ye want to see the new foals.'

Sam giggled and made a beeline for the door, but

it swung open before he could reach the latch, and he was swept up by Sir Alex's arm, beside himself with delight at the unexpected pleasure.

Half-strangled by the constricting little embrace, Sir Alex pretended severe discomfort. 'Where are you going, bare boy?' he squeaked. 'Do you intend to suffocate me first? Good morning, Mistress Biddie. M'lady.' He carried Sam on one arm, but not far. 'You heard about the reivers?' he said.

Sam's euphoria, however, had not quite run its course. 'Did you fight them all, Sir Alex?' he said, sitting up to study him, nose to nose. 'Is that why you were not in here to comfort Mama? Is it?'

Sir Alex's hesitation was well hidden, his glance at Ebony the merest flicker. 'Yes, my wee lad. I was very busy these last few nights keeping the castle safe.'

'Well, now we're all safe and you can come and comfort her again, if you wish. The door—'

'*Sam!*' Ebony whispered, horrified.

'—isn't locked, you know. That's in case I need to come up, but I don't because my bad dreams have gone, so you can have my place. Isn't that kind of me?'

'Sam, for pity's *sake!*' she said.

'What, Mama?'

Unflappable as ever, Biddie came to the rescue. 'Time to get dressed,' she said, firmly. 'Let Sir Alex go now, Sam. You come with me.' She received him into her arms and sat him across one hip. 'I'll fasten you up, m'lady, when you call me.'

'Yes, Biddie. Thank you.'

Sir Alex closed the door after them and rested his back against it, and for the first time Ebony noticed how he slumped, pushing himself away with an effort before walking slowly over to the window-seat. He sat, resting his arms along his thighs with his head hanging low as if he were falling asleep, and she recognised the exhaustion of one who had kept himself awake for too long. But there was more to it than that.

She rearranged the coverlet around herself, wrapping it tightly beneath her arms and tucking the end between her breasts. Then she went to him, peeling away his leather doublet from one arm where it had been slashed from shoulder to elbow, revealing the bloodstain which he had hidden from Sam and Biddie. 'Let me take it off, if you please,' she said.

He was too tired to argue when she removed his clothes one by one, baring his upper half and exposing a nasty gash that still oozed with blood. His hair stuck in dark spikes along the back of his neck and around his forehead, and a red weal encircled his neck where his kerchief had chafed. But his back and shoulders were bruised by blows, and she wondered why he had not worn better protection than a padded jerkin over his doublet. 'God's truth, man,' she whispered. 'Why did you not say?' Had they been as well prepared as Master Morner had said?

The warm water brought up by the chamberlain was still hot, and Ebony set to work in silence to clean the wound, using a paste made of oatmeal and houseleek juice, mutton suet and milk under a soft padding of linen bandages from her simples-chest. To this treatment he neither protested nor showed much interest, but sat with his head resting against the wall, his eyes ringed and closed by shadows, his mind numbed with the need to sleep.

Like a mother with her child, she wiped his face clean of sweat, then his neck, lifting his arms one by one to wash away the toil of the night that had been for her and Sam's protection as much as anything else.

He began a protest, 'You should not be—' But she hushed him, and he made no further objection when she soothed a milky lotion over his sores, little knowing how much pleasure she would derive from the surfaces beneath her fingers, from the first real examination of his huge torso, and from the perverse thrill that, just for a few moments, their roles were reversed. While he was in his own twilight world, she was being the unseen comforter, silently dispensing relief and pleasure to them both.

Almost intoxicated by this newest function, she pulled him gently to his feet, whispering encouragement and steering him towards the bed where he clambered and fell, moving his head obligingly on to her pillow aided by both her hands. With the effort, and the strain on its inadequate fastening, her temporary gown fell open, but she saw little point in bothering about her nakedness while he was unconscious, and now, lingering over the details of his comfort, she carefully lay across his chest and took his face in her hands, caressing and seeing how the bronzed skin moved beneath her fingers and responded to the pressure of her lips. His mouth was firm, scored by tiny lines across the corners, like his eyes, and she wondered how many women had lain in his arms and kissed where she was kissing. There was not a soul to see how she sipped and lapped at the dimpled corners of his mouth, his unshaven chin, his eyelids, or how she nibbled along his hairline to feel the texture of his nut-brown hair. The taste of his throat was delicate and warm, his shoulders cooler where her breasts pressed against them, so she took the coverlet and laid it over him, taking one last kiss from his lips that he would never lack.

Then she set about folding his clothes and soaking the bloodstained shirt, laying the doublet aside to be mended, unable to explain the aura of contentment that settled around her as she performed these mundane tasks for the one who slept peacefully in her bed. Just over a week ago she had been ready to kill him, or, failing that, to sell herself for a place at Sam's side. Now, she was ready to give herself for nothing. And in a few more days he would leave, and she would experience a different kind of hunger that pained her even to think of it.

Preoccupied with these thoughts, she was unaware of a pair of blue eyes that watched from between narrowed lids, or of the smile that almost made it to the surface before it was pulled back into line.

An air of controlled jubilation pervaded the castle that day as the results of the raid were assessed, wounds were tended, the fighting analysed and the prisoners interrogated. There were four of the latter, mercenaries sent by Master Davy Moffat in whose pay they had been for some years. By no means an ordinary reiver attack. More than that neither Ebony nor Meg was able to discover except that the raiders had been more numerous than expected, and very determined.

The two leaders appeared only briefly at mealtimes, both slightly injured, both of the women knowing instinctively who had tended the other's wounds, though the king's men had their own physician. Not by the smallest word did Sir Alex show his gratitude to Ebony for her earlier ministrations, which was what she preferred. But by nightfall her need of him was so intense, her certainty so shaken, that, after Biddie had left her, she waited by the open window rather than climb into the empty bed where he had rested that morning.

Wrapped in the coverlet he had borrowed, she lifted her face to the cool air coming in from the loch and listened to the shrill squeak of bats. In the far distance, the mountains known in Galloway as the Rhinns of Kells disappeared slowly into the darkening sky, and the last reflections faded beneath her high window. The night would be peaceful, for Sir Alex's wound would keep him to his own bed and she to her loneliness.

The door opened so quietly that she heard nothing until the dark figure was well inside, closing it behind him, and so tuned was she to his presence that her heart gave its own cry of welcome, opening her lips in a gasp. Halfway across the chamber he threw off his doublet, reaching her as it fell and catching her in his arms as if he too had had this on his mind for days. She felt the shock as his cool fresh body enveloped her with more urgency than gentleness, his arms cruelly hard across her back, his mouth already taking greedily, putting aside all the differences and quarrels as if they had not existed. Despite her doubts, the joy that overwhelmed her eclipsed her fears, sinking her deep into his kisses as the night closed about them.

By tacit consent, the usual silence was now overcome by Ebony's need for reassurance and, between the ravenous searching of mouths and hands, words emerged as oddly fractured greetings—'Why did you?...I need you...love me...I intend to...I thought...dreadful pretence...sweetheart...' It was the first time she had heard any endearment from him except 'wee lass' and her heart leapt over a beat at the sound of it, lifting her into yet another stage of their strange relationship.

'I've not heard that for so long,' she whispered as their mouths passed each other. 'Say it to me again.'

'I can do better than that,' he replied. Crossing his arms, he lifted them up and over his body, flinging his chainse away over his head to bare himself to her. In the half-darkness, she saw the shine and ripple of his skin as he bent to pull off his chausses. She touched his shoulder, caressing its great expanse before he'd finished, then using him to steady herself when his hands explored the fabric at her breast and unwound her from its folds. Pressed together, their bodies came suddenly alive with a warm vibrancy that made them reach out for more surfaces, her softness cushioning his hardness. 'My black-haired mermaid,' he whispered between kisses. 'My beauty. My sweetheart. Show yourself to me. Let me see you.'

His seeing was done by touch as he took her breasts into his mouth and softly travelled over their perfect fullness while she held his head, trembling and melting with every caress. Her moan became a low wail of desire as his hands slid downwards to lift her, and she was carried to the waiting bed ready to give everything and to take from him only what her limited experience allowed.

As before, it was more than endearments she had lacked, for now as she lay under him she realised that, far from being at the point of consummation, she was being wooed in a timeless and slow void where each advance, though complete in itself, could be taken along a different route. While her lips were kept playing upon his in every key, his skilful hands tuned her body with the most intimate fondlings that made her ache with readiness. Impatiently, she tried to guide him into her, but he took her wrist and held it away, transferring his attention once more to her breasts, biting softly until she cried out for fulfilment. 'Alex,' she moaned. 'Please…now!'

His laugh was one of conquest as his delay ended. He entered her with a swift precision that needed no help from her. 'There, sweetheart,' he said. 'Shall we try to make this last, too? Or shall we…?'

His teasing question was already being answered as a roaring torrent of sensation burst along her thighs, across her belly, shaking her with its force, and she cried out, tossed against the current, lost in its swirling depths. Clinging to his arms, she was taken over by his pulsing invasion that she tried to hold, calling to him to go on, never to cease. But it was too late: she heard him groan as her explosion came, then felt the sweet sigh of release fill her lungs, letting go of her craving. Dazed, she caressed the back of his neck gasping for breath. 'Shall we do what?' she said. She felt his smile with her fingertips.

'I shall have to find a way,' he said, 'of slowing you down.'

Savouring every moment, she knew that, as with Robbie, this too would be lost to her and that she would have only memories to cling to. She snuggled close to him, recalling that morning's picture of him in sleep, his shape and form, the smell and taste of him, his exhaustion, which was not the same as this, here in her arms. He had recovered quickly. 'Your wound?' she said. 'Does it pain you?'

He pulled her closer to him, sweeping a hand over her buttocks. 'Not enough to matter,' he said. 'But have you noticed something, my lady?'

'Yes.' She smiled. 'We're speaking.'

'And that doesn't concern you any more?' His hand continued to stroke.

There was a noticeable pause, then, 'I know it's absurd, but...'

'Go on.'

'But there are good reasons why this should not be happening. In fact, I think I must be mad to have allowed it to happen at all. So to talk of it in the full light of day is more than I can do, at the moment. Do you see that?'

'Yes, I understand what you're saying, though it can hardly be kept secret from your sister for ever, can it? Nor do I believe in your madness. The circumstances were highly unusual, weren't they?'

She was silent at that, for the circumstances, as he called them, had been exploited to the full. Every one of them. And she would be the loser, not he. 'I still don't think it's a sane thing to be doing,' she said at last.

'If it had been left to you, my beauty, it would not have happened at all, would it? Don't be too hard on yourself. I had every intention of getting into your bed, one way or the other, after that offer.'

'You surely cannot be desperate that you had to accept an offer given at such a time under such a misunderstanding?'

The hand stopped its caress as he lifted himself

over her, brushing her silky hair away from her face. 'I was not at all desperate,' he said. 'But offers are one thing and acceptances are another, as you well know. You've rejected offers and would have accepted one only recently for quite the wrong reasons. We both have perfectly valid excuses for accepting offers as they occur, even if they seem strange in retrospect.'

'Then what would you have done if I'd not been crazy enough to attempt to bargain with you?'

He smiled. 'I think I might have found a way round that problem,' he said. 'It would have taken a wee bit longer, that's all.'

'You are arrogant, sir.'

'Yes, sweetheart. That's one of the prerequisites of the job. If I were not sure of my success, I'd not be much good at it.'

She was piqued, and not at all flattered by his overweening certainty of obtaining the thing she had held dear for so long. Turning her head away from his hand, she spoke her thoughts out loud into the darkness. 'Then you must be congratulating yourself on the ease of this particular conquest. Everything fell into your lap, didn't it? Especially me.'

But just when she hoped he would take the last word for himself, some reassurance that all would be well, anything rather than her cynicism, he left the words with her while his hand and lips began another seductive journey over her body, and her last rational thoughts were that, somehow, she and Sam must get away before the damage became irreversible.

Chapter Nine

Each passing day of that week saw an escalation of Ebony's fears that her capitulation would surely have disastrous effects which Sir Alex, probably many miles away in nine months time, would neither know nor care about. A plan to get away from Castle Kells until he should leave seemed like the only sensible action to take, since her nights were not under her control. Nor was her deceit of Meg getting any easier, for although Biddie had already drawn her own discreet conclusions some days ago, it was only a matter of time before the workings of Sam's active mind would succumb to a slip of the tongue. It would take some explaining.

The daytime relationship between herself and Sir Alex had stabilised, reverting to coolness and avoidance for the most part with never a word of their passionate nightly liaisons, and a leaving before dawn that only the guards witnessed. On this particular day, Ebony had gone to the kitchen garden to find some of those herbs noted down in her old recipe book as being useful to bring on a woman's menses, an evasive way of saying something far more serious. With an armful of motherwort, usually prescribed by Brother Walter to calm Sir Joseph after one of his awful rages, Ebony retraced her steps, but reached no further than the bed of dill and parsley before encountering Meg with a note in her hand.

Understandably, Meg registered some puzzlement. 'Who's that for?' she said, looking at the tall spires of motherwort curving over Ebony's arm. 'Whose face has gone purple with rage this time?'

'Nobody's,' said Ebony.

'Then….?' Whether it was the dreadful guilt written on Ebony's face or Meg's inability to think of a good reason why anyone should need this particular medication, no one could have said. But Meg's brain was sharp and, though she might lack literary skills, she certainly knew her simples. Her eyes widened with astonishment rather than accusation. 'Ebbie?' she whispered. 'Eb, what is it? Tell me.'

Ebony's mouth suddenly became dry. 'Come over here,' she said, 'and I will.' They went to sit under the wickerwork shelter where two speckled brown ducks nested nervously not far from their feet, and there Ebony told her silent sister-in-law the whole story from the very beginning, sparing herself nothing, not even her piercing and confused emotions, many of which Meg could see for herself. 'I'm sorry,' Ebony told her at the end. 'I never meant to deceive you. I cannot help myself except by taking drastic measures against it—' she glanced at the herbs at her feet '—and by going away for a while until the king's men have gone. That at least I can do.'

'Ebbie…no!'

'I can't go on like this, Meg. It's been over a week now since Sir Alex first came to my bed, and I could lock my door, I know, but…' Her voice was raw with longing as Meg placed a comforting hand over hers. 'I want him. I want him so much…I need…'

'I know,' Meg whispered. 'I know. It's been so hard for you.'

'There's no excuse. I'm sorry, Meg. I didn't want it to happen, and now it's like a craving. I've thought about it, and I believe I must take Sam and go up to one of the homesteads for a while. I could sneak off with a few of the house-servants and enough food for a week, and you could send more if Sir Alex's men haven't gone by then.'

Meg, her face the picture of shame, spoke carefully. 'I think,' she said, 'that I had better go with you, Ebbie love.'

Ebony rested her head against the wickerwork and squeezed Meg's hand. 'Oh, dear,' she said. 'Oh… *dear*! You too? And Master Hugh?'

Studying the folded parchment in her hand, Meg fanned her reddening face with it and nodded. 'I'm afraid so,' she whispered.

'You're not…he's not…?'

'No,' said Meg. 'He certainly hasn't. Nowhere near. But I have a good idea of how you must be feeling, Eb. It *is* addictive, isn't it? It's been so hard to keep it from you. I was sure you'd be furious with me. Hearing of your problem is quite a relief, in a way, but I can't believe either of them are doing more than pass the time. I expect they do exactly the same everywhere they go, and I'm determined not to help them populate Scotland with their bastards. 'Oh!' She glanced at Ebony's unhappy profile, mortified by her clumsiness. 'Forgive me, Eb. I didn't mean…'

If Ebony needed anyone to voice her fears out loud,

she could have asked for no one more brutally honest
than Meg, though she would have preferred her own
case at least to be unique in some way. 'You're right,
love. It cannot mean anything to them and we must
not allow it to continue, whatever our own feelings
for them are. What's that you're holding?'

'Oh.' Meg looked at her fan. 'Somebody brought
it an hour ago. Here, take a look. It'll be condolences
about Father, I expect.'

Ebony took it and smoothed out the creases over
her knee. 'It's from Dumfries,' she said. 'From
Cousin Jennie. Good heavens!'

'Didn't know she could write.'

'Master Richard can. This will be his writing. He's
telling us, asking us, oh…my God!' The parchment
shook uncontrollably.

'What?' said Meg. 'What's he say, Eb?'

'They think they may have found….ah….my
mother, Meg. They…he knows where…what dreadful writing…where she may be. He says that Jennie
has heard news that…oh dear…she's very ill. She
may be dying, he says.'

'Who, Jennie, or your mother?'

'And that she's been asking for me. He says they
may be able to take me to her. Oh, Meg.' Pale and
shaking, Ebony lowered the letter. 'I must go. This is
the perfect reason to get away on my own. I have to
go to Dumfries, immediately.'

'But Lady Jean was in Carlisle, love. That's much
further on, in England.'

'I know, but they've had news of her, don't you
see?'

But Meg saw what Ebony didn't. 'It's a trap, Ebbie.
You mustn't fall for it. You know what it's all about.

Revenge for what happened here, and revenge on you for not accepting Davy. She's a bitch.'

'I don't care, Meg,' Ebony cried. 'I've been starved of news for so long and I can't let this go without responding. What if there's some truth in it?'

Inexperienced in some fields and wise beyond her years in others, Meg needed no one to point out that her dear adopted sister was not seeing things too clearly. Starved of loving and of news of her mother, Ebony was responding to both with a typical disregard for the facts and for her personal safety, so desperate was she to make good the omissions that had once been the mainstays of her life. It was understandable but highly dangerous, and Meg had no arguments potent enough to counter it, though she tried her best.

Indoors, they began immediate preparations, having sought the co-operation of one of the stable lads to prepare them horses, pack-ponies, and to send up panniers. It did not occur to them that the lad who had been loyal to them for so long was now amongst Sir Alex's most ardent admirers, so when Dame Janet responded to a knock on the door of Meg's chamber, she was not quick enough to lock it before it opened. The timing of the intrusion was not appreciated.

Meg and Ebony looked up from their packing with patent unwelcome. 'What's so urgent?' Meg said to Sir Alex and Master Hugh. 'We're busy.'

'I believe you've had a message from Dumfries,' Sir Alex said, looking about him. 'May I see it, mistress?'

'No,' Ebony said, quickly. 'It was addressed to me. It's private.'

Both couples stared at each other in hostile admiration, the women only half-dressed in old kirtles, the men looking as if they'd been hunting which, in a sense, they had. Like lads brought in from the countryside smelling of woodland and bonfires, their hair was finger-raked, their boots caked with mud. 'If it's from Dumfries,' said Master Hugh, 'it will hardly be a private matter, my lady. I'm afraid we must know its contents. Please, for your safety.'

Ebony saw this as yet one more spoke in her wheel, for now these two would stop any plan she could devise. 'On this occasion, sir, we can manage alone, I thank you. I've had news of my mother and I intend to follow it up. That's all there is to it.' She threw a pile of blankets into a pannier and picked up another bundle.

'From Master Moffat I take it,' said Sir Alex.

'No, from Mistress Cairns. Well, her husband. I'm sure he's—'

'No, he's not! You cannot go. This is a trick. You must see that.'

'I see nothing of the kind. In any case, it's all I have to go on.'

'Yes, and they know that.' He took a step forward, purposely stopping her from continuing. 'Listen, will you just pause for a moment and discuss this rationally? You cannot seriously believe what he's telling you.'

Threatened, exasperated, obstructed yet again, Ebony's veneer of calmness cracked. Her voice was hoarse and breaking with frustration. 'Sir Alex,' she snapped, 'I have had no word of her till now, alive or...or otherwise, nor have I found anyone willing to help me find her. So whether it makes any sense to you or not, I *can* seriously believe it because I have no choice. And I *shall* go to Dumfries and, if necessary, to Carlisle too.'

'Then I shall go with you,' he said, turning to Hugh of Leyland. 'I'll take twenty of the lads, Hugh. Lady Ebony will need her palfrey, but no packhorses. Mistress Meg, Sam and his nurse will stay here with you.'

'No!' Ebony yelped. 'Sam goes where I go! He's not going to—'

'Yes, he *is*!' Sir Alex barked at her. 'Have a thought, woman. You cannot knowingly take the child into danger for your own selfish reasons. You must see that he'll be safer here with the women and Hugh and Josh rather than traipsing cross-country into Moffat's hands.'

'They'd not harm him.'

'Course they would! That's exactly what all this trouble has been about. Getting control of Sam and his property, through you, while he's still a minor.' When she did not answer, he continued in a marginally gentler tone, 'The wee lad will stay here where he can be watched over, and you'll travel with me for protection. If this is a trap, and it most certainly is, then they'll have to get past me and the lads first. And one way or another, my lady, we'll find news of your mother while we're about it. We'll leave at first light and you can unpack that pannier because pack-ponies are too slow. Pack as much as you need into that leather saddlebag. No more.' He spoke to Meg at last as he reached the door. 'You will be perfectly safe with Master Hugh and the men, mistress. I give you my word on it. I trust you won't mind playing guardian to Sam for a while?'

'Not in the least.' She handed him the letter. 'You'd better have this.'

'Good. You'll be kept informed of what's happening. We have our ways of doing that.'

'Thank you.'

He nodded and turned to go, but had to dodge the soft missile that flew past his head and slapped at the door. Expressionless, he picked it up and passed it to Meg, neither men commenting until they were safely out of the room.

Then Ebony's fury erupted. The carefully packed pannier was heaved up into her arms and slung sideways at the door, rattling its latch like a gale and leaving the two departing guests in no doubt as to their narrow escape. Overbearing, arrogant, interfering and loutish were just a few of the words that reached their ears through the heavy wood, but what they missed were the barbs of resentment. And fear. 'I didn't want him to go with me,' she scolded to Meg, 'when the whole point was to go alone to be safe from—'

'Yes, love,' Meg cooed. 'Shh, I know. But now we have no choice in the matter, and we must ask ourselves which is most important, to find Lady Jean, to keep Sam safe, or to protect your virtue. Which you *could* probably manage, love. Is there no chance of you being able to keep him at arm's length? After all, you'll probably not be sleeping together while you're travelling, will you?'

Ebony mopped her face, looked at the remaining pannier-basket and delivered a kick to its side. 'I will, Meg,' she said. 'I *will*. Even if I have to stay awake all night. I cannot allow him to use me like this.' Her words lacked weight, and she knew it, for the concept of using and being used was no longer an honest pretence after the loving words that had begun to pass between them at the height of their passion. Despite Meg's cynicism and her own fears, there were times when she knew all the torments and raptures of love. 'No,' she said, 'that's not quite true. If either of us is doing the using, it's me, Meg.' She sat down upon Meg's canopied bed. 'I know it began as a bargain that became a threat, but I wanted it as much as he did, and I still do. And I believe he must know that. I'm another person when I'm in his arms.' Sadly, angrily, she twisted the wedding ring on her finger. 'He brings me to life. I think of him all the time. It's wrong of me, Meg. I know it's wrong.'

Meg came to sit by her side to place an arm about her shoulders. 'No, dearest. It isn't wrong. If you're thinking of Robbie, then remember how he always wanted your happiness. Didn't he?'

'Yes, I believe so.'

'I know he did. And grieving for ever is not at all what he would have wished. You yearned for his love when he went, then love for its own sake, for comfort. And now you've found it you can't forgive yourself for enjoying it. You're not hurting anyone. I couldn't be happier for you. Honest.'

'You're saying what I wanted to hear, Meggie. Bless you. But the effect of all this is serious, isn't it? Loving doesn't come without its dangers and I dare not ignore them. The king's men don't settle anywhere, and I don't know what his plans are, for him or for me. And I don't know his feelings, though I fear you may be right about just passing the time. What's more, I won't have time to make that infusion properly now.'

'You don't need to, love. There's some left that Brother Walter used to give to Father for his apoplexy, remember? You can take that. When are you due?'

'About a week. Which reminds me, I'd better take my cloths with me. Oh, Meg, I wish we'd been going together.'

'He's quite right about Sam, you know, and you'll need men and speed if you're to find Lady Jean. Sam will be safe enough, don't worry. Janet and I'll sleep up in your room, if you like, so that he can come up and have a cuddle in the mornings. And I'll tuck him up each night and tell him stories.'

'Thank you, dear one. But will *you* be safe?'

Meg produced a new secretive kind of smile. 'Ebbie, love. I've kept myself safe so far, and I can do it for a while longer, believe me. It might be quite difficult for Master Hugh, but if Sir Alex tells him he must behave himself, then he will. Now, we must be brave and reorganise this packing. I'll go down to the kitchen and see about food for the journey. You'll need money, too. Come on, love. No time for recriminations.' Meg was at her managerial best once more, and Ebony was pleased to be managed, for the time being.

Her farewell to Sam was the hardest part but, to her relief, the little lad appeared not to be upset at the idea of losing her for a while, and his merry wave from Master Josh's wide shoulders was the last she saw of him through a blur of tears as they rounded the bend of the track. She had slept alone last night and, whether to check on his kind offer or not, Sam had come to her at first light for a cuddle, to watch her prepare, and to warn her of the possibility of goblins in the dark forests. He was pleased that Sir Alex and the men would be with her, goblins being so un-predictable.

Ebony's confused feelings towards her escort were still unresolved. Relieved to be having his protection, her anxiety about the long-term results were even more real to her while nightly sleeping arrangements would almost certainly be more communal than private. Even the best inns expected travellers to share a room if they were busy, irrespective of gender, a fact that the inexperienced Meg could not be expected to know. There were other concerns to occupy her mind too, about what she might expect from Cousin Jennie, the veracity of her information, a possible ambush, the state of her mother's health, or worse. Sam's goblins seemed like a minor irritation by comparison.

A light shower during the night had washed the dramatic landscape and loaded the white May-blossom with diamonds, dripping on them as the riders passed. Ramsons and early bluebells carpeted the wooded fringes of the loch where herons waited for a catch, knee-deep. Squirrels and stoats leapt across their path, and the distant herds of deer lifted their heads to watch the party ride swiftly by.

On this occasion, the king's men displayed their royal insignia proudly upon the breasts of their padded jerkins, the royal lion of Scotland, red on a gold background, rampant, surrounded by a border and fleur-de-lis. Every head shone with a polished steel helmet, every buckle, chain and rivet glinted in the early sun, every hide and mane gleamed like water. Ebony's black palfrey had been groomed to perfection, though she herself had not ridden for months, and Sir Alex's relentless pace demanded all her concentration over the rough ground. Understanding his

reasons for doing without packhorses, she nevertheless felt as if the sixteen miles to New Galloway were
more like a hundred, the hour's rest at mid-day more
like five minutes.

It was unlikely, he told her, that they would reach
Dumfries that day, but they could arrive at the
Cairns's house by noon tomorrow if they were to
camp overnight by the Urr Water. Still densely
wooded, the countryside here was kinder to travellers,
less rugged and more fertile and, for the first time,
Ebony saw how easily the men lived out of doors as
comfortably as in a castle, organising food, shelter
and safety without the need for a single command.
She was given a place by the fire, roasted rabbit,
cheese and bread to eat and, as darkness fell, a bed
of heather on which to sleep under a canvas roof. She
was too tired to notice the jabs and scratches.

She came awake to see the men already sluicing
themselves in the river, shaving while half-naked,
pulling on boots, rolling up bedding, downing hunks
of bread and ale, chomping on apples, dried raisins,
nuts and slices of cold bacon. She was brought her
share by Sir Alex who had a plan, he said, to which
she must conform. That was the way they worked.

She had already had a day in which to make her
own plan, but it would be no use telling him that.
Politely, she listened.

'You'll enter Dumfries with only one groom as escort,' he said. 'I shall leave you about two miles out
of town so as not to give them any indication that
you are defended. Once you've gone, we shall follow
by a different route and, before you know it, the
Cairns's house will be surrounded and watched.

You'll be in no real danger. I have a fair idea of what they'll suggest, so don't be too concerned, and don't give in to any demands they might make. Your groom will be Perkin; he may look half-baked but, believe me, he's not. He'll stay with the horses and baggage, and he'll let us know what's happening. You can trust him.'

'And you?'

'You can trust me, too.'

'That's not what I meant.'

He grinned, veering her mind away from the day's business to review his rugged good looks, his chin still glowing from his shave. How close to her had he slept last night? What was he seeing with those penetrating blue eyes? 'Nevertheless, my lady, you can. This is a trap, believe me. Do you think you can handle it? Now is the time to say.'

Breezily, she affirmed that she could, wondering if those sharp eyes would identify how her hope of being united with her mother had already taken first place over any threat of treachery. She would not have insisted on coming here otherwise. 'If they have no news of her after all, then I shall simply leave,' she said, licking her fingers.

His reply was heavy with distrust. 'Yes. Well, if that should happen, go where Perkin leads you. He'll know what's best to do.'

The young groom of no particular countenance had turned his jerkin inside-out to hide his royal badge, and Ebony could hardly help being impressed by his sturdy size if not by the sudden transformation from polished king's man into nondescript groom. His helmet had gone, his weapons were well hidden, but his hands were reassuringly strong as he lifted her up into the saddle and arranged the folds of her cloak over her legs, checked the mare's bridle and saddlebags.

Her last responses to Sir Alex on the outskirts of the town were merely nods to his instructions, yet as their hands touched, she knew that more was contained in his lingering fingers than spoken words. Returning the pressure in his caress, she saw the need to remind him. 'I'll be all right,' she said. 'I'll do as you say.'

'Be careful. Go straight there. We'll not be far away,' he said.

She had not been as far as Dumfries for many years, the last time being with Robbie on a visit to the market. Even then there had been early signs of famine, soaring prices, scarcity of food, the absence of imported goods, the rest of Europe having been as badly affected by the flooding. Since that time, the stallholders had ceased to trade for lack of produce, and now her journey over the last two miles took her past sadly ruined hovels where families had once lived cheerfully simple lives.

As the streets ran straighter between dwellings, the appalling poverty became more and more apparent in a way that no secondhand descriptions had ever done. Too weak, or too proud, to call out for alms, the emaciated survivors glowered at the noblewoman's affluence with contempt while their children, gaunt and hollow-eyed, stared despairingly. There were neither smiles nor greetings to be heard as they passed, only angry mutterings and cold shoulders, and a terrible apathy. The disaster was greater than she had dreamed of. These people were starving while her father-in-law had stockpiled precious food until prices rose way beyond the purses of those who needed it most. And she, in her extended grief, had hardly spared a thought for the whole deadly problem.

'Did you know of this?' she asked Perkin. 'Did you know how bad it is?'

'Yes, m'lady,' he said. 'It's not just here, it's everywhere. Thousands have died, businesses ruined, flocks and herds lost. In a way, ye can hardly blame reivers for stealing when it's the only way to get anything nowadays. Law means nothing when families are starving to death.'

For all his appearance, Perkin was articulate, and Ebony was very quiet as he described to her the manner of people's wretchedness. By the time they came in sight of the bridge over the River Nith and the large stone-built house at the end of it, Ebony's conscience was suffering as never before, rousing her anger at the whole Moffat family in general and at Davy Moffat in particular.

They dismounted in the filthy garbage-littered main street where skeletal dogs and rats searched for food between people's feet. The imposing heavily studded door opened to her knock, admitting her at once into a dark passageway, leaving Perkin outside to follow his instructions. Ebony's surroundings might have been in another world, so sumptuous was the house of Richard Cairns, Dumfries's best-known lawyer. The lawyer's wife, Cousin Jennie, was as surprised by Ebony's prompt arrival as Sir Alex had expected her to be, having thought that tomorrow, or even the next day, to be more likely. Which made her invitation to wait a while seem reasonable, at first. But Ebony's assurance to Sir Alex that she would be all right seemed to become less and less likely as the day's

events wore on and as another Dumfries relative was
sent for to lend substance to the Moffat methods of
persuasion.

No country inn, however ordinary, could have
more closely resembled heaven to Ebony than the one
on the outskirts of Dumfries that had been completely
taken over that night by the king's men. It was close
on midnight as she sat packed into their company by
the side of a log fire where a row of boots gently
steamed. The remains of supper lay on the table, the
men sprawled and lounged, and Perkin proudly
nursed a bandaged wrist that had been slashed in defence of the lady. Willingly, he had suffered the inevitable ribbing. Above them, heavy beams flickered
in the warm candlelight while sheeting rain poured
off the thatch outside and rattled noisily into water-
butts. The men were respectfully quiet as Ebony explained to them what had happened at the lawyer's
house on the bridge. Bitterly disappointed, shaken by
fright and anger, then by the sheer force of her rescuers, she hugged her chequered blanket around her,
answering Sir Alex's questions just as his men had
been debriefed at the conclusion of a skirmish.

He handed her a beaker of wine and instructed her
to drink.

'No more,' she said.

'Drink it,' he ordered, putting it into her hand.
'Now, tell me again what happened after Master Davy
arrived?'

She gulped. 'He wouldn't give me any news of my
mother until—'

'Until what? Come on, these lads know all about
coercion.'

'Until I agreed to marry him and…and go to bed with him.'

'Hah! Original. Did he say he had news of Lady Jean?'

'He said he could take me to her, but I couldn't believe him. He wouldn't give me any details. He and Master Richard had drawn up a contract that they wanted me to sign before they'd tell me anything.'

'A marriage contract?'

'That's what it looked like, but it had all kinds of clauses about property, about Sam's inheritance, the castle, handing over guardianship and that kind of thing. I refused, and they began to shout at me. They offered me no refreshment. Nothing. And when they saw I was not going to co-operate, they took me to a small chamber at the back of the house, the one you broke into, and locked me in. There were rats.' Her voice wavered, her hand shaking the wine in the beaker.

'Drink,' he said. 'Perkin knew where you were, wee lass.'

'How did he?'

Sir Alex smiled across at the young man and winked. 'We knew that if no one was going in or out, then it was time for a reminder. Did we scare you?'

'Yes, I thought the house was about to fall down. You certainly gave them a fright. They believed I'd come to Dumfries on my own without you knowing, but now I'm worried that they'll try to get hold of Sam. Do you think they'll try?'

'Hardly,' he smiled. 'They've all been taken into custody in the king's name. We have authority to do that. They'll stay in Cardale's dungeon until the case against them is prepared.'

'Baron Cardale? Not with the sheriff?'

'The sheriff, my lady, is in the reiving game right up to the eyebrows. He used to go out with Sir Joseph. He's in Cardale's custody, too. After retrieving his horses from Castle Kells, the baron's happy to give us all the help we need. Don't worry about young Sam. He's perfectly safe with Hugh, and the next time that crowd will see daylight will be on the way to the assize court.'

'Mistress Jennie too?'

'Yes, her too. I suppose she had no news of your mother for you?'

'No,' Ebony whispered, looking into her wine. 'None of them did. I shall go on to Carlisle. That's where she lived.'

'No.' He leaned back against the high carved settle. 'I said we'd look for her, and we will. But first we must go to Lanercost. I have business there.'

Several of the men exchanged glances, with here and there the lift of an eyebrow in the expectation of fireworks. Sir Alex waited.

'To Carlisle,' she said. 'That's where I'm going. Thank you all for your help. I shall pray for your safe journey and return.'

'Time for sleep then,' he said, quietly.

One of the many advantages of travelling with the king's men was that lodgings were always made available to them for the asking. Ebony was shown to a small private chamber, wood-panelled and cosy, where the sheets were clean and where warm water and towels had been provided for her comfort. Here, she had peace to consider again the seriousness of her situation and how, more than ever before, she must insist on parting company with Sir Alex.

After the fighting at the Cairns's house, she had been required to attend with some urgency the cut to Perkin's wrist. Surrounded by such filth outside the house, there was a need to cleanse the wound immediately, which she did by using the only available safe liquid, the infusion that Meg had given her in case her courses were late. Naturally, the wound was bound up in the next available resource, some of her torn cloths. So now she was without protection, a state not helped by the arrival in her room of Sir Alex.

He undressed and joined her between the cool sheets, taking her into his arms to cradle her head on his shoulder. 'You've done well, wee lass,' he said, sweeping her hair away. 'I'm proud of ye. It all went to plan.'

'It didn't go to *my* plan,' she whispered, angrily 'And now I'm no nearer—'

'Yes, you are,' he said, though he allowed her no more time to ask what was meant by that before his lips began a tender journey over her face. It was equally difficult to tell him that this kind of thing must cease for a variety of very sound reasons when she could not remember even the most basic of them.

The day's expectations, disappointments, tensions and fears spilled out into her loving, a loving that had waited two nights, and in the passionate storm that followed there were moments when she knew that her daytime resolve stood little chance against him. Like a ship on the rocks, she foundered and split apart, completely helpless to follow her own sensible course and knowing that by the light of the day she would have to reconstruct her shattered prudence.

She realised that his intention was to be gentle and persuasive, but her fears were no hindrance to the immediate response of her body to his touch, and he was taken by surprise at the fire that raged through her with sizzling ferocity. Pushing his caressing hand away, she beat at him with soft fists and seized the skin of his wrist between her teeth, her hips almost straddling him as she twisted. She lashed out angrily at her failure while he countered her blows easily, even in the dark, and eventually she was held off, panting and tangled in her hair. One last heave almost shook his mastery, but he rolled her over and over to pin her down as if to prolong the combat, and she was held, excited and expectant.

'That's my beauty,' he whispered. 'There's my fierce black-haired mate. It's been a dark day for you, has it not, my sweetheart? Eh?' He took her without preamble, since that was what she wanted, bracing himself above her, wrapped closely by her legs. Matching her mood, her urgency, his loving was vigorous and as wild as the cries that escaped her lips at each beat of her head against the pillow.

The soles of her feet slid along his thighs and calves, urging him on, her arms at first thrown wide in complete surrender, then searching his working body as if to remind herself of what she intended to forfeit, soon. 'Go on,' she moaned, 'go on…and on. Don't…ever…stop! I need you, Alex.'

Willingly, he obeyed her command as she gasped at his quickening pace. She grasped at his shoulders, her wildness soaring like an eagle reaching for an ecstasy just beyond them both, and he dropped on to her in a last surge of energy, speeding into a meteoric release that took them both far out in space, exploding them like stars.

Swirling, floating, she felt him pulse inside her,

wait, then pulse again. 'Stay,' she moaned. 'Stay there.' She squeezed, holding on to him, wondering whether it might hurt him. He gave a huff of laughter into her ear and she knew that it did. 'Serves you right,' she said, darkly.

'My woman,' he panted. 'Mine. All mine.'

She would like to have asked him for more detail, his precise meaning, but she lacked the courage to risk the laughing denial of any deeper commitment to their brief relationship. He would soon be on his way to Newcastle, his work at Castle Kells all but complete. Relationships were not a part of his life.

Holding back that part of her curiosity, she began a leisurely exploration of his back and buttocks while he rested inside her, her fingertips marvelling at the smooth rock-like hardness, the dips and furrows, the protective warmth of his skin. She felt him move again sending a wave of heat into her throat, rhythmically, deliciously, like a sumptuous dessert.

He raised himself, touching her face with his lips. 'You said you needed me,' he said. 'Did you mean that?'

Hesitating, she felt bound to answer him honestly. 'Yes, I do,' she said. 'I think today has proved that I do.'

'Then come with me to Lanercost.'

'But it's miles beyond Carlisle, and I *must* try to find her.'

'I know. I shall help you to find her. But there's someone I want you to see.' His rhythm became more determined, drawing her mind away from the carefully prepared argument. 'And anyway, I need you. Do you not recall when I said I'd not leave you alone?'

'You were angry when you said that.'

'No matter. I meant it. You're my woman, Ebony. I shall not leave you, and I cannot allow you to leave me. Come with me. We shall have lost no time.'

What was he saying? Did he make sense? Was this just another element of the tender teasing that had begun to creep into their lovemaking as if to compensate for the daytime coolness? 'A challenge,' she whispered into his ear. 'If you can manage it again, now, then you win. I'll come with you.'

'Now that's the kind of challenge I like, sweetheart,' he said, laughing.

But her eyes were closing, and she was nowhere near ready for laughter.

The next day was a Sunday, and Lanercost was almost two days' ride east of Dumfries on the other side of the ancient wall built by the Roman Hadrian many hundreds of years ago. Ebony did not want to ask what business he had in England, nor did he seem eager to tell her, though there was a noticeable swagger in his step as he greeted her the next morning to break their fast, and a teasing grin as he placed a cushion upon her stool with a flourish.

The eastern side of the town and the outlying wastelands brought her thoughts once again to the suffering of villagers. Since yesterday, her new awareness had begun to lodge itself deeply into her conscience and, during the hours of her imprisonment with only rats for company, she had kept her fears at bay by formulating plans for some kind of relief for those within her reach. Castle Kells was in her charge now, at least for the moment, and she was the one who could make good the damage done by her father-in-law's neglect. She was sure Sir Alex was misinterpreting her silence.

As they rode on, however, with the promise of a friendly welcome at Gretna, Sir Alex gave her more details of Davy Moffat's illegal activities that he and Master Hugh had winkled out of the garrulous guests at the funeral. Some of their information had also been supplied by the wounded men who had accompanied their master on his last raid, by the captured men who had raided the castle, from the dishonest estate-steward and, more recently, from sources in Dumfries itself. That she herself had been used as a pawn in Davy's arrest was indisputable, but she could hardly complain about that. What shocked her was the extent of Davy's ambition and the lengths to which he had gone to achieve it.

He had, Sir Alex explained, always intended to marry the fourteen-year-old Ebony Nevillestowe, only daughter of the wealthy widowed Lady Jean. The Nevillestowes of Carlisle were a prestigious family, and any Scot marrying into it would be cementing a new and useful friendship that some cynics regarded as hedging their bets in that uncertain climate when sides changed with alarming speed. But to Davy's fury, his uncle had got there first. Ebony had been sent to live with the Moffats at Castle Kells, while Davy's subsequent marriage had ended tragically when his new wife died in childbirth with their infant.

Meanwhile, Davy had begun an illegal business that hid neatly behind his trade in wines. Into this, he had slowly dragged Sir Joseph by persuading him to store and distribute goods that he did not know had been obtained by smuggling and piracy. Foolishly trusting his nephew, Sir Joseph had believed that his own position as a justice of the peace to be above investigation, as were his reiving activities, his position at Castle Kells geographically invulnerable. He had asked very few questions after Davy had shared some of the spoils with him and helped him to find buyers for the Galloways.

But Robbie Moffat had discovered what was happening and had told Davy to stop, threatening to tell his father the exact extent to which he was being drawn into the network, knowing that he would never have agreed to piracy, to smuggling, or to selling ponies to the English. Reiving he regarded as legitimate. A fact of life. Every man did it. Stockpiling, too, if they could get away with it.

It did not take Davy long to realise that Robbie must be silenced. He sent paid men to Robbie's home one night to frighten them, but they went too far and Robbie lost more than his home.

'You all right?' said Sir Alex, glancing at Ebony's ashen face.

'*He* was responsible,' she said. 'I can scarce believe it.'

'I'm sorry. There's no easy way to say it, sweetheart.'

'No, you must tell me everything. It's time I knew. What else?'

'Well, as you know, Davy planned to marry you after you were widowed. Just as urgently, he wanted closer access to Sir Joseph and the castle, and he wanted to reach Sam's inheritance too, before he was old enough to manage it for himself. So he did his best to persuade Sir Joseph that he'd make a good son-in-law.'

'He didn't have to try too hard. Sir Joseph never

lost a chance to talk me into it. But it was too soon…after…'

'Yes, of course.'

'It would probably have made no difference. I never wanted him, and nor did Sam.'

'Well, he made no progress, did he? Except in his illegal trading. It was not difficult to get the ponies to the wrong armies, and it was easy enough to get the armour and grain and luxury goods to anyone who could pay for it. Smuggled goods, pirated goods, no trace of where they'd come from or where they went except for your father-in-law's benefit. He put his seal to it, thinking it was all legal. The only thing Davy wanted more of was you and Sam. Then apparently Sir Joseph began to hear rumours that all was not as it should be. He'd begun to ask awkward questions and Davy had begun to worry about what he'd do. We heard similar rumours about the ponies at the same time. They'd been seen in the wrong places. We were told to investigate.'

'And I suppose Sir Joseph had to be got rid of.'

'By Davy. I'm afraid so. We were hours too late.'

'So Davy was responsible for the accident?'

'It was no accident. The mercenaries that Davy Moffat hired to get his uncle were the same ones he used three years earlier to fire your home. They ambushed the old man while he was out reiving that night and made sure he was too badly hurt to survive. It was convincing, and no one would have suspected if Davy Moffat had not sent the same men again to raid the castle last week, some of whom we managed to catch.

'The trouble was,' he continued, 'that Davy didn't have the free hand he was hoping for with the king's men swarming all over the place. That was the last thing he'd expected.'

'Nor did any of us, as you know. But it explains why Davy was first to arrive for the funeral. He'd already anticipated the death.'

'Quite. Then it all went askew for him. But another thing you should know about is that Davy also employed men to raid abbeys and churches, Scottish and English. He has casks of salt stored at the castle, stolen from Holme Cultram Abbey across on the other side of the Solway. It's the monks' livelihood to claim it from the sea, yet he'd raided the abbey time and again as the prices rose.'

'Salt! It's worth its weight in gold, literally.'

'That's true. For years, ordinary folk haven't been able to salt their meat and fish for the winter months. And now we're about to find out how many breeding horses the monks of Lanercost have lost to the Castle Kells stables, as Baron Cardale did.'

'Lanercost Priory? But why do you care what happens to English monks?'

'Well, Sam's pony has an L branded on its flank, which may have something to do with it. L for Lanercost.'

'But it's one of Sir Joseph's herd.'

'So there's a mystery for us to solve, wee lass.'

'You know the prior, do you?'

'I know him well, as do many Englishmen. And women.'

She made no reply to that, fearing that it was true and that she might not be the last of them. But the revelations of the last few miles had left her cold and shocked and wondering exactly who, of all the people she thought she knew, to trust.

Chapter Ten

The Springfields of Gretna Manor had seen plenty of raiding from their large fortified house that squatted defiantly at one of the main crossing-points on the border between England and Scotland. It was not difficult for anyone to understand why Leon Springfield and his large household continued to live there, however, for it faced across the wide estuary known as the Solway Firth, a treacherous area of sandbanks, tidal mudflats, salt-marsh, moss, heather and peat that only the locals dared to tread with any confidence and where many a traveller, singly or in droves, had been caught by the fast rush of the tide or a hidden river-channel. From this expanse of sea and sky as flat as a table, Ebony could see northwards to Galloway's mountains and south to the Lakeland hills of England. The westerly winds whipped her face and snatched at her cloak, numbing her ears and deafening her to Sir Alex's observation.

'There,' he called. 'Look over there.'

'What?' she yelled, pulling up the mare as she pecked yet again. They had travelled all day, lashed by sea-squalls that ignored the gentle agenda of spring. Her hair, sticky with salt water, clung to her face. She was cold and hungry and not as exhilarated as she felt she ought to have been. 'What is it?' she said.

He caught at the mare's bridle, pointing to the forbidding outline of a square stone-built manor house that had appeared in the distance, grey against ribbons of land and cloud. Gulls screamed and wheeled above a line of men who stood chest-deep in the sea holding poles and nets in the age-old method of haaf-netting for salmon and sea-trout.

'That's where we'll stay overnight,' he said. 'Gretna Manor. They're friends.'

His cheery words failed to bring the expected smile. Friends would naturally expect the two of them to show a certain regard for each other, after having travelled all this way together, when she would have preferred their hosts to be complete strangers to whom no explanation whatever need be given. Explaining her mission would inevitably lead to more questions.

'What's the matter?' he said.

'Questions,' she said. 'There'll be questions.'

'No,' he said, 'there won't. My friends know better than to ask questions.'

It was not so much the rigours of the journey, or the company, or the irritating delay that occupied the darker side of Ebony's thoughts, but the heartbreaking scenes of hardship in every village through which they had passed where the remains of families clung to life, sometimes the whole population having been lost either to famine or to raiding. Burnt-out hovels had littered their path, skeletons and carcasses of cattle and sheep were picked over by carrion, seething with flies. Plots and homesteads had gone to waste beside the ruins. She had never imagined such destitution, and now she was being required to put it behind her for the time being in response to a friendly reception. The contrast between her own state and the scenes she had witnessed since leaving home would be difficult to dismiss so soon.

Though with little warning of their guests' arrival, the warmth of the Springfield family's welcome could hardly have been greater if they'd known of it weeks in advance. A bevy of well-dressed women rushed through the arched doorway on the heels of the grooms, the three younger ones with heavy unbraided hair swirling wildly across their faces as if to hide their happiness. The elder woman was white-wimpled and just as fair, if her eyebrows were anything to go by.

'Alex…dear Alex,' she said, returning his hug. 'Now this is good timing, indeed. We saw your approach across the moss. Can you stay a while?' She peeped up at Ebony as she spoke, drawing from her at last the smile that had eluded her for most of the day. Though Sir Alex was right about there being no questions concerning the presence of a lady with the king's men, the looks directed at her were full of curiosity as well as admiration.

He held Mistress Springfield at arm's length. 'Good timing?' he said.

'Selena's birthday,' she whispered loudly, as if he ought to have known.

'Of course! And I've brought eighteen of my best-looking men for her, and one each for Helen and Christina. Will that do?'

'Excellent. And the lady? Will you introduce us?'

Ebony immediately suppressed the reservations she had brought with her. It would have been unbelievably bad mannered, she told herself, to dampen the celebrations so unnecessarily for purely private reasons, and there would be better times than this to dwell on the sufferings of others. It was not to be quite so well defined.

Master Leon and Mistress Betty Springfield welcomed all twenty-two of their unexpected guests as if they'd been family, ushering Ebony and Sir Alex into the great hall where the servants were already responding with Scottish stoicism to the new influx of birthday guests. Big and burly, with whiskers resembling coconut fibre, the master of the house yelled superfluous orders to all and sundry until he was hushed by his wife, who had already given them. Sandy-haired and balding, he apparently enjoyed being slightly henpecked over domestic affairs by his four women while grumbling good-naturedly about it to anyone who would listen. Hence, his commands to find a room for Lady Ebony were taken anything but seriously.

Two of his daughters looked exasperated, and the youngest said, 'Oh, Father, what d'ye ken we've been aboot fer the last half-oor? Twiddling oor thumbs, d'ye think?' Selena was his favourite; she could say what she pleased. Plump, bright-faced and blue-eyed, she reminded Ebony of a periwinkle, pert and resilient. Her pretty eyes had already scanned across the dismounting king's men, registering their interest in her, and she tossed her thick blonde mane, ready to make the best of every moment in their company.

Christina, her elder by eighteen months, was taller and more slender, her lovely face chiselled by sadness and a certain desolation around the blue eyes, a wide mouth less willing to laugh than Selena's. Her hair was also fair and abundant, but whereas Selena was still a pretty young lass, Christina was already a beautiful woman. She took Ebony by the hand like a gentle shepherdess and drew her away towards the arch between two huge tapestries where a stone stairway led steeply upwards. 'We're built almost vertically,' she said. 'You can hardly go anywhere sideways indoors. Father says its easier to defend, and he's been right, so far.'

The eldest daughter, Helen, followed on behind them, having hardly taken her eyes off Ebony except to glance at Sir Alex and return his greeting. At twenty-two, Helen echoed her sisters only by the thick rippling texture of her hair which, in her case, was more the colour of ripened corn than pale straw. Like them, she wore it loose like a waist-length cape thrown around her shoulders, part-concealing a beautiful bosom and narrow waist that had shed all signs of puppy-fat. Her bright blue gown clung seductively to her hips and flared out below in a series of cleverly gored panels, a detail that Ebony noted with a suddenly renewed interest.

After a three-day horse ride in the same old woollen gown of lichen-dyed grey-blue, her rain-dampened and crumpled state was not what she would have chosen to wear to a birthday supper. She silently blamed Sir Alex for that. Nor was her hair the way she wanted it to be seen, though she need not have been concerned, both of the elder sisters being eager to lend her their services as wardrobe mistress and maid. Christina lent her a cream kirtle to wear beneath one of Helen's sideless surcoats dyed to a glorious gold with onion-skins.

The more talkative of the two, Christina admired the effect with her head to one side. 'You fill it out better than I do,' she said, holding her breasts.

Ebony smiled. 'Motherhood,' she said. 'That's what it's all about.'

'You have children, then?' Helen asked, her flatly curious tone masking either envy or incredulity, Ebony could not fathom which.

She turned around on her stool to look at the questioner who, according to Sir Alex, should have asked no questions. 'A little boy, Sam. He's six. I left him with my sister-in-law. It's the first time we've been parted.'

'Then he's the same age as—'

'Helen!' Christina's low warning cut across her sister's voice, throwing her off-course before she could continue.

Suddenly, there seemed to be a need to tell them more. 'I lost my husband three years ago in a raid,' Ebony said, surprising herself by the evenness of her voice. 'Reivers came. I expect you've had them close by, living on the border like this.'

'Too close,' Helen said. 'Our father and brothers chased after a reiving band only a year ago. Both our brothers were killed.'

Ebony held her head, feeling the slow advance of an old pain. 'Oh,' she said. 'Oh...I'm so sorry. Only a year! You must still be grieving. Were they older than you?'

'They were our twins,' Christina said, quietly.

The pain seared and flared inside her, taking her breath away. 'Twins! You *both* lost a twin brother?

Then you're only—' She stopped herself, but not quickly enough.

'Yes, we're only half. That's still how we feel. Halved. It's odd. Very odd. But then, you must feel halved too. And heaven knows, we still have a roof over our heads and food to eat, which is more than the villagers were left with.'

'They suffered badly did they?'

'Gretna was wiped out,' said Helen. 'Father is determined not to move, and so far we've been able to defend ourselves. But Mother would leave tomorrow, if she had her way. She's taught us how to be brave.'

'And Selena? How does she feel about losing her brothers?'

'She adored them as much as we did. Feels it as bad as the rest of us. But when everyone else is in the same situation, you can't allow it to rule your life, can you? That's what Mother says. You must have found it difficult too, but these times are hard and almost everyone has lost someone dear to them.'

'Everyone?' Ebony wondered out loud.

The sisters fell silent, looking to each other for a signal, then Christina took an ivory comb in one hand and a length of Ebony's hair in the other. 'Come,' she said. 'It's unusual for us to have well-behaved hair like this to dress. Shall we plait and coil it, or shall you wear it loose, as we do?'

'Like you,' said Ebony, 'if you please. Let's all be maids.'

The birthday supper was a far noisier and high-spirited affair than the Springfields had intended, and it took no great effort on behalf of the king's men to pay Selena all the attention she desired and to have plenty left over for her sisters. But Ebony's brief experience of this courageous family was already making its mark upon her, for none of them appeared to have wallowed in their grief to the extent that she had, nor had they forgotten how to dress becomingly, or to smile, or to think about others' needs. In the presence of these four shining women, Ebony began to feel shame that not even by her appearance had she tried to set an example to others, as a lady was expected to do. Would Robbie have been as proud of her as the two young Springfield brothers of their sisters? she wondered.

There was something else lurking there, too, enough to revise Ebony's first assumptions about Sir Alex's friendship with the family, for the eyes that had trained themselves so relentlessly upon her from the beginning were now just as preoccupied with him. More than once, Ebony noticed how Helen's eyes would flicker away from him, how she blushed when he spoke to her, how they followed his movements when she thought no one was watching. She was in love, and in pain, and there was nothing anyone could do to ease it, least of all Ebony.

Being still so very unsure of him herself, she might have expected to share a similar kind of pain, but found instead that the ache tugging at her heart was more for Helen than herself. Yet for Helen's sake, she took great care to conceal the pride shining in her eyes that evening as she stayed in his company, a pride she had never expected to feel for a man so unscrupulous.

For the first time since their arrival, she found herself suddenly alone with him in a passageway leading to the garderobe. 'Ebony!' he called after her. 'Wait!'

Her heart thudded, but this was no place for them to be alone. 'No,' she whispered. 'Go back. I'm not—'

He reached out and pulled her to him before she could hold him off, taking her mouth and drinking in her kisses, manoeuvring her into a recess of the dark wall to take yet more. His hands delved into her hair, wedging her against his shoulder while the sound of pipes and drums reached them from the hall, peals of laughter, the clash of pewter dishes. 'Well, woman?' he growled. 'Are ye finding this charade to your taste, then? Eh? Is it good to sit by my side like an ice-maiden and pretend to feel nothing when I know how you long for my loving? Do you enjoy the pretence, my lady?'

'It's not for my sake,' she snarled, stung by his misunderstanding.

'Then whose sake is it for? Mine? Are you trying to keep my reputation pure, or is it yours you're still bothered about?'

Enraged, she tried to free herself, abandoning her attempt to reason with him. 'You wouldn't understand, would you? Like all men, you're blind to everything except your own ideas. Think what you like, but I cannot change just like that. Did you think I could? Is that your reason for insisting on coming with me?'

'Yes, I did think it. The Springfields are friends, Ebony. You'd have lost nothing by being yourself, for once.'

'Myself?' she hissed, lashing out at him. 'Stupid, ignorant, churlish, thick-headed…! *Listen* to me for a change. This *is* myself. I *am* being me. Yes, I *do* want to declare what I feel, but I'll be damned if I'll let

you force me into it before a grieving family just to
show them how complete *I* am. There's a woman out
there,' she said, her voice thick with anger, 'who's
twice bereaved. Yes, twice!'

'I know that,' he said, trying to hold her still in his
arms. 'They had two brothers who—'

'Two brothers and…and someone else.'

'Someone else? Who else have they lost?'

'I'm talking about Helen,' she snapped. 'She believes she's lost *you*, you great stupid oaf.'

His hands slackened on her shoulders. 'Eh? *Me?*
She's never had…we've never… God's truth…is that
what she thinks? That I'd…? Oh, *God*!' His sigh was
like a soft gale as he held her gently against his chest.
'There is nothing,' he whispered into her hair. 'There
never has been anything. Honestly.'

'She's in love with you. Any fool can see that.'

'I can't help that. I love only one woman. I love
you, Ebony. You must know that by now. You're the
only one I've given reason to think so. I've never
flirted with her, nor with any of them.'

'What was it you said just then?'

'I said, not with any—'

'Not that. Before.' She took his head between her
palms, the only way in the darkness to feel his words.
'What did you say before that?'

'I said…that I love you.' His declaration emerged
between stretched lips. 'And if you were to release
my face, I could say it more…er…convincingly.'

She relaxed her pressure. 'Better not,' she said.

'Why?'

'Because,' she said slowly, 'I shall be the next to
lose you, and I do not have Helen's courage, and…'
The breath shuddered to a halt, used up far too soon.

'I think I should leave you after all, and go down to Carlisle alone. This would seem like a good place to part.'

Now it was his turn to take her face between his hands. 'Are you saying that you cannot return my love?'

'No, I'm not saying that.'

'What, then? What *are* you saying?'

'That you are the king's man on the king's duty with no fixed place of abode and whose future cannot include permanent relationships. This has gone far enough, Alex. I am at risk. I am vulnerable. I have to protect myself and my child, let alone my reputation.' His thumbs caressed her brow and her cheeks as she spoke, and she knew that, this time, he was hearing as well as listening.

'Do you think I don't know all that?' he whispered.

'That's the problem. I don't know *what* you think.'

'Then we have made some progress. Now you know that I'm in love with you, wee lass.' It seemed natural to punctuate that with a kiss, after which he was the one with enough breath to speak. 'And if you will only come with me to Lanercost instead of Carlisle, you will discover more about what I am thinking. Can you afford to pass up an offer like that?' He waited for her response. 'Ebony?' he whispered. 'Sweetheart? Beloved?'

She gulped back a sob of laughter. 'No,' she said.

'So why are you hesitating?'

'I don't know.' *Because I am changing. Because you said you love me. Because I love you and dare not say it. Because I may yet lose you.*

'That's a sound womanly reason,' he said.

'Alex, will you do something for me out there, in the hall?'

'Anything you wish.'

'Talk with Helen. Show her your interest. Spend some time at her side.'

'Of course I will. And I'll introduce her to Sandy, too. He's been gawping at her all evening like a love-sick calf. Leave it to me.'

It was late when the celebrations drew to a close with a hilarious contest of arm-wrestling between Selena and several of the king's men, all of whom allowed her to win. In her shared bedchamber with Helen, Ebony revived an unanswered question, sneaking it into the tentative attempts at familiarity warmed by several glasses of red wine. She undid the side-laces of Helen's clinging kirtle. 'You said earlier that my lad Sam was the same age as someone,' she said. 'Was that another brother, by any chance?'

Helen slid out of the kirtle and picked it up before answering. 'No,' she said, 'not a brother. I had not realised you didn't know. I suppose I shouldn't have spoken.' She paused, finding the temptation too strong. 'You don't know much about him, do you?'

Ebony sat on the bed and began to plait her hair. 'About Sir Alex? No, I know next to nothing.'

'Why not? Have you never asked him?'

'No.' The answer emerged a mite too sharp, and again Ebony felt the need to explain herself. 'He's been investigating my late father-in-law,' she said. 'We haven't exactly been on good terms, as you can imagine. I had to go to Dumfries rather urgently, and now he needs to go to Lanercost Priory, that's all.'

'Ah, well, then you'll see him for yourself.'

Ebony stopped plaiting to study Helen's expression in the candlelight, but the thick fall of wavy gold concealed it. 'See who?' she said.

'Sir Alex's little son. He'll be about the same age as yours now.'

Something tightened around Ebony's lung, squeezing her voice. 'A son? He has…a *son*? No, I didn't know that.' *Helen was right. She didn't know much at all.*

'Well, I can't see any harm in telling you since you'll see him for yourself tomorrow. He lives with the canons at the priory.'

'Then he doesn't have a mother?'

'Apparently not. I can't see that it's a very safe place to leave a wee bairn, with the raiding so close. They're only a stone's-throw from the wall, you know.'

She had asked, so she could hardly blame Helen for telling her, though there was no way of knowing the exact nature of the satisfaction Helen derived from watching the shock spread like ice across Ebony's face. After the scene in the passageway, Ebony had kept to those parts of the hall less brightly lit where, for a while, she had indulged in the sound of those words she had never thought to hear from the one she could now admit that she loved. Since this news, however, she was hearing them with different connotation attached, as if their meaning carried an extra weight of responsibility, a choice, a proviso. She was glad she had reacted with caution.

Lying by Helen's side in the big bed with the pungent reek of snuffed candle-flames drifting above her, she recalled how once in anger she had asked him how often he saw the bairns he had sired. His reply,

'Not often enough,' had meant little to her except to acknowledge her intended insult. So, was the child left with the Augustinian canons at Lanercost a bastard son? And had he been put there to begin a vocation common with youngest sons or noblemen's bastards? In any case, although the news had stunned her, there was little use in forming conclusions until she had discovered the full story, which was undoubtedly what he had meant by his promise to tell her what he was thinking. First the declaration of love to the grieving widow, then would come the request to keep his child safe and happy while he went off about the king's business. It was not all that difficult, she thought, to know what he was thinking. Perhaps it was a good thing she had been given some warning.

But despite Ebony's scepticism and Helen's heartache, the most extraordinary sight greeted Mistress Betty Springfield when she entered Helen's bedchamber at dawn the next morning, expecting to rouse her guest and daughter. There were four young women, three blonde and one ebony, plucking each other's eyebrows in total silence except for the occasional yelp of pain. 'Well,' she said, tartly, placing herself in the only vacant stool. 'First things first, of course.'

Ebony and Alex had left Castle Kells, believing that Hugh and Meg had reached an uneasy, but reasonably stable, truce with each of them in charge of their separate departments. Despite this over-optimistic belief, hardly an hour since their departure had been free of disputes and squabbles, at first-hand or by proxy, and though Meg felt that this was probably the best way to keep Hugh of Leyland in his place, she also knew that she would not be allowed to get away with it for much longer.

The explosion came on the day that Ebony and Alex set out, only four days since Hugh had taken Meg firmly in hand after the stableyard incident. This time, after a series of petty arguments about the strict observance of mealtimes, about the men pestering the laundry-maids, about who had the right to appoint a new estate-steward and encouraging Sam to pee where he should not have done (over the battlements), the catalyst was to be Brother Walter who, in his innocence, was still unwell. Thinking that the degree of unwellness was being exaggerated, Hugh felt that a week was long enough for the chaplain to escape his parochial duties to the villagers, one of whom needed churching after a birth. Her husband had come to the castle to complain.

Hugh went to see Brother Walter for himself and found that Meg was with him, holding his head under a linen towel over a bowl of steaming friar's balsam. 'When he's finished,' Hugh said, 'ask him if he'll be good enough to come and see me about his duties.'

The chaplain, whose hearing was in no way impaired by this activity, straightened up to speak for himself, allowing the healing steam to escape and Meg's annoyance to return. 'Aye, Mester Hugh,' he said with drips falling off the end of his red nose, 'I'll come to ye reet away. Just gi' me—'

'You'll do nothing of the sort,' Meg scolded, grabbing his head and ducking it once more under the cloth. 'You'll stay indoors and rest. Can ye not see how he suffers?' she snapped at Hugh over her shoulder. 'The poor man can hardly breathe.'

'And you, mistress, can hardly keep a civil tongue

in your head. Perhaps your father kept a scold's bridle somewhere in this place. I may just go and take a look.' Hugh turned back to her with his hand on the latch. 'And if I don't manage to find one, I'll have the armourer make one by tomorrow. Let's see if that will curb your temper.'

Having experienced a foretaste of Master Leyland's ruthlessness, Meg took his threat very seriously, especially so when he had made no overtures to her whatever in the last few days. Now she began to wonder whether he was waiting for her to become more amenable or whether he had given her up as an impossible woman, a result she had not anticipated. Nor did she want it, for now she understood the fears and delights of a first love. But to wear a scold's bridle before members of her own household would be a shame she would never live down. Not ever.

Master Leyland was nowhere to be seen for the rest of that day, nor did he share his supper with her at the high table, but ate in the body of the hall with his own men. He stayed in their company all that evening.

Midday dinner on the next day was the same, when even Sam became alarmed.

'Aunt Meg, why is Master Hugh not speaking to you?' Childlike, he came straight to the point.

Like the others, Dame Janet had noticed something. 'Because he's busy,' she said, her imagination not being geared to the six-year-old mind.

Biddie had discussed the problem with Master Josh. 'Because he has to do Sir Alex's job,' she said, 'and that means he has to talk to the men more than usual.'

'So is that why he's just gone out with Will the armourer?' Sam said. 'Master Will told me he was making something com-per-kated for him.'

Meg paled, and slipped off the padded bench as if she had suddenly remembered something. 'Excuse me, if you please,' she said. She caught up with Hugh and the armourer on the steps down to the courtyard, having no clear idea of what would make the most convincing interruption.

Hugh looked up, surprised to see her behind them. 'Mistress?' he said.

Her usually quick brain failed to come to her aid. 'Er…' she said.

The armourer took the hint and kept on going while Hugh waited for her to speak, purposely not making it easier for her by a smile or encouraging word. He was, she thought, looking very uncompromising. 'Yes?' he said. 'You need to speak to me? Brother Walter must have told you that we've resolved the matter of his duties, surely?'

'Yes…er…no, it's not that.'

'Oh? What, then? Is it Biddie this time, or Dame Janet?'

'Please,' she whispered, looking down at the curious upturned faces in the courtyard below. 'Can we talk…in private…somewhere?' Only a week ago he would have leapt at the chance to be alone with her, but now his almost apathetic and silent agreement was telling her that things had changed and that she must blame herself for it.

She led him across to the towered gatehouse, under the echoing arch and portcullis, and across the drawbridge beneath which a family of swans glided in the hope of scraps. Turning right on to the narrow pathway, they went without a word being spoken into the edge of the forest where Hugh and Sir Alex had gathered their company on that fateful morning almost two weeks ago. Hidden at last from the castle's many eyes, Meg stopped by a large boulder and faced him with more uncertainty and trepidation than she had felt for many a day. She watched her fingers poke at the domes of moss on the boulder, ruffled by his total silence. 'Master Leyland,' she said, 'this is difficult… er…for me.'

'Yes, I can imagine.'

A piece of moss came loose and she tried to replace it. 'Yes,' she said, gritting her teeth. 'It's only two weeks since my father died, and it's not been an easy time for me…for us…for any of us.'

'No, indeed.'

There was something in his agreement that irritated her, though she could not say what. She glanced at his lithe body lounging against the boulder, arms folded, his expression disconcertingly sombre, though his eyes lazily scanned her figure when she would have preferred them to offer her some suggestion of understanding, if not sympathy. 'And so—' she took a deep breath '—so…if I seem to have been… well…irritable, short-tempered, somewhat rude…' At this point she would have liked him to protest that she had every reason to be upset, but he remained still and silent, except that his head tipped sideways as if to see her from a different angle. Her pause had no effect. 'Yes, well, you can probably see what I'm trying to say,' she said, by no means sure that he could.

'I'm afraid I can't, mistress,' he said at last. 'Unless you're telling me that you are about to apologise for your shrewishness.'

'Well,' she snapped, throwing a lump of moss at his boots, 'that's what I *was* trying to say, but—'

'Then why don't you just get on and say it? Go on, try it.'

'Because *you*, sir,' she yelped, clenching her fists by her sides, 'are the most irritating and perverse man I've ever met and I have no more to say to you. I came here to give you the chance…no…to give *me* the chance…oh, for pity's sake!'

But Hugh had seen through her plan from the start and now could no longer keep his face straight. As she stalked away from him, he leaned forward and scooped an arm around her before she could dodge him, pulling her off-balance into his arms where he held her at such an awkward angle across the boulder that she was unable to right herself. 'To give you the chance to what, vixen?' he said. 'As I recall, you've had plenty of chances to come out with a pleasant word or two instead of snapping at shadows like a terrier. Is that how you expect to get co-operation? By snarling at everybody?'

It was unlike Meg to give way to tears, but these last two weeks had been for her exceptionally emotional ones and now, terrified by what he plainly intended to do to punish her, her fright surfaced uncontrollably. A vision of herself having to wear the dreaded scold's bridle taunted her; a contraption of iron bands made to fit over the head with a metal projection to prevent the scold's tongue from wagging, padlocked behind. She had seen it only once, as a child, worn by the village gossip for a few humiliating hours. Hot tears spilled down her cheeks. 'No,' she croaked. 'No, it isn't. I'm sorry. Please…don't make me wear one of those…things. Let…let me explain.'

Easing her up, Hugh took hold of her chin with gentle fingers, his expression betraying nothing of his bewilderment. 'One of…what things?' he said.

More tears replaced those she knuckled away. 'A bridle,' she sobbed. 'You couldn't be so cruel. It won't be needed. I can see you've changed your mind about being smitten, but there's no…no need…need to do that. I shall stay well out of your way, and I'll—'

Without a word of what he was thinking, he hoisted her up into his arms and carried her as if she were no heavier than a leaf to the edge of the trees where the ground fell steeply away to the loch below. There, he sat with her across his knees, cradling her against his chest, smoothing her hair and mopping her tears of tiredness, fright, and the natural reactions to death and new love. 'Come on, now,' he whispered, 'tell me all about it. It's been rough for you, I know, and you've been wonderful. And, no, you need not keep out of my way. That's not what I want. I want you *in* my way, my sweet Meg, and I'm still as smitten as ever. Did you think I don't love you, my little firebrand? Of course I love you. How could you have thought otherwise?'

'Love me?' she gulped. 'Are you sure? You didn't speak to me.'

'Quite sure, vixen. And I didn't speak to you because I didn't fancy walking around headless until I could grow another one. Bad for my image. Course I love you. I'm never mistaken about such things.'

'You've loved before, then?' she asked, softly.

His kisses, so dreamed-of since her initiation, told her many wonderful things about him, one of which was that, whether he had been in love before or not, he certainly knew his way around a woman's garments. As his kiss deepened, her mind was lured away from the concerns she had brought with them to a place where all her sensations were controlled by his lips and one searching hand.

As before, she caught at his wrist, halting his first tender explorations beneath the sideless surcoat that covered her kirtle. 'No,' she whispered. 'You must not.'

His hand stilled and carefully withdrew. 'No,' he said, 'I must not, must I? Then will you allow me to show you something, over there?'

'Where?' She followed his eyes. 'In the loch?'

'No, just down here. There's something I want you to see.' He led the puzzled Meg forward to the edge of the precipice and pulled her down beside him to peer through the fern-fronds at the view below. 'There,' he said. 'What do you see?'

'Nothing,' she said. 'Just the waterfall, that's all.'

'Yes. And who bathed there at dawn on the day we arrived?'

She stared at him. 'We did. Ebony and I. Why do you ask?'

'Well, because you were not as alone as you thought you were, sweetheart, for it was here on this very spot that you had an audience of two. We waited up here before we went to the castle. So you see, I've already—'

'You've *seen*?' Scandalised, she tried to roll away, but his arm was across her in a flash. 'You've seen

me, and Ebony, with no—!' She pushed and
squirmed, but to no avail.

'Without a stitch, my red-haired one. And I fell in
love with you there and then. You were the most…
hold still…the most luscious creature I'd ever seen in
my whole life.'

'*No!* That's disgraceful!' she squealed. 'Peeping
Toms!'

'And I vowed I'd have you. Marry me, sweet Meg.
Please, marry me.'

'No, I won't, sir! I was right. You men think only
of one thing, and now you've taken our privacy without permission. That was *not* well done, sir.'

Whatever else she was about to add about dishonour was lost as his mouth, roving over her neck,
reached her lips at last and held them captive until
she was breathless and quietly forgetful. While her
mind was undergoing a change that she had no control over, his hand eased her garments with a practised
skill over her shoulders and breasts, lingering over
their firm coolness and the small brown buds that
hardened and grew erect under the first stroking of
his tongue. He lifted his head to look into her half-
closed eyes. 'You'll marry me, Meg,' he whispered,
'and we shall make red-haired bairns together like a
litter of fox cubs. No, not here, not yet, but soon.
You're mine, vixen, so you can forget what you think
you know about men's thoughts. You were mine
since the moment I saw you down there in the pool,
and now you'll come back with me like a lamb, and
there'll be no more scolding or snarling. Understood?'

She nodded. 'The bridle…? You'll not…?'

'No, I'll tell Will to put it away for a while,
shall I?'

'Yes. I never meant to…I'm sorry…it's just that—'

'I know. D'ye want to stay here, or are your duties calling?'

'Can we stay here a while, just like this?' She snuggled up against him, this time making no objection when his hand softly caressed every naked surface while the sound of running water accompanied her sighs of delight.

If anyone had told Hugh of Leyland that it would take him almost a fortnight to get as far as this with a woman, he would have laughed with scorn, for it had never done so before. But now the laugh was on him, for he was desperately in love and he would have to convince this woman that, whatever her reservations, he was serious about marriage. Not only that, but he would have to convince Alex, too, and suffer the consequences of dismissal from the king's men, for Hugh would not risk what had happened to Alex.

Chapter Eleven

For the first time in many years, Ebony passed through a demolished part of the massive Roman wall that stretched from the Solway Firth to the town of Newcastle-upon-Tyne on the east coast, taking her at last into England. Lanercost Priory, only a stone's throw from the wall, was a half-day's horse ride from Gretna, but an early leavetaking was difficult and the sun was high by the time they set out, this time as a nobleman and his lady with their retinue of servants and retainers.

Due to the combined assistance of Selena, Christina and Helen, several noticeable changes had affected Ebony's appearance that were enough to make the men's glances linger more than ever. Her clean, newly braided hair had been coiled beneath a silk-covered fillet, a deep band that sat like a crown over a fine net of silk cord with gold studs at each inter-section. A narrow barbette of white silk replaced her former wimple; she must show off her long neck, they told her, now that the sun had reappeared. She allowed them to do whatever they wished, even to apply a touch of rouge to her lips that made her smile at the reflection in the silver mirror. Here was a noblewoman, they said, who would send the canons of Lanercost queuing up for penances.

The canons would not be the only ones to experience guilt, Sir Alex having already expressed true regret at his clumsiness during the previous evening. The only excuse he could offer was that he was driven out of his mind with love and desire for her, and could she find it in her heart to excuse his soldierly roughness? He had been too long away from the domestic scene.

Apologies from men being as rare as rocs' eggs, she accepted it with concealed astonishment, not only because of its unexpectedness, but because his angry outburst had caused him to say what he felt about her, and that was worth weeks of guesswork. His eyes said even more, scanning every detail of the newly polished Ebony, the washed and ironed kirtle, and borrowed surcoat with marten-fur edges. 'What have you done overnight?' he whispered to her. 'Bathed in asses' milk?'

'Yes.' She smiled. 'Rings on my fingers, bells on my toes.'

By coincidence, it was at the gap in Hadrian's Wall where they met Sir Alex's ten men who had escorted Sir Joseph's retainers to the muster of troops at Newcastle. Now on their return to Castle Kells, they found it almost beyond belief that the screaming frenzied woman they had last seen hurling herself like a wildcat at a crowd of men in search of her child could possibly be the same queenly woman who rode demurely by their commander's side.

They expressed a willingness to go to Lanercost with him, but Sir Alex could see the direction of their interest. 'No.' He laughed. 'Go back to Castle Kells and take a bath and a shave, all of you, and be there when I return. And tell Hugh where we'll be. Guard the young laird well.'

Ebony kept her eyes on her recently manicured hands and said nothing, but wondered how many of them knew of his young son and could make a guess as to the reason for their visit. Even more to the point, how many of them would expect to see the young Somers lad riding back with them to Galloway. She was glad she'd been told of the situation well in advance.

Descending into the valley of the River Irthing through a hillside of trees, their first sighting of the pink sandstone priory was like seeing a jewel gleaming in the bright sun, lying in a field of lush greenness. By its side, the river wound like a silver cord, passing fish-ponds and crofts, orchards and outbuildings, rooftops, towers and walls, arches and thatched wooden buildings. Smoke rose in a blue haze from the isolated kitchen, and men crossed the yard while others worked in the gardens.

One group of riders was returning from a hunt with bundles of hares dangling like catkins from their saddles. Seeing Sir Alex's party pass through the large gatehouse and porter's lodge, the leading huntsman waved and rode forward to greet them personally, welcoming them like old friends. Prior William of Southaik, though spare of frame, had a fine bush of white eyebrows and hair that shone like a halo in the sun, an endowment altogether undeserved according to those who knew his ways. Nevertheless, he was popular and large-hearted, hospitable and resilient, and if he looked more like the bailiff than the prior, that suited him well enough. Ebony warmed to him at once, to his smiles and fatherliness, reminding her of something she had never had and something else for which she ought to be searching.

Thankfully, his curiosity about her was well under control, though he was certainly familiar with the name of Moffat, a slight widening of the eyes as they rested upon her, a small delay in withdrawing them, an instant command for her to be shown to the best rooms in the guest-house. The guest-master, Father Andrew, appeared from nowhère to lead them through an extended archway into an open courtyard where a row of thatched dwellings took up the whole of the opposite side. Despite the plain exteriors, the interior of the spacious rooms that were to be hers would have satisfied even the most demanding guest and, although there was little in the way of ornament, there was coloured glass in two of the windows, a stone fireplace and chimney-breast, timber panelling to clad the walls, and even a bath-house next door which the servants would fill for her, if she should wish it. Plainly, his manner suggested that he hoped she wouldn't wish it too often.

'This was part of the lodging prepared for Queen Margaret when she came to stay with the late king thirteen years ago,' Father Andrew told them, holding a hand up to warn Sir Alex of the low door lintel and continuing the gesture to draw back the woollen curtain that divided the bedchamber off from the rest. 'King Edward the First was on his way to Carlisle, but he was very unwell. Had to be carried in a litter all the way. They stopped here for the night in September and stayed till March, so we had suddenly to start a building programme.' He shook his head as if reliving the pandemonium. 'Hundreds of them to house and feed. You never saw anything like it. We had to rebuild this range and a stone-built place for the king, private chapels, draught-proof this, that, and the other. What an expense! Some of them had to live under canvas out there in the meadow, but we had workmen here day and night most of the time. We're still feeling the effects of it all this time later. Great privilege, of course,' he said, hastily, rubbing his nose, 'but very disruptive. Anyway…' he twinkled at Ebony '…it's left us with a fine suite of lodgings second to none. And our inmates are all priests, as you know, so they'll be queuing up to administer a private mass, should you want that.' Which was almost, but not quite, what the Springfield sisters had said.

Left alone to explore her pleasant surroundings and to refresh herself, Ebony felt that it was at times like this when she would have liked a personal maid, though it was to Sam and Meg that her thoughts quickly turned as she tested the fur-covered canopied bed with the small wooden crucifix above it. The white bedcurtains stirred in the breeze from the window that Father Andrew and Sir Alex had opened together with some difficulty and, racked with longing for Sam and the warm feel of his little body in her arms, she went to lean upon the window-sill to look out across the meadow. She could easily imagine him romping and leaping in the waist-high buttercups and ox-eye daisies, sure that he was slaying dragons in an enchanted forest.

Distant figures moved across the landscape into her thoughts and, half-dreaming, she watched them part and reunite like herself and Sam, too far away for any laughter to be heard. A small figure held something up towards an adult, but whether male or female it was hard to tell. They stopped to talk, then there was a brief chase, a quick hug and another parting. Blinking, Ebony realised that they were not her imaginings but real people and that the adult was a woman who had just replaced the slipping veil over her head as only a woman would. They would be village people, to be sure, for these were the precincts of men, not of mothers and children, and Alex's son would be poring over his Latin primer with his tutor.

A young servant came to bring her hot water in a large earthenware pitcher, his eyes modestly downcast. He would have scurried away, but Ebony's query kept him back. 'Are there any other guests staying here tonight?' she said.

'Only two canons, m'lady, on their way to the motherhouse at Carlisle.'

'And who does that field out there belong to?'

He looked beyond her to the sunlit meadow. 'Priory land, m'lady.' The question was an unusual one, coming from a woman. He hesitated, already balanced to flee. 'Will that be all, m'lady?'

'No…wait, if you please.' She went back to the window. 'Just tell me, who are those two people out there on priory land?'

Again, he peered beyond her into the distance, adjusting his eyes to the glare. 'Ah,' he said, relaxing. 'That'll be Master Nicholas and Dame Marie. He's Sir Alex's young lad. No wonder they can't find him. I'd best go and tell them where he is.'

'No,' said Ebony, 'don't do that yet. I'll go and tell him his father's here. How do I get into the meadow?'

'Easy,' the lad said. 'Through the wicket gate next to your door, then across the path. That's all.'

Shedding the formal headgear and the overwarm surcoat, she closed the door behind her and stepped through the little gate, heading into the lush meadow with slow impeded strides that took her towards the hazy pair, sure that this would be the best way for her and the child to meet for the first time.

Halfway there, they saw her and stopped their intimate conversation to stand erect and wait for the space between them to close. Never had she felt more like an intruder, and never had she wished so hard not to be there, disturbing their private idyll. It had been a mistake. A poorly timed unnecessary move on her part. The woman's posture was unwelcoming. Ebony slowed and stopped, still yards away.

The woman was tall and slender, and not at first glance the young nurse Ebony had half-expected. She pulled her veil further forward and took hold of the child's hand in a protective gesture that Ebony resented. Now she could see that the child's hair was a fine shining pale brown that flopped over his forehead and ears, that his skin was peachy and faintly speckled like a wren's egg, and that he possessed the same incredible blue eyes of his father that looked fearlessly into hers. He wore a short tunic of faded brown and some kind of leg-covering half-hidden by the tall grass and, by the height of him against his companion, she judged him to be an inch or two taller than Sam.

'May I join you?' Ebony called, trying to smile.

The woman drew the boy closer. 'Who are you?' she said.

The timbre of the woman's voice held a familiar

ring, but it was to the child that Ebony wanted to speak. 'I'm Ebony,' she said. 'And you are Master Nicholas, I believe? And Dame Marie?'

'Yes, I'm Nicholas,' the boy said, cheerily. He held out a hand to show her a green caterpillar. 'We're looking for things with legs. This one doesn't seem to have any.' His little face, as sweet as an angel, almost smiled, but a movement in the grass caught his fleeting attention and whatever else he was going to say went unremembered in the blink of an eye.

The woman appeared to soften as she reached up again to hold her veil in place with gracefully tapering fingers, and a wide gold band flashed on her wedding finger, bright against the soft grey-blue of her loose old-fashioned gown. Yet there was something in that small movement and in her demeanour that made Ebony wish she would reveal her face and speak to her. She supposed she would have to try again. 'I'm sorry to interrupt your search,' she said, gently. 'I was told that you are Dame Marie. Is that right? Your name *is* Marie?'

The woman nodded, but before she could speak Nicholas pointed excitedly as a butterfly rose out of the grass and fluttered above them, and he pulled at her to follow, hauling her, then slewing her round into the chase. Her veil fell once more into folds around her neck, revealing a sleek head of black silver-streaked hair that coiled behind her in a thick bundle, and she glanced at Ebony in passing with an expression of amused apology. Her eyes, grey as stone and black-lashed, were still beautiful, heavy-lidded but hollowed above into deep cavernous sockets with the haunted look of one who has suffered and was still hiding the trauma at the back of her mind. Her throat was long and elegant, like the hands, yet there was no hint of recognition or interest in her manner, no fragile cord of perception or remembrance showing in her eyes and, for the second time, Ebony believed that either the light was playing tricks with her or that she must be daydreaming.

The boy leapt unevenly away, taking the woman with him, and Ebony was left behind with an eerie and disturbing notion that she was seeing herself as a grandmother chasing after butterflies in a sunlit field. Any moment now they would disappear. She tried to call out but it was like a dream when no sound comes. *Come back*, she wanted to shout. *Stand still! I'm here! Look at me. I'm Ebony. You must know me.* But now there was a faraway feeling in her head, she felt sick, the sun dazzled her and the figures began to fade. 'No...' she whispered, 'come back to me...please! I need to see you. I'm looking for some-one...'

The boy veered sharply, then stopped in his tracks to watch the approach of someone who, multiple-legged or not, was a far better catch. 'Papa!' he squealed. 'Papa...you've come!' Leaving his com-panion behind, he loped lopsidedly towards the tall broad-shouldered figure of the one whose arms were spread wide to catch him, their duet of laughter clos-ing the gap with the soundless collision of bodies. He was swung up high into the air to cling like a limpet, just as Sam had done, and it was only then that Ebony saw the reason for his strange gait. Below the calf-length braies, one leg was white and emaciated, the foot twisted grotesquely inwards towards the other.

For Ebony, the sun slowly eclipsed as the afternoon turned an icy cold, and before she could catch it and hold it still, the field tipped sideways, then reared up to meet her, her legs disowned her, and she slipped quietly into the grassy sleep of oblivion.

She heard a lark singing in her dream. 'Don't wake me,' she said. 'I'm all right here.' A hand smoothed her forehead and faces appeared, dark against the bright sky.

'Ah, sweet lass,' Sir Alex was murmuring. 'I didn't want this to happen. I wanted to be with you. This is my fault. What a clumsy idiot.' He lifted her into his arms and she felt herself roll helplessly against him. 'I'll take her in,' he said. 'She'll be better indoors.'

'Will she be all right, Papa?' a little voice piped.

'Yes, Nick. She'll be fine.'

'She's not going to die, is she?'

'Good Lord, no, wee lad. She certainly isn't. Run ahead and open the gate for us.'

'Who is she, Alex?' the woman said from somewhere behind Ebony's head. 'She said her name is Ebony. Did she come with *you*, then?'

'Lady Ebony Moffat,' he said. 'Does it mean anything to you?'

'Not a thing. I suppose you're telling me it should, are you?'

He didn't reply, but Ebony knew that he was smiling.

The world finally came to a standstill as she was laid upon the fur coverlet of her bed, feeling slightly foolish and absurdly confused. The best thing, she supposed, would be to listen rather than try to talk. She heard Sir Alex's low-voiced instruction to his son. 'With some ice in it,' and guessed that he had sent him for some water.

The bed moved and she felt the warmth as her hand
was taken between two fragile ones, a touch she had
missed for so many years stroking her knuckles with
a thumb. She had hoped to make an instant and eu-
phoric reconnection with the mother she loved, to
hear her story, to tell her own, to confide in her and
seek advice that only a beloved mother can give. And
now, a touch on her hand was to be their only intimate
communication. She opened her eyes and looked directly into a future image of herself that held a tender
expression of concern in the grey depths and a slight
twist to the lovely brows.

'Yes,' the woman said, sitting next to Ebony's
knees, 'I *can* see the resemblance. It's quite remarkable, isn't it? Forgive me, my lady. I feel that in some
way I'm responsible, but for the life of me…' She
searched for the words to explain. 'It was like seeing
myself walking towards me through the grass. Myself
as a young woman. But I can't remember it, you see.'
She shook her head sorrowfully. 'I really cannot remember it. I realise that I'm supposed to know you,
but the truth is that I don't even know who I am,
either. Can you believe me? You are hurt, I can see
that.'

'The boy told me you're called Dame Marie,' said
Ebony.

The ageing face smiled and the gentle thumbs
moved softly over Ebony's skin. 'Yes, all Augustinian houses are dedicated to Mary of Magdalene,' she
said. 'It was Prior William who found me, apparently,
when he was out hunting. I really don't remember it,
but he brought me here, and the canons have cared
for me since then. I do what I can for them in return,

mend their habits and church vestments, that kind of thing. It's very little.'

Sir Alex came to sit on her other side. 'She was half-dead from exposure and couldn't speak for weeks, so they called her Marie for want of a better name. It's most unusual for the canons to keep a lady on the premises, but Prior William makes his own rules about things, and young Nicholas and she took an instant liking to each other. He was four years old at the time and getting a bit of a handful for them. A nurse-governess was exactly what he needed. Dame Marie has been a godsend; far more than the little she claims.'

'We keep good company together.' She smiled. 'Nicholas has taught me how to make a new life.'

'And you taught him how to read and write.'

'As she did for me,' Ebony whispered.

'Ah, so that's how you learned. I wondered,' he said.

'And you,' said Ebony, 'must have suspected that there might be a connection, yet you chose not to tell me about it.' Treading on eggshells was nothing to this, she thought, as the relevance of his discovery began to percolate through every facet of their relationship. Yet she knew that to challenge him was not the answer, that she would have to proceed with care and that she must somehow find strength enough for two women. She could not assume that Dame Marie would automatically switch back to her real self and take on the role of mother to a complete stranger any more than she herself would. Much as she longed to throw herself into her mother's arms and pour out all the pent-up agonies of their missing years, she saw that an act of such selfishness would do nothing but embarrass this lost woman who could acknowledge no blood relationship to anyone. She, Ebony, would have to wait patiently for a change to take place, if ever one did. It was a heartrending state of affairs that she could never have foreseen, yet it was certain that her mother had suffered just as much as she herself, and that the damage might be far more permanent and serious, for she had truly lost a most precious part of her life.

'No,' said Sir Alex. 'I didn't say anything except to Hugh, but he'd seen the resemblance for himself. He didn't need me to point it out to him. We called here a few months ago for Nick's sixth birthday.'

'And when did the prior find Dame Marie?'

Dame Marie looked blankly at Sir Alex. 'August, two years ago,' he said. 'The year after you…'

'Yes,' Ebony said, 'but I'm not the only one to have lost a mate, am I?'

'Prior William has helped me, too. We've known each other for years, since before the worst conflicts started. Being on different sides has made no difference to our friendship, or to his love of Nick.'

Ebony felt that he was evading an answer to her indirect query. 'But isn't it regarded as treachery to befriend the enemy?' she said.

His laugh was dismissive. 'The enmity between England and Scotland is not quite as cut-and-dried as that, wee lass, as you well know. Our two countries were friends until not so long ago, the Scots under English sovereignty, English lords given lands in Scotland. Nick's been as safe here on the English side of the wall as he would have been on the Scottish side, and here I've been able to call on him as I set out on my missions. But he can't stay here for ever, that's certain.'

Unexpectedly, Dame Marie added her opinion. 'He needs a mother and the company of other boys,' she said. 'You know he does, Alex.'

'Lady Ebony needs a mother and the company of a husband,' he said. 'And *her* young son needs the company of other lads, too.'

'No,' Ebony said, feeling that this was going too fast for Dame Marie. 'Wait a while. All in good time. No woman will thank you for pushing her into a situation she may not want. These things must be properly considered.' Her concern was for Dame Marie, not for herself, but Sir Alex placed his own interpretations on her words that seemed to answer a rather different question.

'I'm sure you're right,' he said, standing up. 'Ah, here's the spring water. Well done, Nick.' He took the jug of sloshing water from him and, ignoring the wet patch on the boy's tunic, poured a beakerful and handed it to Nicholas. 'Take that to Lady Ebony,' he said.

'Thank you,' she said, smiling at him. 'You're the same age as my Sam, I believe, although I think you may be an inch taller.'

'Does your Sam look like me?' Nicholas said, endearingly.

'Very much like you. I'm sure he'd like to meet you, one day.'

'Yes,' he said. 'Does he have a pony to ride?' Then, without waiting for an answer, which to him was reasonably obvious, he added, 'I had a pony once, but it was stolen.'

'Oh dear, I'm sorry to hear that.' She glanced up

at Sir Alex, knowing that here was yet another very good reason why Nicholas should be given a home at Castle Kells. How many more good reasons would there be? she wondered.

The father picked up his son and hugged him. 'Now,' he said, 'I want you to take Dame Marie back to your lodgings and get cleaned up ready for supper. I'll come and join you very soon.'

'Promise?'

'I promise.'

The little lad placed his mouth to his father's ear and whispered, with a sideways peep at Ebony.

'Yes,' said his father. 'She is, isn't she? *Very* pretty. Now, off you go.' Hand in hand, the old lady and the child left the room, chattering like schoolfriends and quite heedless of the fifty-year age difference.

Ebony wanted nothing more than to ask about her mother's state of mind, to discuss her future, to talk about her past. Instead, she said, 'Will you tell me about him? He's a dear little lad. And so like you…to look at, I mean. You realise that I knew of him?'

'Helen told you,' he said, returning to the end of the bed. 'Well, no matter. You came, and that's the important part. His mother was English, from a London family. I took her up to Scotland when we married, but she never settled, partly because I had to be away so much. It was a mistake, and stupid of me to think that being married was enough for her. Typically Scottish, I'm afraid. She became pregnant, but I had to go to Flanders on a mission that took far longer than it should. The village was attacked while I was away. The wee bairn was only four weeks old.' His voice became tight with emotion. 'She tried to protect him, and his foot was slashed in the fighting. She wasn't badly injured, but she didn't survive the shock. She was not robust. I should never have left her.'

'Oh…oh, Alex. That's terrible. I'm *so* sorry.' She looked at her hands, finding no adequate words there, or anywhere. He had suffered as badly as she. 'So you brought the child here?' she said.

'Yes, friends would have taken him, and his London relatives too, but I didn't want that. I believed he'd be safer here with men who take no sides. I pay them well enough.' He smiled.

'And Nicholas's pony? That's the one at Castle Kells, I take it?'

'I'm afraid it is. Another victim of the stealing and re-stealing that went on between your father-in-law and his nephew. The prior bought it in good faith from Davy Moffat's contact when it should have been going up to Scotland, but by the time it was stolen back again one dark night, it bore the L for Lanercost on its flank. Poor Nick, he was distraught.' He looked at her more keenly. 'Are you all right, wee lass? Hush, sweetheart. No tears.' He came to her and took her in his arms, gathering her to him like a child and sweeping a hand lovingly over her back. 'Hush, now, it's all right. There…there…'

Unable to contain her anguish for another moment, the gasping sobs racked her body with sadness, confusion and an overwhelming love that could easily have taken in three people if only they had been in a position to accept it. But she was not sure of any of them.

He gentled her with his voice. 'That was a shock,

I know. I never thought you'd find them before I did. It was careless of me. Hush, sweetheart.'

'I can't...ask her...anything.' She wept. 'She can't tell me what happened. How can I help her? How can I insist on taking her back home with me?'

'Prior William will tell you what he knows about her, though I don't think it'll amount to much. Physically, she's whole again, but now the damage to her mind remains, and the physicians here say that only time will heal it. She's not unhappy or in pain. She adores Nick, and the canons treat her like royalty. She goes with them to tend the sick because she seems to know a lot about remedies. In fact, it's strange that she can remember so much of what she learned, her physics and her Latin, but not the important bits like who she is, or how she got here, or where from. But what's most interesting to me is that although she has no mirror to see herself, she realises that she once looked like you. Now I find that very encouraging.'

'Yes, it is. But do you think she'll ever accept me as her daughter again?'

'Well, accepting you is one thing, even if she still doesn't remember, but going back to Castle Kells with you is quite another. I suppose it would depend on what happened to Nick. She'll never leave here without him.'

'Ah,' she said, gently withdrawing herself. 'Of course.'

The evening peace that enveloped the beautiful abbey at Lanercost was almost too heavenly to spoil with a discussion of Ebony's problems, though that was the reason she had been invited to accompany Prior William on his tour of the abbey precincts.

'From what Alex was telling me at supper,' he said, 'it would seem that there's no doubt that you're Dame Marie's daughter and that she is Lady Jean Nevillestowe of Carlisle. That would make sense; she could have walked that distance, or rather *wandered*, in a few weeks. Of course, I saw the likeness as soon as you arrived.' He opened the wooden gate into the orchard and led her slowly along the path to the river and the fish ponds that shone like pink satin in the last of the sunlight.

Ebony had taken supper alone with her mother in a southwest-facing chamber above the king's chapel where the dame was used to sitting with her needlework or her reading, or with Nicholas and his lessons. The two of them had talked on subjects that Ebony hoped might trigger personal memories, and once or twice she thought something had, though she could not be certain.

With a touching perception, the fatherly prior had anticipated Ebony's need for an impartial hearing on a subject that evidently puzzled her, and had come in person ostensibly to show her the tall stone cross erected many hundreds of years ago in the croft. She glanced sideways at his black and white garb, his voluminous cloak and hood, and the fine white hair that lay against it. His deeply lined face showed a lifetime of mental and physical struggle, for the abbey had witnessed terrifying violations and now the brotherhood had dwindled to a mere thirteen. In lieu of a mother, Ebony thought, Prior William would do very well.

'It's a most uncanny experience,' she said.

'To have discovered her at last?'

'Well, yes, Father. Particularly when I least expected to. But what's more unsettling is the need to make an immediate bond with her…you know…to fling myself into her arms, to welcome her to me. I've missed her for so long and never been allowed to search, and now I feel a terrible uselessness, a helplessness, as if I'm not needed, after all.'

They slowed as they reached the large fish pond, its surface bubbling gently with insect-grabbing mouths. 'And you need to be needed,' he said, softly. 'Yes, of course you do. It's a perfectly natural reaction. And this has been quite a shock, I can appreciate that.' He paused, looking down at the greedy lips just below the surface, the sleek flash of silver flanks, the whip of a dark tail. 'Alex tells me that the existence of Nicholas is news to you, too. So, how do you feel about Nicholas now that you've met him?'

Her face shone with a motherly compassion. 'He's a lovely child,' she said. 'He and Sam would—' She was going too fast again. He would think…*what* would he think?

'Would make good brothers? So where is the problem, my lady? There *is* a reservation in your mind, is there not?'

'How can I tell you?' she whispered.

'I am a priest,' he said, 'and we have privacy. There is no one more suited than I to hear your thoughts. Perhaps that's what you lack more than anything, isn't it? An unbiased ear?'

'Yes, Father. Perhaps it is. But you've known Sir Alex for many years, so he tells me. You understand how committed he is to the king's service. He and Master Hugh are exceptionally competent. Did he tell you of his mission to Castle Kells?'

'He did, my lady.'

'So you know how he's hardly ever in one place for more than a week or so, at most. What kind of a father does that make him? I'm quite sure he would like Nicholas to go with my mother to Castle Kells and, in any case, I doubt if she'd leave here without him, so we have to treat them as a unit, don't we? If I can persuade my mother to live with me, Nicholas must come too.'

'Has Alex said as much to you?'

'Not in so many words, Father.'

'He has to me.'

'That he wants Nicholas to be with me? And Sam? Well, that's exactly what my problem is, Father. I feel that he's using Nicholas and my mother as a carrot to get me to be his child's foster-mother. Don't misunderstand me, I could easily come to love the little one. He needs a mother, it's true, but this sounds to me suspiciously like bargaining.' It also sounded similar in so many ways to a previous occasion when she had attempted the same.

'You mean *step*mother, surely?'

'No, Father. Forgive me, but I don't. Nothing has ever been said about marriage and, even if it had, marriage to Sir Alex would be like being wed to a shadow, wouldn't it? Here today, gone tomorrow. That's not what I expect from the father of my children. I've already suffered three years of widowhood. Nor would it be of much use to Sam and Nick.'

'But you are in love with him, are you not?'

'Yes,' she said, watching a grey-brown trout lurking beneath the silvery water. 'Yes, I can't deny it any longer. I *am* in love with him.'

'So you've made attempts to deny it, have you? Why is that?'

'For the reasons I've just given you, Father, and because he appeared to be totally unsuitable, and because I'm not yet ready to love again.'

Prior William was forced to smile a little at that, and his voice was warmed by it. 'My daughter,' he said, 'I must point out to you an important contradiction that you seem to be unaware of. If you were not ready to love again, you would not be admitting to me that you love him, would you? Love doesn't wait discreetly and ask permission to come in, you know, nor is there a set grieving time. We're all different, and the depth of our love for the ones we've lost is no reliable guideline, I'm afraid. There's no internal calendar that dictates the ways of our hearts, my lady. It's our needs that do that, and they're under a higher control than ours. As I said just now, *your* need is to be needed.'

'Not as an occasional mistress-cum-foster-mother,' she replied. 'That's not good enough for me, Father, nor do I want a litter of bastards. Forgive my plain speaking, I beg you.'

'Gladly. Plain speaking is my meat and drink. But as I understand it, you have implied to Alex that you are not yet ready for a proposal of marriage. You do not want to be rushed into a decision of that nature. Could that be why he's not asked you outright to be his wife? Because he knows you'd reject the idea?'

They had moved across to the stone bench, warmed by the sun, and there they sat like father and daughter, though Ebony's face was clouded by a puzzled frown. 'Not be rushed?' she said. 'I don't recall saying that. I don't recall the subject ever being broached, Father. When was this?'

'Just before supper, I believe, when you said that

no woman would thank him for pushing her into a situation she may not want. All in good time? Was that not what you said?'

'Oh dear, no,' she said, leaning her head back with a sigh.

'No? Then what?'

'Tch! I was talking about my mother being suddenly uprooted and having to pretend to be someone else simply because we tell her that's who she really is. As far as she's concerned, she's Dame Marie. All in good time. That's what I meant. Oh dear, did he think…?'

'Apparently.'

'Well,' she said, 'he has expressed his love for me, but I'm still sure that he's not in a position to offer me marriage, Father, and truly I cannot see that it makes much difference in the long run. He must have told you that my sister-in-law and I will have to move out of Castle Kells in a matter of weeks, or even sooner. The keeper of the castle has to be a man of more or less permanent residence, you see, not two single women with bairns, nor even a married one whose husband is never there.'

'So has it not occurred to you, my lady, that you have missed the point somewhere along the line? Has your logic gone astray for a wee while?'

'What… what logic?'

He chuckled into the black folds of his cowl and turned a baleful eye upon her. 'Start at the beginning, then. He would like Nick to live with you at the castle. Yes?'

'Well, that's what I believe. He knows that my mother wouldn't leave here without Nicholas.'

'And the castle must have a resident male keeper.'

'Ye…es.'

'And if he thought that you'd have to move out of Castle Kells very soon, do you think he'd be wanting his son to go and live there? Would he not have already made up his mind to stay there on a permanent basis, especially after what happened to his late wife and infant? He'd hardly want to risk that happening again, would he? And since he loves you, which he also told me, isn't it clear that your objections have no foundation? He cannot hold a castle *and* roam about Christendom on the king's service at the same time, can he? He knows he can't. So could that be why he has to go and see the king at Newcastle? To tell him so?'

For some moments, Ebony digested this line of reasoning that had entirely passed her by until Prior William's patient elucidation. Her grey marbled eyes held his pale watery ones and saw nothing but kindness, intelligence, and an honesty that had won him as many enemies as friends over the years. 'You think he'd be willing to make that sacrifice?' she said at last.

'It's no great sacrifice to exchange one responsibility for another, my lady. Keeping a castle against the English is a step up, not a step down. The King of Scotland himself may want to stay there one day. Eh?' He smiled, levering himself up from the bench and offering her his hand. 'But why not speak to Alex about it? Clear the air. You'll never have a better time than this.'

'Tonight?'

'Indeed. The sooner the better. I've given him leave to come to your room. There's no sin where the intention is lawful and honest. Tell him your fears and listen to him. Move on, now. It's time. Those two lads are growing fast.'

'Yes, Father, I will. Thank you.' On impulse, she raised herself on tiptoe to kiss the cheek and, since no one was around to comment on the correctness of it, he bent down to accept her salute with the delight of a schoolboy.

'I thought it was time,' Sir Alex said without preamble, 'that we had a mediator. Otherwise, we might go on capering around each other in ever-increasing circles and getting nowhere. So I spoke to the good prior. Did I do right, sweetheart?'

He stood on the low threshold of her room that suddenly appeared to shrink in size, though she had thought it large. The light had begun to fade, and Nicholas had been tucked up in bed by three adults instead of one, and the evening had an unreality about it that even Ebony was at a loss to understand. Outside, the last honey-bees returned to their hives and, in the stone fireplace, the flames around the applewood bent and recovered in the draught.

'Close the door,' she whispered. 'Yes, it was the right thing to do. Anyone would think he'd been in love too.'

'Not an impossibility,' he said, closing the door. 'His reputation is colourful, so they say.'

'Do they?'

They had reached each other by that time and no more words were possible between them, so close was their hungry embrace. Hands clung and stroked and searched, lips revived lips with deep kisses like long draughts of quenching wine, and it was some time before they felt the need to say anything that was as important to them as this.

Breathless and laughing, Ebony held him away, drawing him into the bedchamber and to the bed. 'Have I really been getting it all wrong?' she said. 'Why didn't you tell me everything?'

'Because I'm clumsy and rusty,' he said, caressing her face, 'and unused to thinking about how a woman's mind works. And I don't know what comes first, the words or the actions, or the boys, or your mother, or—'

'Yes…yes, there are too many family matters to pull us off course. But you must know how much I love you, Alex. You *must* have suspected it.'

His face took on an expression of childlike vacancy, though his eyes could not lie so well. 'No,' he said, plaintively. 'No, I didn't. You'll have to tell me, sweetheart.'

'Every time I almost told you, I had second thoughts.'

'About loving me?'

'No, about the timing. The darkness seemed to be the best way of hiding it from my conscience. A woman dare not admit her love to a man who'll be gone from her life in a matter of days, never to return. Nor does she go to bed with him, if she has a grain of sense. But, you see, I bargained with my common sense, didn't I? And now I've lost my conscience too. And my heart. I love you, Alex. I adore you. I want to be your wife and bear your children, to take your child and love him as my own, to be your mate. I want to be everything to you, and I want you to be my son's new father. He adores you too. We all do.'

'Sweetheart,' he said, holding her face between his

palms, 'I don't deserve it after the way I've treated you.'

'What else could you have done? It was a mission like any other.'

'Not quite.' He smiled, pushing her backwards. 'They don't end in marriage to the most exquisite creature man has ever seen, to the fiercest and most protective mother, the most sensitive and indomitable spirit. You are every man's desire. A swan,' he whispered, moving his hand over her face and throat, 'a beautiful black swan. Marry me, my lovely thing. Stay by my side. I'll go on no more missions, I swear it. We'll stay together always, you, me and our family. And we'll have more, shall we?'

'As many as you wish. We have no more time to lose, dear heart.'

She had not expected him to take that quite as literally as he did, though she made no pretence at resistance when he undressed her, for by that time her body had come alive, her senses already shifting to a different level.

But now there was something that added yet another aspect to their lovemaking, for the distant glow from the western sky caught upon his great shoulders with a pink sheen, and the flames that licked around the apple-log in the hearth flared its life into both rooms. Ebony's nakedness, warm, flame-washed and rosy with light, was illuminated for the first time since that dawn bathe under the waterfall and her eyes, half-open, were lustrous and deep and wanting him.

He spread her across the bed, able to watch his own hand caressing, to see her responsiveness, and how her soft flesh gave way under his gentle pressure, and Ebony was not to know that he was seeing her as the mermaid, or that he was washing her the way he had imagined at the time, slowly, erotically, sensuously blending sight with touch at last.

For her also there was more to this experience than before, the extra senses extending the delights of his loving into aeons of time that previously had ended too soon. Teasingly, he had told her that she was fast, too fast, too hot to hold, and neither of them had discovered how to slow it down. Yet here in the dim light, Ebony could see the massive hunch of his muscle-bound shoulders and the thatch of hair that spilled like slivers of oak, the glint in his eyes that signalled where his immediate interest would next alight. It excited her to watch him, to taste the moisture in his skin and to see where her tongue had trailed. Her search could not be hurried, so much of it being new.

Languidly, she pushed him back and lay over and beside him so that she could search those intimate parts with which she had already had more than a passing acquaintance, though never like this.

'You can hold it,' he whispered. 'It's yours.'

She took it tenderly into her hand, feeling the throbbing of life through its soft skin. 'Is this the fine sword you don't wield with your eyes closed?' she taunted him, smiling.

Like deep blue gentians, his eyes laughed back. 'Soldiers' talk,' he said, flashing his white teeth. 'We have names, none of them very refined. We can be quite a crude bunch at times.'

'I know. Could you be crude within the next few minutes?'

'Certainly, my lady. I thought you'd never get round to it.'

'I'm learning new skills,' she said. 'Be patient.'

Patience was something they both continued to learn that night in the longest, slowest, most rapturous lovemaking either of them had ever experienced, and if they had thought that their previous couplings were without equal, by dawn they knew that even the excellent can be excelled.

The applewood fire had turned to white ash and the air hung with the sweet scent as Ebony emerged, naked and sleepy, into the light from the window where Alex was sluicing himself from the bowl. She approached softly to girdle him with her arms and to lay her body close along his back. 'This,' she said, 'is to make up for my daytime coldness.' She waited for him to finish drying his face and neck, then said, 'Tell me again.'

He knew what she was asking. His hands covered hers over his stomach before he turned, wrapping his arms around her and taking a fistful of black hair from her face. 'You,' he said, 'are going to be my wife, and you will be known as Lady Ebony Somers, and we shall live together at Castle Kells. My God, woman…let me look at you.' He eased her away from him while she waited and felt the melting of her knees, the urgent ache of her womb. He supported her breasts and moved the hardening nipples against his thumbs, and Ebony's eyes closed in ecstasy. She reached up to make a sling of arms around his neck, and felt herself lifted and carried to the still-rumpled bed, warmed by their last loving.

She had meant to practise her slowness again, in the light, but he had already taken her too far before the whirlwind caught them in its power and tossed them blindly into its vortex. Rudderless, she surrendered herself to the engulfing surge that came from nowhere to possess her and, for those precious moments, to throw her high on to a roaring wave-crest of sensation. Flipped over and over, tumbling through space, she came back to earth, gasping for breath. 'I love you,' she whispered against his cheek. 'Beloved, that was my heart you threw up there and caught. Did you know that?'

'Yes, my love,' he said, 'but you've had mine from the beginning. D'ye want to bargain again, by any chance?'

'No,' she said, drowsily. 'Keep it. You won it. It'll be safe enough with you from now on.'

Epilogue

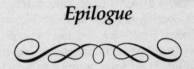

The Castle Kells affair was remembered in Galloway
for many a long year for several different reasons,
depending on whether you were a romantic young
maid, a seasoned knight, or a distant friend of a friend
who knew old Moffat well. Younger men, naturally,
tended to scoff at the tale as being nonsense; soldiers
didn't go round falling in love with women bathing
under waterfalls on Mayday, they said, and, even if
they did, they certainly wouldn't marry them and live
happily ever after with a brood of gloriously handsome children. The young maids not only believed it,
but added their own colourful embroidery to its edges
according to their fancy, sure in the knowledge that
at least some of it must be true. And for the most part
they were right, especially the bit about the widowed
Lady Ebony marrying the king's man she thought was
a reiver.

In fact, Lady Ebony and her bold knight returned
to Castle Kells from Lanercost after several delays,
having been slowed by the addition not only of Lady
Jean Nevillestowe and young Nicholas Somers, but
of several destitute and starving families that Lady

Ebony had insisted on adopting along the way. She had not been willing to leave them to their suffering, and there had been a bit of an argument about it, which she had won. They had been installed at the castle until bothies could be built for them in the village, and many of their line are there still. They called her a saint, even in her lifetime.

Lady Ebony's husband, the laird's stepfather, resigned his vocation as king's special envoy just in time before the conflict between the Scots and the English worsened, for he had been made Keeper of Castle Kells until the young laird should attain his majority. Most of the men who had served with Sir Alex were happy to stay with him as his retainers, though three of them married into the Springfield family at Gretna within the year. The oldest of the king's men, known as Josh, actually married the wee laird's nurse and started a new family, much to everyone's amusement. Sir Alex Somers, however, sired a family of two boys and two girls who, according to hearsay, worshipped the two elder stepbrothers. The two were inseparable, sharing everything, even the old Galloway pony, and although Nick Somers had a misshapen foot, his prowess at archery was legendary. He was a scholar, too. The next generation of villagers never realised that he and Sam Moffat were unrelated, so alike and so close did they become.

The stories that abounded concerning Lady Ebony's mother were as farfetched as any; bewitched by fairies, necromancy, deaf-mute, that kind of nonsense. But those who came into direct contact with her benefited from her natural cures, her skills as a midwife, and her learning. Her memory, lost after a terrible raid on her home at Carlisle, never quite recovered, although it was said that she had moments of partial recall. It seemed to concern her very little one way or the other, having those she loved close at hand, being secure and cherished, a combination of matriarch and tutor to the growing broods of children.

Broods? Well, there was the other couple at Castle Kells too, you see. Master Hugh of Leyland married the old laird's daughter on the same day as Lady Ebony and Sir Alex at the beginning of that July. Meg, her name was, a fiery-haired lass with a temper to match, and a heart of gold. They had a huge family of Leylands with copper hair, and the castle would echo to their shouts, laughter, arguments and fighting. And music, too.

Whether Meg Moffat ever told her sister-in-law about how they had been watched at the waterfall on Mayday morn no one knows, but someone must have, for it became one of the legends surrounding the Castle Kells' affair. It made no difference, however: there were never two people better matched than Lady Ebony and the handsome Sir Alex and, though she had loved her tragic young Robbie, she loved the second one with a staggering intensity that became the talk of the castle guests who saw them, even in broad daylight. Shameless, they said, enviously.

As for the Dumfries branch of the family, not much is known about them except from those who say that King Robert of Scotland fined the wine-merchant and the lawyer so heavily that their businesses were ruined, which no doubt benefited the king greatly. The woman, Jennie Cairns, grew suddenly old. She had a bairn, they say, that the husband refused to recognise, but these were the only sad notes in an otherwise happy ending.

The stories about the Moffats and the Somers will probably continue to circulate and change shape like the eddies of a burn, and though Castle Kells is little more than a ruin now at the side of a lonely loch, there are still wild Galloway ponies grazing the hillsides, progeny of that much-travelled and long-suffering pony with an L branded on its flank.

* * * * *

Savor the breathtaking
romances and thrilling adventures
of Harlequin Historicals

On sale September 2004

THE KNIGHT'S REDEMPTION by Joanne Rock

A young Welshwoman tricks Roarke Barret into marriage
in order to break her family's curse—of spinsterhood.
But Ariana Glamorgan never expects to fall for the
handsome Englishman who is now her husband....

PRINCESS OF FORTUNE by Miranda Jarrett

Captain Lord Thomas Greaves is assigned to guard Italian
princess Isabella di Fortunaro. Sparks fly and passions flare
between the battle-weary captain and the spoiled, beautiful
lady. Can love cross all boundaries?

On sale October 2004

HIGHLAND ROGUE by Deborah Hale

To save her sister from a fortune hunter, Claire Talbot offers
herself as a more tempting target. But can she forget the
feelings she once had for Ewan Geddes, a charming
Highlander who once worked on her father's estate?

THE PENNILESS BRIDE by Nicola Cornick

Home from the Peninsula War, Rob Selbourne discovers
he must marry a chimney sweep's daughter to
fulfill his grandfather's eccentric will. Will Rob
find true happiness in the arms of
the lovely Jemima?

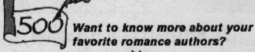

FALL IN LOVE WITH THESE HANDSOME HEROES FROM HARLEQUIN HISTORICALS

On sale September 2004

THE PROPOSITION
by Kate Bridges

Sergeant Major Travis Reid
Honorable Mountie of the Northwest

WHIRLWIND WEDDING
by Debra Cowan

Jericho Blue
Texas Ranger out for outlaws

On sale October 2004

ONE STARRY CHRISTMAS
by Carolyn Davidson/Carol Finch/Carolyn Banning

Three heart-stopping heroes
for your Christmas stocking!

THE ONE MONTH MARRIAGE
by Judith Stacy

Brandon Sayer
Businessman with a mission